ONCE MORE FROM THE TOP

NAN REINHARDT

Once More From the Top

Copyright © 2013 Nan Reinhardt

Published by Fine Wine Romances

ISBN-13: 978-0-9893968-8-2

ISBN-10: 0989396886

Cover art by Chipperish Media

Cover art and logos Copyright © 2013 Chipperish Media

For my Dee—Thanks for always believing in me. We had a wondrous thirty-three years, my friend. I miss you every day.

CHAPTER 1

Carrie Halligan's fingers tickled the keys of the ebony grand piano, finding the notes almost without conscious volition. She'd played "Misty" so many times in this bar, she didn't even have to think about the music. Instead, she focused on the low rocks glass just to her right. One last slip of paper, only one more request, and her shift was over.

The click of silverware against plates, the chink of glasses being bussed, and the murmur of a dozen conversations overwhelmed her music. Didn't matter. Carrie wasn't there to be the center of attention. Her job was to provide the background and that suited her just fine. A smattering of applause broke out as she played the final notes and tossed a smile over her bare shoulder. If it weren't for the can lights shining down on the piano, she'd have been freezing in the strapless black dress.

She pulled out the last slip of paper and unfolded it; Jim Croce's "Time in a Bottle." She recognized the spiky handwriting —the Dugans were in the audience. The couple came in every other Saturday and stayed for hours listening to her play. Sometimes they danced, snuggled close in each other's arms. Their obvious infatuation warmed Carrie's heart. That kind of devotion was rare these days.

"This one's for Suz from Peter," she announced and began the haunting ballad amid a collective sigh from the crowd.

"Thanks, Carrie," a deep voice called and she smiled as she played on.

Tired and ready to go home, she frowned when Rudy, the bartender, appeared over her shoulder and dropped another slip of paper into the glass. Holding up one finger, he backed off the tiny stage, mouthing, "One more?" With a nod and a wink, she played the last notes of the old ballad.

It happened sometimes. A late-night request, usually from a sad barfly dredging up old memories or some couple who wanted one last dance.

She rolled her neck and stretched her fingers before reaching into the glass. When she opened the slip and peered at it under the soft glow of the piano light, her breath caught.

Haydn's Concerto in C Major.

Her pulse pounded in her ears, shutting out the chatter in the bar as she gazed uncomprehending at the paper. She squinted, blinking at the square black letters unable to make sense of what was written there.

Dear God in heaven. Who requested this?

Her fingers shook and the words on the paper blurred. Only one person would ask her to play that particular piece, and there was no way on earth *he* was in this bar. She tensed, afraid to even turn around. Closing her eyes, she released a long, shuddering breath before glancing as casually as she could at the crowd.

Is he here? Is it possible?

Heat rose into her cheeks and perspiration dampened the back of her neck as she scanned the room. The lighting was so dim she could barely make out individual faces in the crowd. People were already beginning to stand up to leave, assuming, no doubt, that she'd finished playing for the night. Carrie didn't see him, but would she even recognize him? It had been so long—a lifetime ago.

"I–I'm sorry." Her voice was barely a whisper. "I don't know this one."

"You knew it once. Play it."

An icy chill settled in the pit of her stomach as she recognized the voice coming from across the bar. Her head whipped around and she peered into the shadows. A tall figure stood silhouetted in the entrance.

She didn't need to see his face. Even in the dark, his towering height and that unmistakable halo of dark red hair identified him.

Maestro Liam Reilly.

He stepped into the light and their eyes met. His mouth curved into a hint of a smile that sent a spasm of longing through her. The cacophony in the bar dwindled to distant background noise as she gazed dumbfounded across the room. It *was* him. Silver threads shone among the thick hair that swept back off his forehead, except for that one stray strand that still fell to his brow.

He's older.

The inanity of that thought occurred to the logical part of her stunned mind even as she tried to comprehend that he was standing less than thirty feet away.

Of course he's older. It's been sixteen years.

Helpless to do anything but gape, she closed her fingers around the scrap of paper, crumpling it into a tiny ball. Her stomach churned, and although the urge to flee was overwhelming, she knew her trembling legs would never hold her up long enough to escape. Not without tripping over the piano stool and falling flat on her face.

What is he doing here?

Heart pounding a rough rhythm, Carrie sat perfectly still for a moment, caught in his mesmerizing gaze. His smile broadened and that dimple, oh God, that killer dimple, creased his cheek as he gave her the barest nod.

A challenge.

At last she managed to pull her eyes from his and swallow the panic that rose in her throat. She could do this. She was a pro. Didn't matter who walked in off the street. Hell yes, she could do this and without freaking out.

Hands trembling, she dropped the bit of paper, squared her shoulders, and began to play—tentatively, then more confidently as her fingers remembered the notes. First the *Vivace,* and suddenly his brawny frame, arms raised as he conducted, flashed through her mind. Her first glimpse of him standing tall on the podium in that little auditorium at McGill University. He took a group of musicians through a Rachmaninoff chamber piece while she watched, spellbound.

She banished the memory and focused on the *Adagio—Un Poco Adagio*—but there was their first kiss, gentle, just the touch of his mouth before turning deliciously erotic. They'd stood beneath a streetlight on the campus in Montreal, so wrapped up in each other they didn't even feel the raindrops. Her memory conjured up such a clear picture that her lips burned and tingled as she bent over the keyboard.

No!

Biting her lower lip, she leaned in, and the music poured from her fingers. Finally, she got to the *Rondo*, the *Allegro*. Memories of his bare chest, heaving as he rose over her, crept into her head, nearly causing her to lose focus. His whispered words, the fierce kisses… but she played on, shaking that scene from her mind as sweat prickled her ribs and plastered the curls to the curve of her cheek. By the time she was done and the piece flawlessly played, her carefully managed control snapped.

A moment of silence reigned before the burst of applause and whistles from the few remaining patrons. Panting and breathless, she searched the handful of people left in the bar.

He was gone.

She stood, craning her neck to see over the shadowed heads of the patrons as fear gripped her. The piano bench scraped when she shoved it back and raced off the stage and out the door. Wringing her hands, she peered around the hotel lobby, past the front desk and then to the bank of elevators, watching for his tall frame, his broad back. She didn't see him anywhere.

But he *was* here. Liam was here... in Michigan.

Five minutes later, she careened out of the parking lot, blinking back hot, stinging tears. Gulping them away, she wrapped her damp hands around the steering wheel, trying desperately to concentrate on the road as she sped toward Willow Bay and home. Straightening in the seat, she drove with grim determination. Once she reached home, she could breathe again.

Lights shone in her apartment above the old boathouse at Dixon's Marina. It was only a little after eleven, so of course Jack was still awake, probably playing games on his laptop. She raced up the steps as fast as her high-heeled sandals allowed and threw open the door. Following the sounds of pinging and electronic explosions to his room, she tapped on the door jamb.

"Hey. Get packed. I'm taking you up to camp tomorrow morning." She slipped out of the shoes and pressed her ankle where the strap had rubbed a raw spot.

Jack glanced up. "Why? You said I couldn't go 'til Monday."

"I changed my mind."

"Why?" He'd mastered the fifteen-year-old's exasperated eye roll, but she ignored it this time and tossed her shoes on the loft step.

"What does it matter? You're the one who wanted to go a day early. I'm taking you up a day early." Hurrying into his room, she yanked a big canvas duffle from the top of his closet. "Here. Start packing. Did you get your laundry done?"

"The last of it's in the dryer." Jack closed the laptop and set it next to him on the messy bed. "Mom. What's going on?"

"Nothing." Struggling to keep her voice calm, she was determined not to let him see her panic. "I just got to thinking there's no reason to make you wait when all the other counselors are going to be there tomorrow. Isn't that what you told me?"

"Well, not *all* of them, just some. Max and Sean and... Mom, stop." He stood up and took a pile of socks and underwear from her hands. "Come on, what's up?"

"I can't win, can I?" She forced a grin. "First you're ticked because I wanted to keep you with me an extra day before you leave for the whole summer. Now you're balking when I agree to take you up a day early."

"I'm not balking." Jack stuffed the clothing in the duffle. "Just curious why you changed your mind."

"Ever hear the old saying, 'Don't look a gift horse in the mouth'?" She patted his cheek as he nodded, still eyeing her with suspicion. "Well, don't. Get packed. We're outta here at nine in the morning."

Running up the stairs, she stopped dead in the center of her own bedroom as cold fear overtook her. She dropped down on the end of the bed and buried her face in her hands, then bent over, fighting nausea, trying to keep from flying into a million pieces. When she could breathe again, she yanked off the dress and slipped into yoga pants and an old t-shirt. In the bathroom, she smeared cold cream on her face, wiping off the smoky shadow and black mascara as her thoughts tumbled and turned.

What in holy hell is he doing here?

What does he want?

What does he know?

Carrie's heart plummeted as she stared at her stricken visage in the mirror. Eliot brought him here—that was the only explanation that made any sense at all. The nausea subsided as anger began to simmer in its place. Yes, this thing reeked of Eliot Raines's fine hand. For years, he'd been more than a godfather and old family friend. He'd been the one person she could count on to support her. Confidant. Surrogate father to her, and grandfather to Jack. And the one person in the world who knew her deepest secrets.

Why on earth had he betrayed her now?

She grabbed her phone.

"Damn you, Eliot," Carrie said through gritted teeth when he answered. "He's here. How in the hell could you do this to me?"

"I can see that talking to you tonight is going to be quite pointless." Eliot showed no surprise that she'd called him so late. "Go to bed. We'll have coffee and talk in the morning."

"No. We'll talk *now*." Panic made her throat tight. "Why is he here?"

"I needed a big name." When she didn't respond, he continued. "You know I'm chair of the Lawson fundraiser. I needed someone who could draw a crowd full of deep pockets."

"You *promised*," Carrie choked out the words in a whisper. "You promised me you wouldn't tell him."

"I haven't told him a thing."

"Not yet you haven't. Don't, Eliot. Please." Carrie begged and then hated herself for it.

Eliot sighed. "I told you. He can draw the kind of crowd I need for Lawson. This isn't about you. That camp needs money… money for kids like your son, and I won't let it go under because you can't face your past."

Carrie opened her mouth to object, but snapped it shut as she caught sight of Jack sprinting up the stairs. "Don't think we're done, Eliot. We're not." She ended the call just as Jack appeared in the doorway, his red hair gleaming in the light from the ceiling fan above the bed. "Hey, babe, what's up?"

"I'm packed." He flopped onto the bed and stared at the fan circling lazily above his head. "Who was that?"

"Just Eliot asking if we wanted muffins for breakfast. He's been baking again." Carrie smiled, surprised at how easily the lie slipped from her lips.

"Yeah? What kind?"

"Dunno. I told him we were on our way to Lawson tomorrow morning." She groaned as she pulled him up to a sitting position. "Time for bed, dude. We've got an early day tomorrow."

"You sure about this?" Jack rose and headed for the door. "I can wait till Monday."

"Nah, it's alright. I'll be fine, and you're gonna have a great time." She gave him a quick hug before he loped downstairs. When his door closed, she released a shaken breath, and curled up on the bed, wrapping her trembling body in the old quilt.

CHAPTER 2

L iam Reilly zipped the empty suitcase and set it in the passageway outside his stateroom. He'd take it down to the hold later. For now, he fell back on the bed and heaved a sigh. God, it was good to finally be settled for the summer—good and settled with three whole months in which to do anything he chose. No rehearsals or galas, no long plane rides, no hotel rooms or lousy room service suppers. Instead long days on the *Allegro*, cruising the Great Lakes with his friends Will and Tony. Just the guys, fishing, swimming, drinking beer, and being tourists for a change instead of the main attraction.

The past year had been a bear. He loved conducting, but it had been a long season. His agent Marty had overbooked him—*again* —even though Liam begged him to limit the tour to ten or twelve European cities. Twelve stops meant two to three weeks of rehearsals with each orchestra, at least three performances, some-times four or five if they did matinees. Marty had booked sixteen cities that included a whirlwind of rehearsals, opening night galas, parties, and performances.

He'd been plenty pissed when Liam reminded him that he was taking time off for a few months. Marty had already started booking the summer concert tour in the States. Three missed calls and four texts proved he was still upset, but Liam didn't care. He was sick and tired of fighting with Marty about his career, particularly when the real argument was *whose* career it actually was.

Marty showed no signs of giving up. The last text he'd sent reminded Liam that he had a standing date at Tanglewood at the end of July to conduct part of the Pops series. He'd been their big summer draw for the last ten years. Did he really want to disappoint all those patrons? But Liam knew what Marty was actually asking was, *Do you really want to give up all that money?*

He didn't want to disappoint anyone; he simply needed a break. A vacation. Something he hadn't had in years. Screw the money. He'd earned more than he'd ever use in his lifetime, and his friend and accountant, Will Brody, had invested it so well he could step off the podium tomorrow and never look back.

But Marty wanted more. Liam had been a hell of a gravy train and his agent clearly hated for it stop, even for a short while.

Stretching his arms above his head, he rose and wandered to the window to stare out at Lake Michigan shimmering in the morning sun. His mind drifted back to the bar and the music and Carrie. He hadn't intended to go into the bar when he passed through the hotel lobby. Frankly, all he'd wanted was a hot shower, a minibar, and cool sheets after the long drive from Chicago to Traverse City. But the music drew him in. Hoagy Carmichael's "Georgia on My Mind" drifted out over the chatter of the patrons and the clink of glasses. He stood in the open doorway, his eyes locked on the shapely brunette at the piano.

He knew her. Her dark curls were short now, but her shoulders still appeared soft and freckled in a strapless dress that emphasized her luscious, womanly curves. But that wasn't how he knew it was her.

No. What he recognized was the way she played—leaning into the piano, her slender fingers dancing lightly across the keyboard, emotion caressing each and every note. Only one person in the world played with such passion and effortless grace.

He'd sent the request up with the bartender on a whim, then sat stunned by her dismay when she read his request. Her eyes had widened in panic as she gazed out into the audience. Then she'd played it so exquisitely she stole his breath away, exactly as she had the very first time he heard her play it in Montreal. He hadn't been ready for that, and he'd bolted rather than face her again.

Chicken shit.

He scowled as he watched a freighter chug into the harbor, his mind awash with memories of Carrie Halligan. She wasn't the only woman he'd ever loved, but she was the first to break his heart, and he'd never forgotten her.

Even after all these years, the pain of her rejection still stung. Liam didn't want to admit how often he thought about her or how much she'd affected every relationship. Oh, he'd moved on after Carrie dumped him, and his career had skyrocketed. He was in demand to conduct orchestras all over the world. There was plenty of work, plenty of money, more than enough celebrity, and always lots of women.

The classical conductor whose sex appeal is bringing a new, younger audience to the symphony hall—Marty Justice had done his job well, and Liam went along without protest. He loved drawing the music from an orchestra, working with musicians all over the world, and teaching seminars and workshops, but he was tired.

Shaking his head, he left his stateroom and pulled out his phone to send a simple text message to Marty. No, he wouldn't be doing Tanglewood this summer. The only orchestra he intended to conduct in the next few months was the Traverse Symphony Orchestra.

"Company!" Tony called down to him as he was shoving his suitcase into a rack in the hold.

Company? Maybe it was her...

Liam took the companionway stairs two at a time, hurrying to get up on deck, where he found Eliot Raines coming up the short gangplank.

"Welcome to Michigan, laddie." The old man's handshake was still firm, even though he was nearing eighty.

"Eliot, so glad to see you." Liam was pleased to see his former teacher looking so spry. "Come sit down for a while. Sorry I can't offer you any coffee, but I've got water and soft drinks. Maybe tea. We just tied up and need to hit the grocery store."

"Thanks, but I can't stay." Eliot seemed a little jumpy as he laid a large manila envelope on the table next to the railing. "Just dropped by to bring you the paperwork for the benefit. I think you'll like this marina. Noah and Margie Dixon have a fine operation here. Been on the bay for years."

"It's a beautiful harbor and they've been very hospitable." Liam attributed the awkwardness between them to the fact they hadn't seen each other in years—until Eliot's next comment.

"Hope you found the hotel I suggested comfortable." Eliot's gaze wandered out across the wide expanse of water before coming back to meet Liam's.

Liam was certain that particular hotel recommendation had been deliberate. Folding his arms over his chest, he gave him a wry smile. "It was fine. I, um, enjoyed the entertainment in the bar."

"Did you?" Eliot raised one bushy white brow and smirked.

"Does she live in Traverse City?" He couldn't have stopped the question if his life depended on it.

Eliot shook his head. "She lives right here in Willow Bay." Turning, he pointed to an apartment above a big white boathouse about a hundred yards away. "She's the Dixons' niece."

Liam's stomach flipped over as he stared up at the boathouse gleaming in the sun that peeked through the pines behind it. When he glanced back at Eliot, the old guy wore a rather self-satisfied expression. "What are you up to?"

Eliot shrugged. "Just trying to keep Lawson Music Camp afloat. I can't thank you enough for taking this on, especially while you're on vacation." He patted Liam's shoulder. "Gotta run. Oh, hey, if you need a cup of coffee, I'd recommend you walk up to the village. The Daily Grind on Main makes great coffee and scones. Perry Graham, the owner, is a platinum-level supporter of the TSO."

"Eliot—" Liam began, but Eliot was already halfway down the gangplank. He moved damn fast for a man approaching eighty.

"We'll catch up later, my boy," he called over his shoulder as he hurried up the dock.

Liam shook his head and smiled. It wasn't exactly an admission he'd been set up, but Eliot Raines could've gotten any conductor for this gig—Palmer, Dudamel, even another former student like Raymond Curry. Any one of them would've signed on for a cause like Lawson Music Camp. The old man may or may not have had an ulterior motive when he invited him to conduct, but Liam's curiosity was piqued.

Remembering the flare of heat as he watched Carrie play last night, he thought, *Why not?* Looking up an old lover suddenly made the idea of spending time in Willow Bay even more appealing.

∽

Carrie rubbed the back of her neck and shifted her purse from one shoulder to the other as she waited in line for coffee. She'd barely slept last night. The house was so quiet without Jack—and then there was Maestro Liam Reilly. She'd deliberately left the house early to avoid a conversation with Eliot. It didn't matter what he had to say. Liam was here, and although she'd gotten Jack away before Liam discovered his existence, she still had to face him sooner or later. Anyone who stood in the same room for longer than thirty seconds with Jack and Liam would figure out the truth.

Not exactly rocket science…

"Hey, kiddo."

She started at the light touch on her shoulder and glanced back to see her best friend Julie Miles cutting in line behind her. "Hey, Jules."

"What are you doing here? I thought Jack had to be up at Lawson at nine." Julie waved away the protests of the other patrons in the queue. "I'm not getting coffee, I'm just here to chat." That perfect grin and shapely body bought her a lot of good will from the men she'd moved aside.

Carrie shook her head. "I took him up yesterday."

"Why? I thought you guys were going to do one last day together."

"He really wanted to go up when Max did, so I caved." Carrie kept her tone casual as she met her friend's curious gaze.

"You okay?"

"Yep." There was no hiding anything from Jules, so it was best to keep her answers succinct. She could be relentless as a terrier and Carrie wasn't in the mood to be grilled.

Kelly, the barista, gave her a nod and Carrie placed her order. With a raised brow at Jules, she pointed to the counter. "You want anything?"

"I'd better not." Jules shook her head, making her long blonde hair shimmer in the sunlight streaming that streamed in the window. "Don't make a liar out of me."

"Oh, for God's sake, just order her a venti white chocolate

mocha and get it over with." Ben, the owner of the hardware store, grinned good-naturedly from his place in line.

"Yeah and put her damn bran muffin in the microwave, Kelly," Al, the barber, added from the doorway. "Whose turn is it to pay?"

"I think I'm up." This from Gary, who owned the bookstore next door.

Julie held up her wallet. "Not necessary, guys. I actually remembered my money today. Coffee's on me." She nudged Carrie to one side. "Hey Perry, run me a tab for these guys, okay?"

A cheer went up from the men in line and Carrie rolled her eyes. At fifty, Julie was still a knockout and her career as a catalogue model made her a celebrity in Willow Bay. But it was her sense of fun and vivacious personality that made most of the men in town lust after her. Alas, she was hopelessly devoted to her husband.

"Let's find a table." Scanning the room, Carrie spotted one near the back window.

"I can't stay more than ten minutes. I've got a mani-pedi at nine." Julie set her coffee and muffin down and plopped into the chair across from Carrie. "Was it as tough as you thought it would be? Leaving him for the whole summer?"

"Worse. I lost it. He stood by the car and patted my head like I was the kid and he was the parent. So in addition to being painful, it was also embarrassing." She shrugged. "But I know this is the best thing for him."

"It is. He needs to feel free to explore where he's going and what he's about. You were right to ship him up there." Julie added a packet of raw sugar to her latte as Carrie cringed. Julie's sweet tooth was notorious in the village. "And hell, don't apologize for crying. I'm still a mess when I leave the twins at school, and they're in college. Why do you think they asked Charlie to take them back Ann Arbor for summer session today? They know their dad won't lose it. They hate it when I cry during goodbyes, but it's a mom thing. We're allowed."

Julie had been Carrie's dear friend for ten years and was one of her first customers. When she brought her twins in for portraits, the two women clicked immediately despite the fact that their lives, and their personalities, couldn't have been more different. Julie was bubbly and flamboyant, adored Elvis and Brooks & Dunn, and had three grown kids and a successful surgeon husband, Charlie Miles. Life at Julie and Charlie's house was chaotic and noisy and hectic.

Carrie was quiet, private, and settled into a routine. She adored Jack, her photography studio, and her orderly apartment above the boathouse at Dixon's Marina. Her life was low-key and modest. But she and Jack shared a love of music, movies, swimming, and sailing on Willow Bay. She worked hard to keep life simple and full of love.

That life was about to get very complicated, and she wanted to spill the whole story of Liam's reappearance to Jules, but she couldn't do it in five minutes at the coffee shop. They'd need a quiet place to talk, several bottles of wine, and chocolate.

"He'll have a ball working with those little kids, don't worry about him." Jules took a big bite of the muffin before washing it down with a gulp of coffee.

"It's not him I'm worried about." Carrie said. "It's me. I'll be lost without him."

"The experience will be great for you too, if you let it. Maybe it would be a good time for you to try getting a life. Like, I don't know, dating?" Julie arched one brow. "You're forty and—"

"Hey, you've got me by ten years, so watch it. And my life is just fine, thank you." She waved away Julie's concern like an annoying fly. "I have two weddings to photograph this summer, the church directory photos, and senior pictures. I can help Uncle

Noah at the marina, sail, swim, and do my thing at the bar. I'm well into the *middle* of my life, so don't start that 'begin your life' crap again. I'm going to miss him, that's all. And by the way there's more to life than men, Jules."

The conversation was old territory. Jules had been fixing her up with various men practically from the moment they'd met. Carrie enjoyed dating, but Jack was her focus and she never brought men home. It was an unwritten rule that she kept her dating completely separate from her home life. She'd experimented with relationships, but the encounters left her unfulfilled and vaguely dissatisfied, as though something she couldn't define was missing.

"I'm just saying—"

"Don't you have a mani-pedi in about two minutes?" Carrie interrupted.

"Oh shit." Julie stuffed the last of her muffin in her mouth, swallowed, and grabbed her coffee. "Call me later."

"Want to grab a pizza tonight?" Carrie asked hopefully. It would be good opportunity to talk to her about Liam.

"Thanks, but no. I'm planning an empty-nest celebration of champagne and hot sex with my husband." She waggled her perfect brows as she backed away from the table.

"Ah, Julie, you're killin' us here," Ben said while Al and Gary elbowed each other and snickered.

"Sorry, guys. TMI." Julie swung past the counter to settle up with Perry before breezing out on an audible sigh from the group at the table by the door. "Enjoy your coffee, gentlemen."

Carrie watched wistfully, half-wishing she had the time to join her friend at the nail salon. An hour of self-indulgence would go a long way toward easing the knot in her stomach. She nibbled her scone, and the crowd dissipated as the merchants headed out to begin their days. Senior pictures started today, but her first appointment wasn't until ten-thirty. She had time to finish her coffee and read the paper.

The headline jumped out at her as she shook the *Record-Eagle* open to the Arts and Entertainment section, hoping to find dates and times for performances at the local playhouse of *Belle of Amherst,* a play she'd looked forward to attending. There it was in bold black letters. THE MOST INFLUENTIAL CONDUCTOR SINCE BERNSTEIN. The article ran two columns above the fold, hailing the virtues of Maestro Liam Reilly, but as she tried to read it, the print jumbled together over words like *dramatic flair* and *intellectual vigor.*

"Don't believe everything you read in the papers, sweetheart."

She gasped as her mind registered the identity of the man standing beside her. He hadn't changed much—a little brawnier, a few gray strands threading through his dark red hair, some lines around his eyes. The gray-streaked goatee was new, but basically he was the same Liam.

What a crummy thing to do, blindsiding me in the coffee shop in front of the whole town.

"Mind if I join you?"

She shook her head since he was already pulling out the chair opposite hers. When she was finally able to speak, her voice was raspy. "What are you doing here?"

"Getting coffee?"

She gave an exasperated sigh. "I mean what are you doing in Willow Bay?"

"Vacation… with a little work thrown in." He eyed her over the lid of his cup before taking a sip. "How are you, Carrie?"

How was he so cool and calm, while she was about to burst apart at the seams? Folding the newspaper back into a neat rectangle, she laid it carefully in the center of the table.

"Good. I'm good," she replied with a tight smile. "How about you, Maestro?"

"I'm good, too." The quaver in his voice was so slight, she'd have missed it if she hadn't been so attuned. It gave her courage.

"Great. I'm glad to hear it." She rose. "Well, I've got to run. Enjoy your stay."

He stopped her with a hand on her wrist, his eyes locked on hers. "Wait. Don't go. Can we… catch up? It's been a long time."

That simple touch sent her pulse into orbit. Damn the man for having any effect on her at all. He was still too sexy for his own good. For *her* own good. Beltless jeans rode just below his waist. His tucked chambray shirt was unbuttoned at the collar, the sleeves rolled back to reveal the soft hair on his arms. Why couldn't he have been bald or sporting a giant pot belly? Anything but still *her* Liam?

Frightened and frustrated, she was dying to touch him. Instead she gripped her purse, slipped into her chair, and gave him the most casual smile she could muster. "I only have a few minutes."

"So, what've you been up to?" His smile nearly melted her into the floor of the coffee shop. "How did you end up here?"

"My aunt and uncle live here. I came up after my dad died and I liked it. Now it's home."

"You cut your hair." He leaned back in the chair, assessing her with narrowed eyes.

Heat rose in her cheeks. Dammit, she hated blushing. It was so juvenile. She chuckled, trying to cover her discomfort. "Several times. As you said, it's been a long time."

"You still look fantastic." His deep voice caressed her, just as it had so long ago.

"Thanks. So do you."

He *did* look good. Better than good. All the photos and television appearances didn't do him justice. With a strong jaw, gray eyes, and thick hair, he looked more like a cowboy than a musician. He exuded sex appeal—which was exactly how he'd been marketed to the public. As classical music became a hot commodity, Liam rode that interest right to the top. According to the press, he mingled with musical celebrities and Hollywood types alike, drawing crowds of star-struck women into concert halls around the world.

Tugging the lid off her coffee cup, she shoved the napkin containing a bit of leftover scone into it and snapped it back on before meeting his gaze straight on. There was no point in letting him reduce her to a silly school girl. They needed an even playing field. "Life on the road certainly agrees with you."

"It's been a hell of a ride." He sipped his coffee. "What're *you* doing these days?"

Dimples showed around the beard when he grinned, and his resemblance to Jack startled her speechless. "Um... I'm a–a photographer. I own a studio a couple of blocks from here." She cocked her head toward the front of the shop. "I do weddings and portraits... that sort of thing."

"A photographer? Wow, I had no idea you were even interested in photography." He seemed truly surprised. "Your own studio? How wonderful."

"Thanks." She nodded with a smile. "It pays the bills."

He dipped his head and that stray lock of hair fell across his forehead. "What about your music? I thought you were headed to Carnegie Hall like your mother." His question was hesitant, as if he wasn't sure he should bring up the topic. "Now, you're playing jazz in a hotel bar on Saturday nights? What happened?"

"Just didn't work out."

Carrie rose, unable to sit still for another second. What a surreal situation! Liam here, sitting across from her, the two of them exchanging pleasantries like a couple of old classmates. There was so much he didn't know, so many things she'd do over if she had another chance, but this wasn't the time or place. His questions were too probing and she wasn't ready to tell him.

Not yet.

"I need to get going, I have stuff to do. Really good to see you, Liam."

"I'll be here a while." His gray eyes raked her body before returning to her face. "Let's get together for dinner one night. Maybe you can show me around."

Carrie's palms were sweating and she longed to hurl herself into his arms with a *Yes, yes, let's have dinner.* How wondrous would it be to simply confess all her sins to him? But instead she stood, dry-mouthed, fidgeting with her purse strap.

His gaze held hers, a question in his eyes.

She wasn't prepared to answer any more questions, so she simply shrugged. "Maybe. We'll see."

And she walked away.

CHAPTER 3

Liam smacked his palm on the steering wheel of his Mercedes roadster as he sat in the parking spot in front of the Daily Grind sipping his second cup of coffee. The plan had been simple when he saw her sitting in the coffee shop. Drop by and check out an old lover. Maybe share a few memories that might reveal why she'd dumped him so unceremoniously. That was it—nothing more. He expected her to be wary, but not so coolly polite, as if they'd never been more than passing acquaintances.

What he truly hadn't counted on was her effect on him. She still had that haughty tilt to her chin that was such a turn-on when he first met her, mainly because it was contrary to who she actually was. And she'd bolted when he asked about her music, never even acknowledging his presence at her gig at the bar. The way she kept him at arm's length piqued his interest even more. What happened to the open, passionate girl he'd known? How had she become this closed-up, cool woman he barely recognized?

Instead of driving back to the marina, he got out of the car, wandered out into the street, and took a turn toward the lake shimmering in the distance. Rounding another corner brought him to Waterfront Drive, where he settled on a bench by the water's edge to finish his coffee. Boats filled the public harbor docks, and he craned his neck to catch a glimpse of his own yacht, docked at Dixon's Marina. Everything was so close in this town. Eliot was right. He could have walked it in no time—which probably would've been better for him in more ways than one. Now his mind was a morass of memories and emotions.

Reminiscences of Carrie washed over him. The two of them had been together every moment for an entire week. Endless walks across the McGill campus, talking for hours. Passionate kisses at the end of an evening. Time spent watching each other's rehearsals. From that first moment, he had wanted to know more of her, wanted desperately to touch her—perhaps because she appeared so untouched. Her quiet grace and innocence had surrounded him with a warm glow that held none of the pseudo-sophistication and artifice of other women he had known.

When he'd attended her audition, the music wrapped around him, the technique perfect, the emotion of the allegro coming through as she played the piece superbly—exactly as she'd played it at the bar. By the time the audition was over, his self-control was gone. They'd barely made it to his apartment, where he took her straight to bed. He hadn't had a sexual experience like that before or since. Carrie gave herself to him freely, without a moment's hesitation. When he loved her, he knew he had all of her.

But now she's closed up tight... unreceptive. What the hell happened in the intervening years?

He finished his drink and tossed his cup into a nearby recycling bin. Still too restless to drive back to the boat, he explored the town, which was just waking up. The shops might not be open yet, but Willow Bay was already abuzz with activity. Sailboats skimmed across the surface as charter boats docked and offloaded their morning fishing parties. He wandered down Main Street, pretending he wasn't looking for Carrie's studio. It was closed up and there was no sign of her. But when he passed it, he peered in the window, checking out the portraits there. She was damn good if her storefront display was any indication.

The townsfolk were friendly but not intrusive, smiling and nodding as he passed by. It was a pretty little village that seemed to be doing a thriving tourist business even this early in June. From what he'd discovered in his online reading, tourism *was* the area's main industry. Willow Bay was known for being a four-season destination, offering everything from snow skiing to bicycling to boating and fishing.

Just as he found himself back at the harbor side park, his phone vibrated in his pocket.

Marty. Again.

With a sigh, he reined in his growing resentment and answered the call. "Hi, Marty."

"Where are you, man?"

"On vacation."

"Liam, do you think these orchestras are going to invite you back if you snub them this year? Do you?"

"I've already spoken to Karen at BSO about Tanglewood—she understood perfectly, and she's already invited me back next summer." A dull throbbing started above Liam's eyes, so he took several deep breaths as he paced along the wharf. How many more times were they going to have to have this particular discussion? "And Will's been in contact with ISO, National, Atlanta, and the rest. They're all fine with it. Why can't you be?"

Liam heard Marty light a cigarette and take a deep drag. He pictured him on the deck of his house in Malibu, sipping coffee and smoking.

"What the hell are you and Will doing making calls to BSO or any other orchestra? That's *my* job."

"You aren't *doing* your job, Marty."

"My job is to get you booked, Maestro. To keep you working." He coughed as he said it.

Liam shook his head at the phlegmy sound. Marty had been a heavy smoker since the day they met, something that caused Liam great distress for the first few years they'd worked together. He finally figured out that he wasn't going to stop his agent from lighting up, so he'd simply laid down some ground rules about where and when Marty could smoke. Not in Liam's presence, basically, was the rule. "No, your job is to manage my career. *My* career, not yours. If I tell you I need a break, your job is to honor that request."

"Where are you?" Marty took a new tack, his voice softening to that persuasive timbre he'd used too many times in the past. But even over the phone, Liam could hear the anger simmering below the surface.

"I'm cruising on the *Allegro*, exactly where I told you I was going to spend the summer."

"Hang on a minute. How the hell does Will know who to talk to? He's a goddamn bean counter for Christ's sake."

"He's not just my accountant and financial advisor, Marty— he's also my friend. I gave him the list. He made the calls. I had to head you off somehow. You weren't listening to me." Liam pinched the bridge of his nose in an effort to stave off the headache that always occurred when he tried to reason with Marty. "I need a break, okay? And not just from conducting."

"Then why are you doing the benefit in Michigan?"

"It's a favor for an old friend."

"What friend? How much are they paying you?" Marty's voice rose a half step. "Where's the contract? I need to go over it before you sign."

"There *is* no contract."

"You can't perform without a contract. I don't care what the reason is, you—"

"I'm hanging up now, Marty. Enjoy your summer. I'll talk to you later, okay?"

"Goddammit, Liam, wait—"

Liam disconnected and shoved the phone in his pocket, heartsick at how their relationship had deteriorated. The summer concert circuit was only one more thing in the list of differences between him and his agent of nearly twenty years. Ever since… since the cancer scare six years ago, Liam had come to realize that he and Marty were poles apart about his career.

But he couldn't think about that now, not while his mind and heart were elsewhere. He made his way to his car, drove back to Dixon's, and headed for the boat. Stopping on the dock, he stared up at the boathouse apartment for a long moment. It didn't go all that well in the coffee shop earlier, but she'd had time to process his reappearance in her life. Maybe he could try again.

When he knocked on her door, he received no answer, and when he tried the knob, it was locked. Her studio had been closed, too. He gazed around the marina, squinting in the bright sunlight that reflected off the water. The big red barn where he'd filled out the papers for the slip had a bait shop. Maybe Carrie's Uncle Noah would know where he could find her.

"Hi, can I help you?" The young man behind the counter gave him a smile as he scooped night crawlers into a container.

"No, I'm just wandering around, getting acquainted with the place." Liam extended his hand. "I'm in berth thirty-eight. Liam Reilly."

"Brandon Mc—oh. Oh!" The kid's brows rose. "Very nice to meet you, sir. My mom's gonna freak when she hears I met you in person. She's a huge fan. She and Dad already have their tickets for your concert."

"That's great. Tell your parents Lawson appreciates their support, okay?" Liam gazed around the shop. "Where's Mr. Dixon?

"He's out gassing up a boat." Brandon jerked his head toward the docks. "He'll be right back in."

"Okay, thanks." Liam wandered among the aisles of fishing gear, amazed there was so much paraphernalia available just to catch a fish. When he and his brothers fished in the farm pond as kids, they had cane poles with balsa wood bobbers.

He walked back to the door and peered out at Noah, chatting with a customer as he filled the tank on a fishing boat rigged out with antennas and fishing poles of all sizes. A bright green bulletin board covered with photographs of people and their catches drew his attention. Right in the center was a print of a young man at the tiller of a wooden sailboat and a girl riding in the bow.

Liam squinted at the photo before pulling his glasses from his shirt pocket. Slipping them on, he plucked the thumbtack and took the picture over to the door to get a better look. God, the kid looked almost exactly like his nephew, Jamie—dark red hair, long, lanky limbs... the boy wore sunglasses, so he couldn't see the color of his eyes.

How weird.

He shook his head with a smile. Didn't they say everyone has a twin somewhere? Jamie would probably get a kick out of knowing that his doppelganger was here in Michigan.

He started to pin the picture back up when his heart began to pound in his chest and his mouth was suddenly dry. He knew the girl in the front of the boat. It was Carrie—wearing the same gauzy flowered shirt she had had on at the coffee shop. Stepping out into the sunlight, he stared at it again. Yeah, it was Carrie alright. The boy looked to be about Jamie's age, fifteen.

Fifteen...oh, Jesus, no way!

His hand shook as he tried to swallow the panic that welled up
in his throat and attempted some quick calculations in his head.
Fifteen years and nine months ago, he and Carrie Halligan had
been in his bed in Montreal.

CHAPTER 4

C louds played tag with the early afternoon sun as Carrie walked along the hard-packed sand of the Lake Michigan shoreline, her thoughts consumed with Liam—and Jack—as they had been most of the day. She didn't keep regular hours at the studio, so when she finished her appointment, she'd locked up and run to the one place she knew she'd find peace—the lake. The lake, the beach, and a camera could always soothe her when she was stressed or feeling blue.

Rounding a curve in the shore she spotted the old lighthouse in the distance. This was her favorite stretch of beach because it was usually quiet and deserted. A freighter moved along the horizon and she watched for a moment, her hand shading her eyes. Lifting the camera, she took several shots of the boat and then turned to get some pictures of the lighthouse.

She had hundreds of photographs of Willow Point lighthouse —shots of the water, the rocky shoreline, the old lighthouse perched on the top of the cliff. But still, she always took pictures whenever she came out to this spot. Each time the light was a little different or the clouds created new shadows on the dunes where the Queen Anne's Lace and beach grass she loved grew wild.

Carrie spread out her beach towel and plopped down on the sand, dropping her canvas bag beside her. Rummaging through the bag, she found the water and apple she'd packed when she got home from work. Not much of a lunch, but her stomach was still uneasy from her encounter with Liam. All morning, she'd replayed the brief meeting, wishing she'd been braver and simply told him everything. Then it would be over and maybe the knot in her belly would subside.

She'd seen him peering in the studio window as she hid in the back room, peeking around the curtained doorway. What a coward she was. Hell, she hadn't even mustered the courage to talk to Eliot yet. No, she'd escaped to the beach the minute she finished for the day, ready to let the lake work its magic on her frazzled nerves.

She munched thoughtfully, unable to get her mind off Liam. She had to tell him about Jack—and probably soon—but not now. And there was more… the whole mess with Marty and the money…

Dammit.

What a tangled web she'd woven by not revealing her pregnancy to Liam from the very beginning. Would it have been easier? Maybe. But what did it matter now?

She finished the apple, took a sip of water, and pulled off her sweatshirt. Using it as a pillow, she lay back in the sand, closing her eyes against the bright rays of the sun. Until a few hours ago, she would have denied vigorously that she was torch-carrying for Liam Reilly, but she *had* lived almost like a nun, never allowing another man to get close to her, devoting herself entirely to her son. His effect on her was beyond disturbing. She hated that he could still stop her dead with just a smile. Too much to think about right now…

The sharp tingle of sand on her bare legs woke Carrie. Opening one eye, she squinted sleepily at the silhouette towering over her, blocking the afternoon sun. Both eyes flew open when she recognized the fiery highlights in Liam's hair.

"Don't you think it's dangerous to fall asleep alone on an empty beach? Anyone could attack you or steal your stuff." His voice was rough.

"I'm on this beach almost every day." She pulled herself to a sitting position, wishing she'd worn something nicer than crumpled denim shorts and a faded yellow T-shirt. "No one bothers me. *Usually.*"

He'd changed into khaki shorts and a green polo shirt under a lightweight navy windbreaker. Worn leather sandals showed his long feet, and his tanned legs were dusted with gold-red hair. A memory of those legs tangled with hers came unbidden to her mind. She sent the picture packing. "What can I do for you, Liam?"

"This morning when we bumped into each other at the coffee shop, I... um... I thought we could get to know each other again." He sat down in the sand a few feet away from her. "We moved so fast in Montreal, it was crazy, but I believed it was real. Then you just... blew me off. I never knew why. When I saw you playing Saturday night, it all came back to me." Pausing, he gazed out across the lake. "I was also pretty surprised by the fact that when I sat down at your table this morning, all I could think about was kissing you."

Carrie's jaw dropped as he continued in a monotone. He wasn't even looking at her. "Ten seconds in the same room and I wanted to drag you away and—well, you get the picture." His mouth twisted. "But you were so cool. You acted like we didn't even know each other."

She dropped her gaze, unable to look him in the eye. Not while she lied through her teeth as she was about to do. "It was a long time ago. I don't remember everything, but I do remember feeling that I *didn't* know you back then. I didn't want to follow you all over the world, waiting in hotel rooms or backstage like some groupie. That wasn't who I wanted to be."

"Really? You certainly had me fooled when you let me send you a ticket to London." His voice was cold. "Yeah, we fell fast and hard. But I opened up to you like I never had with any other woman. We might've made it."

Her heart was pounding so hard, she was amazed he couldn't hear it. "Liam, listen, I—"

He held up one hand as he stared out across the water. Even though they weren't touching, she could feel the tension coiled in his body. Why wouldn't he look at her?

"That's my boat at your uncle's marina and Eliot told me where you lived. When I walked around town earlier, your studio was closed so I came back to your apartment. I guess I thought maybe we could try it again, but you weren't there. So I went down to the bait shop to see if your uncle might know where I could find you."

Now, he was eyeing her. An inkling of fear niggled at her as he continued with almost deliberate indifference. "He was out with a customer, so I wandered around."

Her heart hammered, and her mouth went dry. Still she managed to remain outwardly composed.

What had he seen?

She tried to picture the shop, but her mind was a jumble of fear as he went on, his voice rising.

"You'll never guess what I found on the bulletin board next to a flyer for the fish taxidermist." He pulled a photograph from his pocket and tossed it in her lap.

She already knew what it was. The photo of Jack. Margie had

taken it just last week when they launched the *Penguin,* the sailboat he and Noah had refurbished. Apparently, Noah had pinned the picture on the bulletin board. She sat in silence, trying to calm the clutch of fear in her stomach.

"Where's my son?" Liam demanded. "And don't even bother denying he's mine. My half-blind granny would recognize that boy as a Reilly."

Carrie raised her eyes to his, expecting anger. Prepared for fury. And clearly, he *was* furious, but the pain in his expression shocked her speechless—pain so raw it cut through her like a knife.

"Why would you do that?" His voice was so quiet she had to lean closer to hear his next broken question. "Why? Why would you have my child and not tell me?"

There was no point in denying any of it. "I considered telling you." She slid her eyes away from his rage and anguish to stare at the photo. "More than once."

"What the *fuck,* Carrie?" He was trembling. "It's been fifteen years. You've hidden my son from me for *fifteen years.*"

"I was afraid." Her response was barely audible above the water lapping on the shore. Liam put one finger under her chin, forcing her to look at him.

"Afraid of *what?*" Tears shimmered in his eyes, and bewilderment triumphed over outrage for second.

She bit the inside of her lower lip, trying to control its tremor. She couldn't speak.

"Jesus!" Liam's grip on her chin tightened. "What did you think would happen? Why didn't you tell me you were pregnant?"

"I–I didn't want you like *that*—not forced into a relationship with me because we spent one afternoon in your bed. We'd only known each other for a week. It would've changed your career. Everything you'd worked for. You–you'd end up hating me," she stammered, twisting her head away.

"But you didn't think I'd hate you if you had my baby and never told me?" His hands clenched into fists, turning his knuckles white. "What the fuck is wrong with you?"

Carrie swallowed hard, determined not to let the tears flow. "I don't know. I thought we were over. Then when Jack was born, you were becoming this—this celebrity. I knew we'd never fit into that life, not a wife and a baby." Pausing, she searched for words to defuse his anger. "Later, I suppose I could've called you. Okay, I *should've* called you, but there was no right time. I was so scared of losing him. He's all I have."

"What the hell are you talking about?" Confusion and fury flashed in his eyes. He shoved his fingers through his hair, pressing it back against his head.

"I couldn't have a custody battle with you," she said. "I knew you'd win. I didn't have anything to fight you with. The best I could hope for would be joint custody, and how could we have done that? Where would *you* fit a child in your life? It seemed impossible." Breathless, she wrapped her arms around her knees and stared out at the lake.

He rose, and she raised her head to watch him through blurry eyes, half hoping he'd simply walk away. Anger showed in his stiff frame as he paced the beach, head down, hands fisted at his sides. Finally, he stopped and plopped down. "How in the hell could you do this? Didn't I at least deserve a chance to be in on the decision?" He peered into her face. "Dammit, Carrie, I just want to—" His fingers curled into a fist.

She shifted away from him.

Dropping his hand, he rested his forehead on his bent knees. When he raised his head, he closed his eyes, the muscles working in his jaw. He swallowed hard. "That's his name? Jack?"

"Jackson Michael Halligan." Carrie forced a wan smile.

"You gave him *my* middle name?" Liam's face lit up just for an instant as she nodded. "And why Jackson?"

"Jackson was my father's first name."

"And he was born... in late January?" She could see him calculating in his head.

"January thirtieth, actually."

"God, that's my brother Duncan's birthday."

There didn't seem to be a good response to that so she sat quietly. He stood again and walked up the beach a little ways. She wished she could read his mind, know what he was thinking. He walked back to her and she leapt up, sliding Jack's picture into her pocket. When he reached out for it, she handed it to him.

"This is the real reason Eliot called me to do the benefit, isn't it?" He waved the snapshot before pocketing it himself. "Why did he decide to come to me now?"

"I don't know. He believes I should have told you from the beginning, but I made him promise to stay out of it. He's getting older—almost eighty and his health isn't great. Maybe he's tying up loose ends or crossing this off his bucket list." She gave a little shrug when her attempt at lightening the mood fell flat.

"This is one hell of a loose end."

"Don't blame Eliot for any of this." She reached out to touch his arm, but snapped her hand back before she made contact. One touch and any chance of clear thinking would be gone. "He's been by my side since the day Dad died. His choices came from a deep devotion to me." She exhaled a long breath. "Including coming to you now, I guess."

Liam shoved his hand into his jacket pocket, kicking at the sand as he withdrew the picture. "Tell me about Jack." He held up the photo, staring at it with an intensity that sent a shiver racing the length of her spine. "He could be my nephew Jamie's twin. That's actually why this picture stopped me. He's sixteen, Duncan's youngest."

"Jack's beautiful," she replied, not guarding her words for the first time since she'd seen Liam. "And smart and completely charming." *He's you.* She only wished she dared say those words out loud. "He'll be a sophomore at—" She hesitated a fraction of a second. "—in the fall. He loves to swim and read and sail. He's funny and curious about everything." The breeze off the lake raised gooseflesh on her arms.

He reached down and grabbed her hoodie. After shaking the sand out, he tossed it at her. "Get your stuff, let's walk. By God, you're going to tell me *all* of it."

Carrie zipped on her sweatshirt and then picked up her belongings. "You want lunch?" She slung the canvas tote over her shoulder.

"Lunch?" He stared at her aghast. "Are you kidding? I want to see my son. Where is he?"

"He's away for the summer." Brushing the sand off the back of her shorts, she started down the beach at a brisk pace.

He followed, jogging alongside her on the hard-packed sand. "Where is he?" Suspicion darkened his eyes. "Are you hiding him from me?"

"Oh, for God's sake, Liam." When she stopped short, he almost ran into her. "I didn't even know you were going to be here, how could I be *hiding* him from you?"

"Actually, that's exactly what you've been doing his whole life." His hair ruffled in the breeze as he rubbed the back of his neck. "I'm still dealing with seeing *you* again. Now I find out I have a fifteen-year-old son I never knew existed. Why don't you cut me some slack and just tell me where he is?"

"He's at camp," she snapped. "He'll be there until the end of August."

"I want to meet him. I want to talk to him. Where's the camp?" He started walking toward the marina, but she didn't follow him. He turned to face her. "Where's the camp?" he demanded through gritted teeth.

"You need to let me talk to him before you go charging up

there." She caught up to him. "He's not prepared to meet his absent father out of the blue like this."

"*Absent father?* What the—that's not *my* fault, is it?" His voice hardened. "*You* are the reason I've been *absent*. That certainly would never have been my choice!" His eyes narrowed into tight, angry slits. "What exactly have you told him about me?"

Chewing her lower lip, she turned away from his intense scrutiny. "Nothing."

"Surely he's asked about his father once or twice in his lifetime. Did you tell him I was dead or that I abandoned you?"

"Of course not!"

"It's a legitimate question." He sounded perfectly reasonable in spite of the rage simmering near the surface. "How the hell am I supposed to know what you've been thinking or doing the last fifteen years? Exactly what *have* you been telling my son about me?"

"I haven't told him *anything* about you, okay?" His fierce expression had her backing up several steps, and she eyed him warily. "Look, I told him things didn't work out between us—that I was young and I chose not to tell you about being pregnant. He doesn't know who you are or how I met you. All he knows is that *I* wanted him more than anything."

"So *he* knows *I* don't know anything about him?"

Carrie nodded.

Liam threw up his hands. "He knows that he has a father out there somewhere, who doesn't even know he exists, and he's totally okay with that?"

"I seriously doubt he's *totally okay* with it, but it is what it is. He's not the only kid in town being raised by a single mother. You don't understand. This is the way our life has always been—just him and me." Tears of frustration stung her eyes. "Would you rather I'd told him you were dead or that you didn't want him?"

"Goddammit, Carrie, I would've preferred that you'd told *me* you were pregnant to begin with!" He didn't hide his fury as ruddy color rose from his collar. "Were you *ever* planning to tell me? Or was I going to find a thirty-year-old, red-headed stranger on my doorstep one day saying, 'Hi, Dad'? Did you ever think about any of this, or was it easier to be stupid and pretend none of it mattered?"

She turned away and then spun back, blinking back tears. "For God's sake, it's all I've thought about since the day he was born! I knew the time would come when I had to tell you both. It's a moot point now, isn't it?"

"Damn straight."

They walked toward the marina in stilted silence, Carrie's own aggravation building as he strode several feet ahead of her. He had a right to be mad, even furious, but couldn't he try to see her side? Even just a little? Her conscience nudged her.

Give him a break. He just found out he has a son he never knew about. Let him cool off. Especially since he doesn't know everything yet.

She picked up her pace, intending to leave him to work through the anger. Then they could talk.

He stopped her with a hand on her shoulder.

"It was real big of you not to make me out the bad guy in this. Thanks. Thanks a bunch." In spite of his words, his voice wasn't quite so harsh.

Carrie stared up into eyes so filled with hurt her heart ached. "Liam, I'm... sorry. I didn't make this choice to hurt *you*. Please believe me." She stopped, placing a hand on his arm. "I made it to protect *me*. And Jack. When I found out I was pregnant, I didn't know what else to do. I thought we were over." She tightened her grip. Although his jacket was warm from the sun, he was trembling. "You were in Europe. We hadn't known each other long enough to—" She didn't know what she was trying to say, so she shrugged and gave up.

His expression hadn't softened, but as he gazed down at her, confusion clouded his eyes. Suddenly his mouth closed over hers. Without a second's hesitation, Carrie swayed toward him as his lips moved fiercely on hers, his tongue tracing her lower lip. He yanked her body to his almost brutally, and yet she lifted her arms to circle his neck. His big hands moved over her back and down to her hips, claiming her as he pulled her against him. She curled her fingers into the thick hair at his nape. Her tongue met his in an intimate duel that left her shaken.

His lips softened to a gentler kiss, and she tasted the salty tang of his tears as well as her own. At last, he lifted his lips a fraction of an inch.

"Dear God, Carrie. What's happening?" he whispered. Tears shimmered in his eyes when he pulled back, but he simply allowed them to roll down his cheeks.

CHAPTER 5

Her wide-eyed innocence and purity did Liam in—the same expression that messed with his mind from the first moment he saw Carrie Halligan. The very look that heated his blood the afternoon they spent in bed in Montreal. When she'd gazed into his face and whispered, "I'm sorry," that was it. He was a goner—the anger momentarily overcome by desire so strong he nearly took her right there on the sand. How could a woman live in this world for forty years, raise a son, run a business, and yet seem so completely untouched? And Christ almighty, why couldn't he stop thinking about touching her?

Walking along the shore in silence together, the yard or so between them seemed vast. When they reached the docks, they agreed to go to neutral corners for a little while. She had an appointment with a client, while he and Will were expected in Traverse City to meet with TSO's artistic director. He was dying to hear everything about Jack, but he and Carrie both needed time to regroup. Tonight would be soon enough. Drained mentally, emotionally, even physically, he was still as pissed as he'd ever been in his life, but also exhilarated.

I have a son—a teenage son!

He'd believed he would never have a child—since the cancer, that door had been forever closed. And now, here was a miracle. His son.

Liam ached to meet him, to see him, to talk to him. The picture from the bulletin board burned a hole in his pocket. He pulled it out again and again, examining it for—what? He didn't know. Himself, perhaps?

Sitting on the hood of his roadster in the marina parking lot, he gazed out across the bay, waiting for Will. After the meeting in Traverse City, they were driving by Interlochen Arts Academy to tour the concert venue. He was grateful to have his friend along. The morning had been so overwhelming, Liam wasn't sure he could focus on any of it.

He gave the picture another moment or two of scrutiny before footsteps crunched on the gravel.

"Hey, whatcha got?" A lively breeze tousled Will's blond hair as he approached.

"Take a look." Liam handed him the photo.

Holding the photo up to the sun, Will squinted at it and then grinned. "Geez, that kid's getting tall. When did Duncan get a sailboat?"

Liam pulled himself up with effort and slid into the car, surprised at the toll emotion had taken on his body. Suddenly, he was exhausted and more than anything, wanted go back to his warm bed on the *Allegro* and sleep. "That's not Jamie."

"It's not?" Instead of opening the passenger door, Will hopped over it and dropped into the red leather seat, still clutching the picture. "Sure looks like Jamie."

"It's *my* son, Will."

Will's jaw dropped and for a moment, he was speechless. "*Your* son? Who sent you this?"

"I found it on the bulletin board in the bait shop." Liam inclined his head toward the red barn at the bottom of the hill.

"Where? How? Wha—"

Liam couldn't help grinning. Will was clearly flummoxed, his reaction pretty much summing up his own feelings. "He's Carrie's. Well, Carrie's and *mine*."

"Carrie? Carrie from McGill?" Will threw up his hands. "Jesus! Okay, back up and start at the beginning." He glanced at his watch. "But drive." Then his eyes narrowed as he eyed Liam, slumped in the driver's seat. "Or would you rather we postponed these meetings? I can do that. We can go back to the boat and have a drink. Seriously, you look like you could use one."

"No, I promised I'd do this, and I will." Liam took a deep breath. "Would you mind driving?"

"Sure."

They switched places, and Liam rode silently for a few minutes, grateful to have a friend like Will Brody. They'd met when Liam conducted *The Nutcracker* for Chicago Ballet and Will was a supernumerary in the production. A chance conversation in the green room about investments developed into a business relationship, which quickly became a friendship. More than once, he'd thought about asking Will to take over as his agent. He knew Marty would be ugly about it, even though Marty himself had relinquished most of the day-to-day career management.

Maybe it was time to make a change. After all, it was Will, not Marty, who'd been there through the cancer battle, staying at the hospital with him for radiation and driving him to doctor's appointments. Marty had been house hunting in California. While Will brought him food from Chicago's finest restaurants in an effort to tempt him to eat, Marty took a trip to Hawaii with his latest girlfriend.

Will had picked up Liam's parents at O'Hare, sympathized as Liam overshared his frustration with Marty, and listened without judgment one long night as he confided the story of Carrie Halligan. Will was the one who hung out backstage during concerts and ran interference for him. Marty rarely made it to a concert anymore. The Internet and cell phones had made his physical presence unnecessary. His focus was to keep Liam on the podium, and he could do that from his home in Malibu—a house that Liam's lucrative career had made possible.

Even as he told Will what he'd discovered about Jack, he still couldn't wrap his mind around the fact that he had a son.

"Did she say why she never told you?" Will asked, turning onto the highway heading east to Traverse City.

"Apparently, she was scared I'd try to take him away from her."

"Oh, come on," Will scoffed. "That's crazy."

"I know." Liam leaned against the headrest, letting the sun warm his face. "Don't ask me what she was thinking. She's an enigma. But by God, I'm gonna know my son and he's going to know me."

"So he's at camp all summer?"

"That's what she said. I think she was telling the truth. We're having dinner on the boat tonight to talk."

Will glanced at him with a smile. "Want Cap'n Tony and me to make ourselves scarce?"

"Yeah, that'd be great."

"No prob." Will's grin widened as he guided the car into a parking spot near the symphony offices. "Actually Noah and his wife, Margie, invited me to go night fishing. I'll take Tony with me. Feel free to call if you need to be rescued."

The meeting at the symphony went well as the artistic director agreed to their music selections. Eyeing Liam with concern, Will stepped in to take charge of the details, asking all the right questions about the orchestra and verifying schedules. Liam, whose head still throbbed, appreciated his friend's assistance. Everything seemed right on track.

By midafternoon, Liam's headache had all but disappeared as

they drove onto the Interlochen Arts Academy campus to tour Corson Auditorium. Dave Lawson and his music camp board had pulled out all the stops for the event—it was already nearly sold out despite being set for the last Saturday in July. Patron tickets included a wine and cheese reception in the lobby before the concert, and a post-concert gala would take place on the lawn.

Short, round, and hyperactive, Dave bubbled over with enthusiasm, obviously thrilled with Liam's decision to conduct. "Thanks so very much for agreeing to do this, Maestro! You're a huge draw for our event!"

"My pleasure, Dave. Your summer program's one of the finest. I'm glad to be a part of it." He couldn't help but grin at the balding man, who reminded him of Mr. Toad from the books of his childhood.

"I know this is also a vacation for you, Maestro, but we'd love to have you come up and tour our camp while you're in the area." Dave smiled. "The kids would get a kick out of meeting you, and you could see what you're raising funds for. As a matter of fact, we're doing a recital this Sunday afternoon for the junior piano campers. I think you'd enjoy it." His smile expanded. "The five-to-seven-year-olds are getting their feet wet onstage, and the counselors get to see their students shine. Very casual, but fun." Stopping for a breath, he wiped his brow. "A couple of the older ones will perform, too."

"Call me Liam, please. And yes, I'd like to see the recital, thanks." A glance at Will's furrowed brow made him add, "What time? I could slip in when everyone's seated and meet folks afterward."

"It starts at two. Eliot can give you directions. Oh, and tell Eliot his star is closing the recital with Jelly Roll Morton. That'll get him up there." Dave extended his hand to both men, then trotted off.

Will shook his head. "That man's energy could light up a

small town. I'll bet he's good with those kids. He's a big kid himself." He reached for the passenger door as Liam slid into the driver's seat. "You okay to drive?"

"Yeah, I'm better, thanks." Liam started the engine and headed back toward Willow Bay. "I've been thinking… what would you say to taking over as my agent-slash-manager?"

Silence from the seat next to him drew Liam's eyes from the road for a brief moment.

Will seemed pensive. "Are you sure you're ready to let Marty go? He's been managing your career for twenty years." Will shifted in his seat, clearly uncomfortable with the turn of events that could suddenly change his own career. "Don't get me wrong, I want the job. Hell, I'm practically doing it now. But are you *sure* this is what you want?"

Liam didn't hesitate. "Absolutely. This isn't a whim, it's been coming for a long time. Marty disengaged when he left Chicago for LA five years ago. We never see him. Besides, you've seen the schedules he's put together the last few years. He seems to think I'm running out of time—like he's afraid he can't sell me since the cancer and so he's trying to milk the last of my appeal. Sometimes I think he never really believed that my talent took us this far."

"Well, *I* know it's your talent. But he did create the image, Maestro, and it's been a helluva profitable ride—for everyone."

"True," Liam agreed. "But I'm done being manipulated. I'm sick of being Marty's… puppet. His stupid toy."

Will nodded as Liam went on. "I let him create this illusion around me and went along with it because all I wanted to do was conduct. And frankly, after Carrie, I didn't care who was on my arm—or in my bed for that matter—at first."

Embarrassment heated his cheeks as he recalled the early years before he'd become friends with Will. Long tours, a different city each week, hotel rooms, dressing rooms, women—

women whose names he didn't remember, whose faces were a blur. Even if they weren't in his bed, they were on his arm.

Until the cancer. After his treatments were over, he'd opted out of the glittering parties and glitzy events, and the battles with his agent grew more frequent, more intense.

He blew out a frustrated breath. "I just can't be the guy Marty created anymore. I haven't been able to be him for a long, long time. You know that. How many arguments have you refereed between us?"

"Quite a few, but he's never going to let go of his own agenda. Not at this late date, my friend."

Liam stroked his beard as he drove. "You're right. He was pissed as hell when I told him I wasn't going to tour this summer and that I accepted this gig for Lawson."

"I was there for the fireworks, remember?"

The sun hovered low in the sky as Liam drove into town. "If I'd paid attention to Carrie and not gotten caught up in Marty's agenda, maybe I could have been in my son's life. I don't know that for sure, but I do know I'm sick of fighting with Marty. You know as well as I do that *this* news will send him right into orbit."

"Yeah, it will." Will smiled. "Okay, so now what, Maestro?"

"I haven't got a clue," Liam groaned as he turned down Waterfront Street. "That woman can still drive me out of my mind with one look, despite making me so mad I could cheerfully shake her stupid. She's locked up so tight I may never get to her, but I've got to try. I'm not losing her again. At least not without finding out what might be possible."

He scanned the street, peering at the storefronts. "And if nothing's possible between us, there's still Jack—my son thinks I don't know he exists. I gotta fix that, even if his mother and I never figure out how to communicate. And while I'm doing all that, I have to decide what I want to do with the rest of my damn career." With a weary sigh, Liam pulled up in front of Carrie's studio. "What do you say, Will? How about we figure *that* part out together?"

"I'm in." Will hopped out of the car. "I've had some great ideas, but Marty never seems very open to talking."

"Like what?"

"Like a movie score." Excitement colored his tone. "Marty's kept you on the podium, but hey, who knows? I can start looking around. Make some calls."

"A movie score? Damn, that'd be great!"

"You've been composing practically your whole career. You've got *tons* of music. Why not see if it can work somewhere?"

Will's enthusiasm was contagious, and Liam couldn't help grinning. His career had been stalled on the podium for years because Marty Justice had been afraid to let him spread his musical wings. Conducting was wonderful, but he was more than ready to try new outlets for his talent.

"Didn't you tell me Marty turned down invitations to do conservatory workshops and summer seminars after your diagnosis? Well, you're past your five years clean, so I think you should go for that, too. You're a terrific instructor." Will stopped to take a breath. "What do you think?"

"I think I could get excited about my job again." Liam clapped his friend on the shoulder. "Say you'll represent me. I'll handle Marty."

CHAPTER 6

C arrie slumped at her desk, clicking mindlessly through the proofs of Mariette Hollister's twins. The morning played in an endless loop in her head. First, Liam at the coffee shop and then later on the beach. Damn the man for still having the power to make her feel helpless, foolish, and utterly irrational. But, oh God, it was so good to be in his arms. His hands still set her on fire. His mouth was still magic, his kiss still a heart-stopper.

That was the upside.

The downside? Her organized, tidy, everything-in-its-place life was in chaos. Last week, her precious son spending the summer away at camp was her biggest issue. Today, it was figuring out how to tell that cherished kid who his father was.

Oh, and by the way, he's on a yacht fifty feet from our door.

The bell above the front door jingled as Liam walked in with a tall blond guy in tow. "Hey." There was that slow, sexy smile Carrie still fantasized about. "Carrie, this is my friend, Will Brody. I told him about you and Jack. We thought we'd stop by on our way back from Interlochen so he could meet you." The message was loud and clear—Will Brody was someone he trusted with the intimate details of his life.

"Hi there, Carrie." Will's blue eyes crinkled at the corners as he took her fingers in a warm grip. Definitely the all-American surfer type—tanned, muscular, and handsome with streaky blond hair, carefully mussed. "I'm very glad to meet you."

"Hello, Will." Carrie returned the smile. "Did you drive up with Liam?"

"Actually no, I came up on the boat."

He and Carrie discussed the cruise from Chicago to Willow Bay while Liam walked around the studio, studying the photographs on the wall. He stopped before an eight-by-ten of Jack taken by the lighthouse at sunset and framed in ebony—an extraordinary photo Carrie was particularly proud of. The setting sun gleamed red and gold on Jack's hair, creating a shimmering halo effect that Eliot had always referred to as the "angel shot." Liam bent to examine it more closely, his eyes narrowed.

"He was about ten in that photo," Carrie offered. "It's one of my favorites. The sun was exactly right and I happened to have my camera. Poor Jack, I shoot him relentlessly—along with the lighthouse. I'm in heaven when I can get them both in the same frame." She hoped her breezy explanation would lighten the heavy atmosphere created by Liam's thundercloud expression.

"Mind if I take a look?" Will asked. Carrie nodded and Liam stepped aside. "Good Lord, he really is all Reilly, isn't he?"

"That he is," Liam replied quietly, meeting Carrie's eyes in the deepening shadows of the studio. She felt the look all the way to her toes—a mix of apprehension and sensuality.

Will ambled around the studio. "Do you use a digital camera?"

Carrie tore her eyes away from Liam's. "No... um... I mean, yes, I do use one when I'm just out taking pictures or for news-paper shots or–or when I'm not in the studio." Her answers stumbled under the intensity of Liam's piercing gaze. Was it anger at seeing the photo or something else? "I prefer traditional film for portraits. I use both for weddings. It depends——" The back door opened and Julie's voice interrupted her.

"Hey, kiddo!" Julie called out from the back room of the studio. "You aren't going to *believe* who I saw coming out of The Grind this morning."

"Oh, I bet I would." Carrie glanced at Liam and Will who exchanged curious smiles. Apparently her friend hadn't bothered to shut the door while using the washroom.

Carrie went to the curtained doorway and stuck her head in. "Hey, Jules——" she began, but the older woman rushed on as she flushed and turned on the water to wash her hands.

"That hunky symphony conductor from Chicago," Julie announced, tearing off a couple of paper towels. "Perry says he's here for the Lawson benefit. Hot damn, Caro! We saw him conduct in San Francisco last August when we went out to see the kids. That man's butt in tails made two hours of Mahler almost bearable!" Her dramatic sigh was pure Julie. "Those shoulders and that hair? Yum! Think a younger Jeff Bridges in that movie he did with Barbara Streisand. You know the one? God, he was so *hot* in that film." She still hadn't stopped to take a breath.

Carrie tried again. "Jules, hey——"

But Julie talked right over her, much to Liam and Will's amusement. "Do you remember the name of that movie? Lord, if Charlie ever kicks it, I'm calling this conductor guy. I could use a little sexy culture. Perry says he's staying at Noah's—that he came on a *yacht* or something. Do you believe that? Have you seen it yet?" She waltzed into the studio, her blonde hair flying. "Have you seen him?"

"Yeah, I've seen him."

Julie stopped short, giving Carrie a long curious stare. Then her blue eyes squinted as she spotted the two men standing by the window.

"Oh crap!" Julie came around the desk. "Holy Mary, mother of our Lord. It's *you*."

Both men burst out laughing as Liam came forward, extending a hand. "Hi there. I'm Liam Reilly, and this is Will Brody." He nodded toward his friend. "And you are?"

Julie closed her eyes and swept her hair behind her ears. Her face flushed, but she carried it off with her own brand of panache. "Julie Miles, Carrie's big-mouthed and very embarrassed friend. Nice to meet you." She shook hands with Liam and glanced at Carrie. "Thanks a lot, pal!"

Carrie put her hands up in a helpless gesture and shrugged. "I tried to stop you."

"So you're not a big Mahler fan?" Liam crossed his arms over his chest while Will and Carrie snickered like kids.

"Not at all. How do you know Carrie? Through Eliot?" She stood in the center of the studio, her eyes shifting from Liam to her friend and then back again. Carrie still hadn't said a word. Suddenly Julie's eyes widened. "Oh, good God! Carrie?" She turned, a huge question on her face, and Carrie knew she'd doped it out within ten seconds.

"Liam is Jack's father." Carrie watched her friend assess the Maestro.

She walked back and forth, arms folded under her perfect breasts, looking him over as if he was a used car and she was considering kicking his tires. She shook back her blonde mane. "Well... he certainly is. Where the hell've you been, bucko?"

Liam and Will both straightened at the about-face in Julie's attitude, glancing at one another, wide-eyed.

Will shook his head. "I think she's going to kick your ass, pal." He gave the words a corner-of-the-mouth delivery without even *attempting* to lower his voice.

"No, wait." Although Carrie put her hand up, she was curious to see exactly how far Julie would go to defend her friend's honor.

Will was probably wrong about the ass-kicking, but Julie was sure to give Liam a serious piece of her mind. "Liam didn't know about Jack. I never told him."

"Are you kidding me, Caro?" Julie shot Liam a puzzled look. "Why not? What's wrong with this guy?

"What happened to all that admiration for your great butt?" Will muttered.

Liam shrugged as Carrie spoke to her friend, who was still eyeing both men with open curiosity. Carrie gave her the two-minute version, promising more details at the earliest opportunity.

"This isn't pure coincidence, is it?" Julie asked. "Do I sense Eliot's fine hand in this reunion?"

"You do. He's the one who brought Liam here."

"Good for him. Who'd have thought the old cuss had it in him?" Julie grinned. "God Almighty. Who'd ever believe *your* life is a damned made-for-TV movie?"

"I didn't plan for it to be." With a grim smile, Carrie jerked her head toward the back of the shop. When it came to her friends, Julie could be as unrelenting as a bull terrier. Carrie really didn't want her questioning Liam—or revealing things she and Liam hadn't discussed. "How about I catch you later, okay?"

Julie turned to Liam. "So what *are* your intentions, Sparky?" Carrie's frustrated sigh drew a glance, but Jules stood her ground. "I have a right to ask, Carrie. You're my dearest friend."

"First of all," Liam began, "I intend to meet my son."

"You married or engaged or anything?"

"Nope." Liam shook his head slowly while Will let out a whoop of laughter.

Julie glared at him.

Liam elbowed him in the ribs.

"Come on, it's okay. Truly." Carrie put her arm around her friend's shoulders. With a grimace, Julie allowed herself be led to the back door of the studio. "I'll fill you in later, I promise."

"Are you *sure* you're okay?" Julie asked. "We really need to talk."

"I know we do. Believe me, I know." Carrie hugged her. "I love you, Jules."

"We are *so* getting together. I'll call you in the morning."

As soon as Carrie closed the door, Liam and Will hooted with laughter. Returning to the studio, she stepped around them to flip the sign over and lock the front door, rolling her eyes at their antics.

"God, Carrie, I think I'm in love." Will was practically breathless with glee. "She's a knock-out."

Liam nodded his agreement, doing a rotten job of keeping a straight face. "A knock-out alright, but kinda scary." He finally let go with a giant guffaw. "She really wanted to hurt me."

"She probably could've taken you." Will leaned against the counter. "She struts like she's on a Paris runway. Damn, she's hot!"

"As it happens, she *is* a model." Carrie couldn't help laughing. Julie always made a serious first impression. "And she *is* hot, but she's also fiercely loyal. Let that be a lesson to both of you. We take care of each other in this town."

After reassuring Liam she would meet him on the boat for supper, she shooed them out.

Julie was the best, ready to protect her friend at the first sign of trouble. Her attitude wasn't the problem—Carrie treasured that. No, the problem was the fact that in no time at all, she'd realized Jack was the connection between Carrie and Liam. Perry's imagination had to be working overtime as well, and since his coffee shop was the town's gossip hub, the entire population would have the scoop by noon tomorrow.

Maestro Liam Reilly is Jack Halligan's long-lost father.

Just thinking about it made her head throb. Was there any way to get home and into the tub without running into a single townsperson? Maybe—if she scooted out the back door and zipped down the hill behind the boathouse. Despite his smile, she knew Liam was still furious. Why had she *ever* agreed to dinner? Her shoulders sagged. *That* event was going to take every emotional resource she possessed.

And her resources were in very short supply.

CHAPTER 7

"Carrie, where *are* you?" Julie yelled up the loft steps.

"Up here. I'm in the tub." Carrie had settled into the bubbles, hoping to relax. Closing her eyes, she laid her head back against the rounded edge of the bathtub.

Julie pounded up the stairs, appearing in the doorway a few seconds later. Their camaraderie still amazed Carrie. She was perfectly comfortable with her friend coming in to chat while she was in the tub. Even in college, she hadn't been one run to around the dorm clad only in a towel or take a shower in front of the other girls. Somehow she'd never developed the confidence to be so unselfconscious. But Julie brought such matter-of-factness to all things that having her make herself at home in the bathroom felt entirely normal.

"Okay, every detail and don't even *think* of leaving anything out." Julie dropped the toilet lid and plopped down, her legs extended out in front of her on the fuzzy yellow rug. "Talk, kiddo."

Carrie gave her a long look, but Julie's stern stare told her she was brooking no argument about this discussion.

"C'mon," Julie prodded. "You didn't really think I was going to wait until tomorrow morning to hear this, did you?"

"Foolishly, I thought you might." Carrie reached through her bubbles for the glass of wine sitting on the edge of the tub. "Do you want some wine? It's in the kitchen."

"Wine? Hell no. Right now I need information."

"I think you've pretty much got most of the story." Carrie sipped her wine. "Liam Reilly is Jack's father."

"My God, girl. That man's to die for. If *he's* the high water mark for your love life, no freakin' wonder you hardly ever date." Julie's eyes sparkled. "How did you keep this a secret from me all this time? Oh, and by the way, don't *ever* do that again."

"I kept it a secret from everyone but Eliot. I couldn't talk about him. It was—too hard."

"Why didn't you tell him you were pregnant, you idiot? I don't get that at all. He's Jack's father. He had a right to know. It's not like he's a serial killer or anything."

"We'd only known each other for a week when I got pregnant. By the time I found out, he was in Europe. I couldn't face him, not with a pregnancy. He's a decent guy. He'd have wanted to marry me, and his whole life would've been completely messed up." She set her glass back on the edge of the tub.

"Oh, and yours wasn't?"

"My life was already in chaos with Dad's death and our farm going up for sale because of his gambling debts." Carrie squeezed creamy shower gel onto a bath sponge. Lathering it up, she spread some on her leg and reached for her razor. "By the time I found out I was pregnant, I knew I wasn't going to be playing in piano competitions. It wasn't what *I* wanted anyway—it was Dad's dream for me to be a concert pianist like Mother. I'd lived it for so long, I didn't even have any dreams of my own."

"You'd had sex with *that* man and you say you didn't have any dreams? Cripes, Carrie, what about him? *He's* a dream."

"Jules, we'd known each other a *week*." Carrie drew the razor up her calf. "I didn't want to be following him around the world, waiting in hotel rooms and backstage until he got tired of me and moved on. That's exactly what would have happened if I'd told him. I especially didn't want that life with a baby. There's no way we could have made it work."

"Why didn't you have an abortion?" As usual, Julie went for the blunt question.

Carrie didn't hesitate. "I couldn't. That was never an option."

"You were in love with him?"

Meeting her friend's probing gaze straight on, Carrie admitted, "I was nuts about him. It was heaven, and I love—um—*loved* him so much it hurt. But we never would have made it. Love wasn't enough. With a baby, I needed security, and he needed to follow his dream. It was doomed from the start."

"Why?" Julie leaned forward earnestly. "Look at you. You're already glowing and he hasn't been in town twenty-four hours." She sat back with a knowing smirk. "He's already kissed you, hasn't he?"

"The glow is from this hot bath, dummy. Get real." Carrie busied herself with the other leg.

Julie's eyes narrowed. "Shit. Now you're blushing. He *did* kiss you, didn't he?" She stamped her feet, chortling. "Oh, good God!"

Carrie's cheeks burned. She focused on the razor.

"Was it hot?" Julie persisted.

"Okay, he kissed me on the beach this morning. But first it was anger and then sympathy, nothing more." Carrie confessed without raising her eyes. "I told him about Jack and of course, I cried. He was furious, but I also think he felt sorry for me."

"Did he use his tongue?" Julie asked, standing up to look through the assortment of makeup on the vanity.

"Oh, my God, Julianne. Are we in junior high here? I *cannot* believe you asked me that." Carrie glowered at her friend. She finished shaving and dropped her leg back in the sudsy water.

"Ha! He did. I knew it. I saw how he was staring at you earlier." Julie looked at her in the mirror and winked. "It wasn't sympathy, honey. Sympathy never involves a man putting his tongue down your throat." She opened a compact of blusher and brushed pink across her already faultless cheekbones. "How did he react to the news about Jack?"

"Pissed beyond words. Then he cried." Carrie's saw Julie's eyes on her in the mirror. "Well, not sobbing or anything, just a few tears."

Very touching and sexy tears.

"Seriously? How'd you even tell him? Was he freaked?" Julie smudged shadow onto her eyelids, but Carrie could tell she was measuring her reactions.

"He was freaked alright." Carrie rolled her eyes. "*I* didn't tell him. He found Jack's picture in the bait shop. But that was *after* I saw him in the Grind." Bubbles floated as Carrie expelled a breath. "I just acted casual this morning. I never even mentioned Jack. So when he dropped that bomb on the beach later, I was ready for him to be furious—and he was. But I never expected him to be so *hurt*. I mean stabbed-in-the-heart hurt"—she put her hand on her chest—"because I'd kept Jack from him. Even more hurt that I've never told Jack who his father is."

"Do you blame him?" Julie sounded infuriatingly reasonable. "After all, how would you feel if you found out you had a fifteen-year-old son you knew nothing about? Who knew nothing about you?"

"I'd be mad as hell and hurt," Carrie admitted. "I guess I don't blame him." She *didn't* blame him, but she hoped he'd see her reasoning soon. He was Jack's father and keeping them apart was wrong. She regretted it, but she had no idea how to make it up to either of them, except to try to make the transition from strangers to father and son as easy as possible. Liam had every right to be furious with her, but now that he was here, she couldn't bear him being unhappy with her.

Not when he can still light a fire in me with a look. Dear God, I have to get myself under control.

And there was so much more she had to confess, she really hoped he could cool off and understand.

"How do you think Jack's going to react?" Julie sat back down on the toilet seat.

Carrie blinked and shook her head. "I have absolutely no clue. None."

"I think he'll be thrilled to know his father. Margie told me a couple of months ago that he said something to her and Noah about trying to find him when he turned eighteen."

"He said *that?*" She was floored. Jack had never mentioned anything about finding his father to her, even though she knew he had to be curious.

"Well, yeah. Did you think he never wonders?" Julie's blue eyes darkened in the artificial light of the bathroom. "You'd get Mom of the Year anytime, Caro, but it's only natural for him to wonder about his father."

"I assumed he thought about it. I've considered telling him, but I'm such a damn coward." Carrie wrung out the plushy net sponge and hung it over the spigot. "Mostly, I couldn't face Liam again. He makes me feel so... I don't even have a word for it." She gave her a friend a little helpless shrug.

"Turned on?" Julie offered with a grin. "Horny? Hot?"

Carrie couldn't help laughing. "Yep, all those things and more. But you know, our issues are still the same as they were before." She shoved the drain open with her toe. With a loud gurgle, the tub began emptying. "Nothing's changed. I'm still not gonna follow him around the world, waiting backstage, even if he might *possibly* want me to. And I'm most certainly not going to allow him to take Jack anywhere with him."

"Carrie, he just got here, and you're already borrowing trouble. You're still in love with him." Julie tossed her a bath towel. "Don't deny it. After all this time, you are still as hot for him now as you were then."

"What if I am? What good is it going to do me?" Carrie caught the towel and wrapped it around herself. "Noah said he's only rented that berth until the end of July. I have no idea how he even feels about me right now. He's pissed, but he's being decent —only because he wants to see Jack."

"So when does that happen?"

"Actually, I'm hoping I can convince him to wait until Sunday. I'm having dinner with him tonight on that boat." She jerked her thumb in the general direction of the docks as she stepped out onto the bath mat. "I need to get a feel for what Liam's thinking about *me* before I bring Jack into the picture."

Julie gave her a puzzled glance and then sighed. "You aren't going to convince him of anything if you intend to wear those khaki pants and that powder-blue granny twin set you have laid out on the bed." She opened the glass door of the shower stall that butted up to the garden tub. "Hop in the shower, rinse off, and wash your hair, kid. I'll find you something to wear that will knock his socks off."

Carrie dropped the towel and slipped into the shower, turning on the water full blast. She pivoted slowly to rinse the bubbles off her shoulders. "What's wrong with the blue twin set? I just bought it."

"Yeah, well, it isn't exactly enticing." Julie's voice floated in from the bedroom. Carrie imagined her rooting through the closet.

She shampooed quickly, wrapped herself in a terry robe, and wandered into the bedroom, using a small hand towel on her dark curls. "I don't think I'm going for *enticing*, I'm thinking more of *grown-up*. He accused me of being a selfish child this afternoon. I need to present as a mature adult tonight."

"You need to present as a sexy mama tonight if you want to convince him to wait 'til Sunday to meet his son." Julie pulled several dresses from the back of the closet. "Besides, enticing can be very mature. Here, this one." She held up the black strapless cocktail dress Liam had seen her in at the hotel bar.

Carrie sat on the edge of the bed and shook her head. "No, he's already—" She stopped. This was no time to go into the fact that Liam had showed up at her gig a couple of days before or that she'd bolted like a frightened deer. Julie would have a field day with *that* information. "This is supper on a boat, not dinner and dancing."

Using her fingers, she styled her curls as Julie held up and rejected several others outfits. Too long. Too wintery. Too brown. Too frumpy. Then she pulled the dry cleaner's plastic from a sleeveless red linen scoop-neck sheath that Carrie had worn only once last summer.

"This is it," Julie cried triumphantly. "It's perfect and those red strappy sandals I brought you from New York will make your legs look long and lean."

"I can't walk in those sandals," Carrie complained, going to her dresser for underwear.

Julie stopped her. "Tough. You won't be doing much walking tonight. Put away that slip, the dress is lined. And don't even *think* about white cotton undies, you big nerd."

"Look, I'm *not* sleeping with him tonight." Carrie backed up as her friend shouldered her out of the way. "Even if I wanted to, I have no idea if he's interested." Yet all of her womanly instincts told her Liam was *more* than interested.

But why? Maybe it was to seduce her into letting him get to Jack, or maybe it was to salve his ego. She was probably the one and only woman ever to break up with him.

No doubt he thinks he's got something to prove.

But her conscience prodded her before that thought was even fully formed. *That's completely unfair. Liam's not the kind of man who has anything to prove.*

"He has a pulse and a pecker, doesn't he?" Sorting through Carrie's lingerie drawer, Julie missed the eye roll. "He's interested. Besides, the way he was looking at you this afternoon, it won't take anything more than these"—she held up red satin French-cut panties and a matching push-up bra that she'd brought Carrie from a photo shoot in Chicago—"to get him all hot and bothered."

"I'm not sure I *want* him hot and bothered." Carrie stroked on body lotion. "I don't know if I even remember what to do with a hot-and-bothered man."

"Geez, you *so* need to get laid, and this is the perfect opportunity." Julie pulled a shoe box from the closet shelf and dangled the red sandals temptingly from one finger. "This guy's gonna be in your life forever. Why not let it be a good experience? Maybe you can pick up where you left off. You know, like a do-over."

"Where we left off was him in Europe with female string players hanging all over him, and me in Louisville, broke and pregnant." Carrie grabbed the underwear and went into the bathroom. "I sure as hell don't want to do *that* over."

"That's not what I meant and you know it." Julie followed her. "Here, let me do your makeup."

"Okay, but nothing extreme." She sat on the toilet seat and looked up expectantly. "Keep it simple and natural, please."

"Hey, that's actually a great idea—simple and understated." Julie picked up a foundation brush. "We'll let the dress do all the work."

She started on Carrie's face, applying a light base of powdered foundation and a stroke of blush to each cheek. Then she highlighted her dark eyes with shimmery taupe shadow and added a touch of lip gloss.

"There. Perfect. And not a lot of bling either. Just wear your diamond studs. Add the red undies, the sandals, and the dress and —*bam*. The guy's a goner."

CHAPTER 8

"I like your friend Julie, but she's a little... um... intimidating." Liam poured wine into two glasses and set one in front of Carrie.

The lake air was light and cool as they sat on the deck of his boat. The sun floated on the horizon, turning the sky dark orange while Norah Jones played softly in the background. His hair rumpled from the breeze, he looked fantastic in cotton khakis and a white dress shirt with the sleeves rolled up. She was dying to stroke back the errant curl that always fell over his forehead, but she reached for her wine instead.

Settling into the deck chair next to hers, he tipped his glass toward her in a silent toast.

She touched her glass to his and took a sip. "This is good. What is it?"

"A cabernet sauvignon from the Sierra foothills—about three hours northeast of San Francisco. I go wine-tasting wherever I travel—and I *love* northern California wines."

They were both making an effort, a tentative give and take. Carrie wrapped her hands around the bowl of her wineglass, resisting the urge to touch the soft hairs on his arm. The setting sun created an aura of red-gold light around him that ignited a flame of desire low in her belly.

"Julie's a good friend." Carrie switched back to his original observation when she caught herself staring. "She's not really scary. She just speaks her mind, which I always appreciate."

She turned as footsteps sounded behind them.

A very male arm appeared as someone set a tray of appetizers on the table between them. "Hi, I'm Tony, captain of this tub. You must be Carrie."

When he came into view, she blinked. Built like a bear, Tony was all muscle and dark hair and dressed in shorts, a Hawaiian shirt, and sandals. He towered over Carrie as they shook hands.

"Nice to meet you, Tony. She's a beautiful boat." A wave of her hand encompassed the whole sleek vessel. "How long have you been in charge?"

Tony reached for an appetizer and popped it in his mouth. "Actually, I came with the boat, so I've been her pilot for about ten years—the last two with the Maestro here. I'm also chief cook and bottle washer, and I know every inch of her intimately. Would you like a tour?" When he offered his hand, she accepted, dropping her sweater on the chair.

"*I* can take her on a tour." Liam popped up from his chair.

Tony tossed him a cell phone. "You've got a call." Taking Carrie's hand, he led her away while Liam frowned after them.

The boat *was* elegant with plush carpet, shiny stainless steel fittings, and satiny teak and mahogany wood. The salon was furnished with an overstuffed sofa and chairs and dark wooden tables. A built-in bar and a state-of-the-art theater and stereo system were tucked into carved wood cabinets. An electronic keyboard and laptop sat on a table behind the sofa. The master cabin boasted a king-sized bed, a private bath, and an exercise area with a treadmill and free weights. There were three smaller quarters, each with a full head, plus a complete galley that seemed more like a gourmet kitchen.

After taking her below to see the engine room and storage areas, Tony brought her back up on deck. Smiling, he gave her shoulder a friendly squeeze. "I'm outta here. Dinner's warming in the oven. Good to meet you, Carrie." He jumped over the rail onto the dock and headed off with a salute to Liam, who was still on the phone.

Carrie sat down and picked up her glass, trying hard not to eavesdrop.

"I miss you too, Ella. Give Dana my best. Yeah, yeah, I will, I promise. Goodnight, babe." He shut the phone off and dropped it in his pocket. "So you got the nickel tour?"

"I did. It's like a traveling household." She allowed him to pour more wine into her glass. As she sipped, she tried not to think about who he may have been talking to.

Ella? Who's Ella?

Okay, stop. Ella is none of your business. His personal life is none of your business.

Oh crap, was that Ella Grant? That hot actress he was with at the Grammy Awards?

Carrie gave herself a mental shake and refocused.

"—and we take her out every chance we get," Liam was saying. "We've stuck to the Great Lakes so far. I bought her in Chicago when the former owner moved to Arizona."

"Has Uncle Noah had a tour yet? He'd get a huge kick out of this."

"He got the grand tour before you came down this evening. He's made fast friends of Will and Tony. They're both crazy fishermen. Here, we'll have dinner on the port side." With a hand on the small of her back, he led her to a table on the other side of the deck.

She shivered at the light touch of his fingers, feeling his heat through the linen of her dress.

"Let me get your sweater." He pulled the chair out for her. "If it's too chilly out here for you, we can eat inside."

"No, no—this is fine, thanks." Carrie sat down. "I don't need the sweater."

Get a grip. You can't react every time he's within two feet of you, every time his hand brushes against you.

She helped herself to the appetizers, savoring the delicate crabmeat and artichoke dip on crackers. "This is delicious."

"Yeah, Tony's gone all out for you. We aren't usually this fancy." Sitting across from her, he lit the hurricane lamp. As their eyes met over the flame, the atmosphere instantly became more intimate. "Citronella," he said with a shrug. "Probably too early for bugs, but why chance it?"

They chatted—carefully, politely— as they ate Tony's delicious meal, and Carrie gradually began to relax. The wine helped, but it wasn't simply the alcohol's effect—Liam also loosened up. His eyes sparkled with curiosity as she talked about Willow Bay, her life, and her studio. She told him about coming to Michigan after her father's death, about how photography changed her life, and she talked about Jack. He asked questions, but didn't push, even though she could tell he was hungry for information.

She loved watching him. He still used his hands when he told a story, almost as if he were conducting as he spoke, and his smile made her heart pound. But long days on the road, traveling from city to city—endless hours of rehearsals and performances—had left their mark on him. His face was older. Lines showed around his eyes. Gray threaded through the auburn hair above his ears. The young eager musician had been replaced by a mature, balanced, and if possible, sexier version of the man she remembered.

This is Jack in thirty years.

He'd stopped talking and now eyed her expectantly.

"I'm sorry," she said. "I got distracted for a second."

"What were you thinking about?" He took a sip of wine.

"I was thinking how much Jack looks like you."

"He does, doesn't he?" Liam was actually blushing and in that one moment, Carrie might have been sitting with Jack.

But Liam was here now. He was Jack's father, and he was back in her life. What that might ultimately mean terrified her, but tonight she wanted to savor the sensation of feeling beautiful and desirable again. The sexual tension was evident in his smoky eyes —a tension that had been intensifying since he kissed her that afternoon.

Was it only five hours ago?

God, how she wanted him. But she needed to set boundaries and find her limits before they went any further. "May I ask you a favor?" The words were out before she could change her mind. She held her breath, watching him closely.

"What?" He seemed cautious, but those eyes promised her anything.

Almost.

"Will you wait until Sunday to see Jack?"

His jaw dropped and he started to object.

Knowing she'd picked the one thing he wasn't willing to do, she put her hand on his arm. "Please, just listen."

He nodded, but she could tell he was already closing his mind, so she hurried her explanation.

"I've been thinking. I want him to have at least this week before we turn his life inside out. He's been looking forward to camp all year."

"Don't you think there's a chance he's been looking forward to meeting his father *all his life?*" Liam pulled his arm away from her. Standing, he walked over to the railing, staring down into the bay.

Carrie swallowed hard and sat staring at her hands for a long moment before she answered. "Yes, he probably has. But I'm only asking you for one more week—five days, really—and then we'll tell him. Together."

"Why?" he asked. "Why not tomorrow?"

Slipping out of her chair, she went to stand beside him. "Because I need to know if we're going to be able to get along, you and me. If we can't be in the same room without biting each other's heads off, how will that affect him?" She hoped he couldn't hear the tremor in her voice. "I'm sorry, but I can't—I won't—throw all this at Jack until *we* have some sort of understanding. Can we figure *us* out first?"

"In five days?" His face was unreadable. After a moment, he sighed. "I'm so pissed at you, but dammit, the chemistry is still there. Aside from finding out about Jack, that one thing amazes me most, and frankly, scares the unholy crap out of me. I never imagined seeing you would make me feel like–like *this* again." Lifting her chin with one finger, he forced her to face him. "I thought it was all gone. It's been so long—" He stopped, his eyes boring into hers.

"I know. I'm surprised too." She closed her eyes against the heat of his gaze. "I never meant to hurt you. I didn't. Protecting *my* heart was the goal. I thought it was over, too, but all this—" Palms upward in a helpless gesture, she stammered. "—whatever *this* is makes it im–impossible for me to think clearly."

His eyes widened and he raised both hands to cup her face. "God, Carrie," he whispered.

His mouth came down on hers, soft and gentle at first but the pressure increased when she opened her mouth. Sliding her hands up his chest, she put her arms around his neck as his hands grasped her waist. It was a kiss born of anger, of desperation, of lust, but it didn't matter. As he hauled her against his hard body, moving his hands to her hips, she wanted to crawl inside his skin. She couldn't get close enough.

His tongue plunged seeking hers, his fingers tracing each vertebra through the linen of her dress. Her own hands sought his waist, untucking his shirt to find the warm muscles of his back. She needed to feel his skin, and he shivered at her touch as he pressed her hips against the rail. Pulling his mouth from hers, he dropped fierce kisses and tiny nibbling bites on her face, her jaw, her throat.

Too much. No.

The thought surfaced even as her own fingers continued to seek the heated flesh beneath his shirt. He ran his hands over her back, obviously feeling for a zipper, and as she dropped her head back, his tongue drew a path of liquid fire down her neck. She started to guide his hand to the side zipper, but he slid one hand down over her behind, bunching the fabric until he reached the hem. Slipping his hand under it, he found the skin of her thigh, his thumb barely brushing her red satin panties.

His lips claimed hers while he pressed her against the rail, fitting his erection into her belly. Moaning into his mouth, she brought her hands around to his chest, her fingers working the buttons of his shirt. When his other hand moved to her breast, her eyes flew open.

God, oh, God, what am I doing?

Grasping his wrists, she twisted away from him. "Liam, please. Stop."

He dropped his hands immediately and stepped back, breathing heavily, his eyes dark with emotion.

Smoothing her dress over her hips, she crossed her arms and leaned forward for a moment, trying to catch her own breath. "*That's* why we have to sort this out," she said, taking air in great gulps. "Don't you see? We have to figure this out or we're going to have some frustrating months ahead."

"Months?" He rubbed his face and blinked. "Wait a minute, what are you talking about, *months?*"

CHAPTER 9

C arrie wandered to the table, obviously dawdling over a sip of water before she spoke. "You're gone after the benefit, right? This boat sails out of Willow Bay, and you go back on tour. Back to *your* life. Then what?"

Breathing heavily, Liam leaned against the rail, struggling to keep a lid on his feelings, which were caught somewhere between dazed and belligerent.

She started again. "Look, we're two reasonable adults—"

"*There's* an arguable point," Liam interrupted, his heart still hammering.

Barely twelve hours, and she's already driving me insane.

His groin ached, and her red dress and lovely round breasts distracted him from her words, yet he fought the urge to shake her silly. Turning away, he focused on the water lapping against the *Allegro*, trying to force the heat to subside while getting the anger under control.

"I don't see why we can't make this work," she said, clearly ignoring his snarky comment. "Thousands of separated parents do it all the time."

Her words were like ice water dumped over his head. Shoving away from the rail, he crossed the deck in two strides. "Are you suggesting we think of ourselves as... as *divorced*?" Grabbing the bottle of wine, he splashed some into his glass and swallowed it in one gulp.

"I think that would be best." Her eyes darted away before meeting his glare head on. "That way you can have time with Jack while you're here. When you leave, we can both go on with our own lives. Later, if you want to see Jack, we'll work that out."

"And we come to some amicable arrangement about visitation and child support?"

"Well... okay, yeah." She squared her shoulders. "I can call my attorney in the morning. He can draw up whatever papers we need to sign about visitation, and as far as child support goes, no thanks. We don't need your money."

Liam watched her for a long moment, hardly believing what he was hearing. He walked away, pacing the length of the deck and back again. Conflicting emotions boiled up in him as he stared across the moonlit lake. He should hate her for keeping Jack from him. He should hate her for dumping him. He should hate himself for still wanting her so desperately.

But he didn't have any hate inside him. Only anger and confusion and a longing to discover what the future might bring—with both Carrie and Jack.

As a mist rose over the bay, he counted to ten... and then to twenty. Finally, he took a deep breath, and without turning, spoke quietly and in measured phrases.

"Listen to me. No lawyers. No papers to sign. No talk about visitation rights. Because I don't intend to give up my son before I even meet him." He spun around, heading for her with purpose. "What's more, I have no intention of giving *you* up, either. We're going to find out what could have happened if you hadn't run away." He took her shoulders in his hands, struggling to be gentle.

"Rehashing the past isn't going to accomplish anything." The conviction in her words made him tug her around to face him. "We've both changed so much. We're older, wiser—"

"Wiser?" Liam would have laughed had she not been so absurd. "You're not one single moment wiser, Carrie. The naïve girl I met in Montreal has become a damn recluse—closed up in a box. Where's all that glorious passion and curiosity I fell in love with?"

Trembling, she twisted away from him, anger flashing copper glints in her eyes. She stood there trembling, silent.

"Once upon a time, you were brave—brave enough to audition for the Ecklund Competition. Brave enough to agree to come to Europe with me. But you lost it somewhere. How? Hell, you couldn't even work up the courage to tell me I had a son. You made all the choices for both of us." His laugh was harsh and guttural to his own ears, but he'd stopped caring how he sounded to her. "Well, baby, guess what? I'm back and it's my turn. I'm opening up the box."

"You self-righteous son of a bitch." Carrie's hands curled into fists at her sides. "How dare you make judgments about my life? About *my* choices? You have no idea who I am or what I've become." Her rage must have calmed the trembling. Now she seemed just plain infuriated. "Frankly, I think this is all about your ego. You're pissed because *I* left. *I* wasn't there drooling all over you. *I* wasn't hanging around backstage, waiting for you to grace me with ten minutes of your very expensive time before the next performance. Excuse me if I haven't lived the glamorous, exciting life you have all these years, Maestro. I had a child to raise!"

"You made the choice to do that alone," he retorted. Shock and hurt filled Liam as she continued mercilessly, clearly unable to stop the flow of angry words.

"Jack and I were *never* going to fit into the image you and

Marty spent so much energy creating. And I knew it. I wasn't as stupid and naïve as you seem to think I was. I did what I *had* to do given the circumstances and—" She stopped suddenly, then drew a deep breath. "I'm willing to let you get to know Jack. But you and me? Not happening. We need to stay separate because I *still* won't fit into your world."

"Jesus!" He grabbed the wine bottle with unsteady fingers. Liquid sloshed in the bottom as he pulled his arm back and threw it furiously over the rail where it fell with an unsatisfactory plop into the bay.

Swallowing hard, he smacked his hand on the table. "Good God, woman. This morning, I only wanted to get to know *you* again, that was all." He pointed an accusing finger. "Jack had no part in it. I didn't even know he existed. This is *not* about my ego —at least not the way you think. I guess I needed know what happened to us. And because you"he lowered his voice"you never left my mind—not once in all those years. And trust me, I tried *damn hard* to get rid of you." He picked up her wineglass, drained it, and wiped his hand across his mouth. Shoving his fingers into his hair, he dropped heavily onto the bench by the rail.

Too emotionally exhausted to speak or move, Carrie stared at him in disbelief. Had she truly been on his mind all this time?

Damn him for saying that!

Now how was she ever going to tell him about Marty and the money? If he'd known, he would've forgotten her in a heartbeat. Dear God, had they really had the same fantasies? Somehow being angry at him was easier than wanting him so desperately. She was afraid to say anything. Afraid everything—the whole truth—would come pouring out and then he'd truly hate her. Afraid she'd throw herself into his arms. Afraid she'd never have another clear thought again.

Liam sighed. "Okay, Carrie, maybe I *don't* know you now. But you have to give me that same point. You *think* you know who I am because you've watched PBS or read *People* magazine or some saw some website or heard a backstage interview on NPR." He exhaled a short angry laugh. "Everything moved so fast in Montreal, we never knew what hit us. Come on. Let's give it a shot. Maybe we'll work out, maybe we won't, but we'll never know if we don't try."

Despite her resistance, his heated gaze drew her in, and his words kept her from tripping over the lines to flee the boat.

He pressed on. "Don't think for moment that I won't be seeing Jack as often as I can, no matter what happens between us. But you and I can't possibly stay *separate*. That boy binds us together as surely as if we'd figured everything out years ago."

"How do we go back, Liam?" She whispered the question, her face hidden in the shadows.

"I'll give you your five days." He moved closer—so close she could feel the heat of his body and smell the crisp masculine scent of him, although he didn't touch her. "I don't want to, but we have to figure this out. I'll wait until Sunday to see Jack on one condi- tion. You agree to–to *dating*, for lack of a better term. And I'm *not* going to beg. You have to meet me halfway. Can you do that?"

His endearing little smile sent a frisson of desire zinging through her. The deep cadence of his voice caressed her as he continued. "We don't go back. We go forward."

Crossing her arms, she walked slowly to the other side of the boat, watching the lights at the bait shop flicker between the swaying branches of the ancient pines. Uncle Noah was up there, probably sorting through the box of new lures and laughing with Will and Tony. A few days ago, Jack would have been with them, his gray eyes—so like Liam's—sparkling as he unpacked new fishing gear. Nothing would ever be that simple again.

But Liam was Jack's father, and didn't she owe it to her son to at least try?

A noble concept.

She glanced over her shoulder. Just thinking of his kisses turned her insides to mush and made heat build low in her body.

Who am I kidding?

Boundaries. I need to set some boundaries.

"Okay," she agreed warily, still not facing him. "But we have to lay down some ground rules. I can't think straight when you— when your hands are—"

Liam's seductive chuckle stopped her stammering as he pulled her back against him. "Don't ask me not to touch you. I can't promise that." His voice was soft and sensual. "I'd be a liar if I did." His lips caressed the sensitive skin behind her ear and then found her throat. She felt his warm breath against her skin when he whispered, "And you'd be *so* disappointed if I never touched you."

Carrie gave up. Turning, she slid her arms around his waist, settling into his embrace. He was right. Incredibly, wonderfully right. She *longed* for him to touch her everywhere, to kiss her, to stroke and suckle her. She wanted his hands on her. His mouth on her. "Oh God, Liam," she murmured. "What am I going to do with—"

His lips hushed whatever she was about to say. She returned the deep kiss, loving the urgency of his hands on her back. Finally he lifted his head, his mouth hovering over hers. "Tell you what," he said, his warm, wine-sweet breath mingling with hers. "I promise we won't do anything you don't want to do. How's that?" Even in the dim light of the deck, his eyes gleamed.

"And *I* get to decide what it is *I* want, right?" she asked before she pulled his mouth to hers in a searing kiss.

Liam's eyes were smoky when he broke contact. "Oh yeah, your choice all the way, sweetheart."

Chuckling, he took her lips again.

CHAPTER 10

"These were on the bench by your door." Eliot handed Carrie a bouquet as he and Aunt Margie sauntered into her apartment the next morning. Depositing a basket of scones on the granite bar by the kitchen, he dropped a kiss on her cheek. "Have you forgiven me yet?" His tone was grave, but Carrie noted the gleam in his eye.

"You've opened up a very large can of worms, Eliot." She frowned before turning to Margie for a hug. "Hey, Aunt Margie." Then she tugged the florist's paper from the bouquet to reveal pink roses bound up with a white ribbon.

"My goodness." Margie fingered the delicate blooms. "How gorgeous." She gave them a sniff. "Don't they smell heavenly?"

Carrie pulled a card from the center of the bouquet. No message, simply a bold black scrawl, *Liam*. That signature sent pinwheels and rockets ripping through her veins. How did he know she loved she loved pink roses? As she buried her nose in the flowers, the scent propelled her thoughts back to the previous night.

Thank God, Tony and Will had come strolling down the dock,

or she'd have had Liam flat on his back on the deck of the *Allegro* —or he'd have had her there.

Who knew?

When she raised her head, Margie and Eliot were smiling at one another. Sighing, she took the flowers into the kitchen to find a vase.

"I saw Perry at the farm stand this morning, so I've heard some of the story." Margie sat down at the table, eyeing the piles of albums and pictures covering the surface. "And Eliot was kind enough to tell me what he knows. I think he may have brought me along for protection." She winked at Eliot who was at the kitchen counter gathering napkins, butter, and plates.

Carrie rolled her eyes as she set the flowers on the chest in front of the sofa. Perry owned the local coffee shop, which also happened to be the best place in town to catch up on the latest news. "Jeez, Perry's in gossip heaven, isn't he? Well, there's nothing like being the topic of the day." At the table, she closed her laptop and set it aside, stacking up pictures and albums to make room for the impromptu breakfast. "The jury is still out on whether or not I've forgiven you, Eliot. But I love you too much to stop speaking to you. Besides your scones are to die for, and I've got a fresh pot of coffee."

He smiled and patted her shoulder. "I consider it a fortuitous merging of necessary events. I needed him and frankly, it was time you dealt with all the baggage. A win for both of us."

Carrie rolled her eyes. "We'll see, won't we?"

With a flourish, Eliot buttered a scone and set the plate in front of Margie. "Here you go, Margie, enjoy." Buttering another one, he offered it to Carrie. "Tell us everything."

They nibbled on scones and sipped coffee as she shared the events of the last twenty-four hours. She couldn't stop smiling, although she kept the details of the intimate encounter on the boat to a minimum.

"So where do you go from here?" Margie leaned back in her chair. "What happens next?"

"I don't know. He wants to *date*." Carrie scrunched up her face. "It all feels backward. *Dating?* After all this time?" She gestured at the albums and photos on the table. "Anyway... he agreed to wait until Sunday to actually meet Jack, so I'm putting together a quick photo album for him." Handing a black leather album to Margie, she chuckled at the first page. "Look at this one. Jack's like two minutes old. Oh, and here's one with Eliot and Uncle Noah right after he was born."

Margie turned the pages slowly, examining the chronicle of Jack's young life as Carrie followed along. After the first few pages, almost every one included shots of Jack at a piano. Jack playing in a recital at Lawson Music Camp. Jack at Eliot's beautiful Steinway with Eliot standing over him. Jack at the piano in their apartment, intent on a sheet of music.

The last page was an eight-by-ten, black-and-white photo taken last winter. Carrie had been experimenting with duotone film, and the light in the apartment had caught her eye. In that instant, Jack sat at his Grandmother Beth's old baby grand, his head thrown back, his eyes closed, long lashes touching his cheeks, and his fingers stretched over the keys.

Margie gasped. "That's beautiful. He looks like Beth Anne, doesn't he? So dramatic. Liam will love this one."

"That looks like a publicity shot." Eliot peered over Margie's shoulder.

Carrie gave him a scowl. "Not deliberately." She yanked the photo out of its plastic sleeve and tossed it down on the table. "Don't say that, Eliot. If I had a choice, I wouldn't even tell Liam that Jack plays."

"Why on earth would you not tell his father that the child plays piano like an angel? 'Specially considering who his father is?" Margie rose to take dishes to the sink.

Carrie handed her a mug and plate. "That's *exactly* the reason. Who knows what he'll do with the information? What if he wants to take him out on tour or something?"

"And what if he does?" Eliot piped in. "Why would that have to be a bad thing?"

Carrie shook her finger at him crossly. "He's not taking Jack anywhere. I don't want that kind of life for my son. I won't allow it." Reaching for another photo of Jack—one of him with several friends playing basketball in the yard behind the marina—she replaced the one she'd pulled earlier. Expelling a breath, she started shoving pictures in envelopes, moving quickly to clean up the table.

"You're not the only one in this anymore," Eliot's tone was sober. "The sooner you recognize that, the better off you'll be."

"What's *that* supposed to mean?" Carrie stacked the albums back in the bookcase beneath the stairs, glancing up as Eliot and Margie exchanged a meaningful look.

"He means that you can't allow Liam into Jack's life and yet refuse to let him participate in decisions about him." Margie arranged framed photos on the baby grand in the corner.

"You know what? I can't think about that right now." Carrie strode across the room and grabbed more photo albums. "My life's completely upside down. I don't know where things are going with Liam. One minute he's furious, the next he's all, well… never mind." Heat suffused her cheeks. "And I still have to tell Jack and pray the kid doesn't hate me." Tears started to form, but she blinked them back, refusing to let her tumbling emotions take control.

"You knew you'd have to tell Jack about Liam sometime," Eliot said. "It's not like you're handing him some worthless bum for a father. My God, why would he hate you?"

"I don't know, maybe–maybe because I kept him from Liam for such a long time."

"Now you're borrowing trouble." Gathering up his basket, Eliot headed for the door. "Have a little faith in your son and in his father. Things are going to be *different,* but that doesn't automatically mean they're going to be *bad.*" He elbowed open the screen door. "Margie, walk up with me? I want to steal a couple of your tomatoes if you have some to spare."

"Sure, I have plenty." Margie gave Carrie a quick squeeze. "He's right, you know, sweetie. Change often turns out to be a very good thing."

"I guess." Carrie walked them out to the deck, unable to keep her eyes from the massive boat in berth thirty-eight. "Or I could get my heart broken again, couldn't I?"

"Maybe," Eliot nodded. "But better a *broken* heart than a *frozen* one."

"A little fortune cookie wisdom, old friend?" Carrie offered him a wry grin. Resting her elbows on the deck rail, she tracked Margie and Eliot's progress to the docks below. The sound of their laughter drifted back up the stairs.

It was early—not even nine yet.

Where did he find those beautiful flowers?

Their delicate scent filled the room, intoxicating her senses as she came back into the apartment. Suddenly, calm, peaceful, orderly Carrie was a morass of feelings. Tears threatened and yet she couldn't stop smiling. Her heart ached one moment, then sang in the next. A twinge of—*okay, Carrie, let's call it what it is, lust* —weighed heavy.

That particular sensation had been buried so deep for so long she barely recognized it. Oh, she'd handled the feeling readily enough when it surfaced through the years, but the memories of Liam were nothing compared to this new reality. Now her lust simmered, clouding her thoughts with its intensity. She'd barely gotten off that boat last night without dragging him down on the deck and making love to him until they both ached.

Can we build a relationship—a family—on the basis of heat?
That was the big question.

Carrie's immediate reaction was *no way*. Heat had no staying power. Heat cooled quickly when the dishwasher broke down, the toilet backed up, or the car doors froze in winter. Heat faded when a teenager grew sullen and sulky because he couldn't stay out past eleven on a Friday night. Heat disappeared when a husband and father traveled far and wide, away from home for weeks at a time.

But the heat is still there, even after sixteen years.

And oh, God, she was so ready for some heat. So ready for Liam's arms, his hands, his mouth. So ready for the fulfillment of years of fantasizing and waiting, even though she'd never realized she *had* been waiting. She hadn't dared believe she would ever see him again, let alone touch him, kiss him. Shivering, she pressed her hands against her belly, almost as if to hold that feeling in.

Her cell phone sang "Maggie May" on the bar. A check of the caller ID revealed a number she didn't know, an area code she didn't recognize. But there was no name. "Hello?"

"Are you hungry? Would you like to have breakfast with me?" asked a deep, sexy voice.

Her stomach did a crazy flip. "How did you get my cell number?" Moving to the window, she glanced down at the boat, where Liam sat in a canvas deck chair, his feet resting on the stainless steel rail. He waved up at her.

She backed away from the window, embarrassed that he saw her looking for him.

"It's on your business card. I picked one up yesterday when Will and I were in your studio."

"Oh–oh–um, well…" she stammered, tongue-tied and foolish.

He chuckled, almost as if he knew the effect he had on her.

Closing her eyes for a second, she took a deep breath. "Actually, Liam, I have coffee and blueberry scones. Why don't you give me thirty minutes and come on up?"

"Do you have eggs?"

"Yep," she said. "Thirty minutes. Okay?"

So it begins.

Change begins today, and I can open my mind and heart, or I can kick and scream.

Either way, life is going to change.

CHAPTER 11

E xactly a half hour later, Liam tapped on the screen door.
Carrie had barely had time to shower and change into a
pink polo and white capris. Still barefoot and detangling her
damp, loopy curls, she held the screen door open. "You're up
early."

"I'm always up early." Clad in jeans and a faded plum-colored
T-shirt, he flashed that killer grin as he eyed her up and down.
He'd already gotten some sun in the couple of days he'd been on
the boat, and the color suited him.

Carrie's heart stopped for second, but amazingly, resumed
beating as he ambled in, fingers tucked in his pockets. She headed
for the kitchen. "I like mornings too. How do you like your
eggs?"

"Scrambled, if that's okay." He stared around the big open
space that served as living room, dining room, and kitchen for her
and Jack. "Nice place."

Nodding, she began work on breakfast. It was better to keep
busy. If she didn't, she was sure to humiliate herself since she
longed to touch him. Longed for him to touch *her*.

He roamed around, peering at the paintings on the walls,

picking up pictures from the baby grand. "What a beautiful piano." He ran his fingers over the keys.

"It was my mother's. One of the few things I brought with me when I came up here."

"This is her, isn't it?" With a smile, Liam picked up a gilt-framed photo of Beth Anne Halligan sitting at a piano. "She was a knockout."

"Yes, she was. I don't really remember her, only that my father was heartbroken when she died. That's Dad with her in the blue frame." Carrie turned on the gas under a skillet. "Are you okay with butter or are you a low-fat kind of guy?"

"Butter's great—that's how I always make them." One by one, Liam took photos off the piano—her father, Margie and Noah, Jack in the sailboat, she and Julie on the beach. He gazed at a picture of Julie, her husband Charlie, and their kids, taken last Christmas. Eliot at his piano. Carrie and Jack by the lighthouse. He examined each photo intently. That was how he did things, she remembered from Montreal. Always scrutinizing. Studying.

"You cook your own eggs?" Somehow that wasn't a picture she had of him. She'd never thought of the man as holding an ounce of domesticity.

He looked up and laughed, a warm, sexy sound, and a quiver shot through her. "I cook. How do you think I eat when I'm home?"

"I guess I figured you had people for that, like servants or a maid or a cook." A warm flush crept up her neck.

Grinning, he continued his tour of the apartment. "A service comes in to clean once a week when I'm home, and I send my laundry out. Otherwise, I take care of myself." He passed by Jack's closed bedroom door under the open stairs, then glanced out the back window at the pines. Leaning his elbows on the bar, he watched her pour golden, frothy eggs into the sizzling skillet. "I think you have me confused with some rock star, sweetheart.

I'm a symphony conductor. I don't have servants. I live a pretty simple life in Chicago." He gestured to the stairs. "What's in the loft?"

"A bedroom and a bathroom. Uncle Noah remodeled this old place when Jack was about three. Before that we lived in the big house with them. I love this apartment. It's perfect for us." She stirred the eggs gently, smiling up at him, noting that he'd wandered back to Jack's door. "It's okay if you want to go in and take a peek."

"Are you sure?" Hand on the knob, he hesitated. "I'm dying of curiosity, but I don't want to trespass."

She paused. Jack's domain was his own, and they were always conscious of one another's privacy. How would he feel about a stranger in his room?

But this isn't a stranger, it's his father.

"Go ahead, it'll be okay." She prayed the tour wouldn't set off the anger she was certain still smoldered in him.

Liam drew a bracing breath, turned the knob, and shouldered the door open. Sunshine streamed in from the open shutters over the south-facing window. His eyes swept the small room that held some of the clues to his son's personality. Carrie watched from behind the kitchen bar, picturing Jack's room in her head, most likely slightly messy but not so much that she needed to be concerned about Liam checking it out.

One wall was a huge window that looked south across the bay. Posters covered the other walls—one from Willow Point Light-house, another from Sleeping Bear Dune. The colorful Beatles Sergeant Pepper poster, a movie poster, and a picture of the Milky Way with a tiny red arrow and the words, *You are here.* Some young and fabulous starlet, whose name Carrie couldn't remember smiled from above the bed while next to her, Eric Clapton bent over his guitar. A Chicago Bulls team picture was tacked up above a cluttered desk, along with a bulletin board covered with ticket stubs, photographs, and playbills from area theaters, many of them from Interlochen.

She set the skillet aside and moved to the open door, breathing in scent of teenaged boy—sweat and dirty socks mixed with Irish Spring soap and pine from the trees outside. When she leaned against the jamb, she saw that the bed was neatly made, but the open closet door revealed shirts and pants hung haphazardly on hangers, some even spilling onto the floor. A small flat-screen TV and a stereo sat at the end of the bed, which was on a platform that contained drawers. A T-shirt sleeve peeked out of one of the drawers. CDs and DVDs marched in orderly rows above several shelves of books below the stereo.

Liam leaned down to squint at the collections and Carrie couldn't help smiling. Some of the books were obviously from his younger years—the Hardy Boys, Harry Potter, even Dr. Seuss and Mercer Mayer nestled next to the story of Ernest Shakleton's exploration of the South Pole, Stephen Ambrose's *Undaunted Courage*, and several Clive Cussler adventure novels. The CDs were a diverse mix of rock, classical, and everything in between, including Bob Marley, Daft Punk, the Beatles, Alicia Keyes, The Kinks, BB King, and John Legend. She grinned when Liam's brow furrowed at a CD of the music from Baz Lurhmann's *La Bohème,* as well as Jack's newest fascination—Broadway musicals. The soundtracks to *Rent, Cabaret*, and the original Broadway production of *Camelot* were stacked on top of the other CDs on the shelf.

He glanced up as she backed out of the room. "Quite an eclectic music collection," he said, following her to the kitchen to accept a plate of eggs.

"There's really not much he doesn't like when it comes to music." She was grateful he still seemed to be in a good humor. Either that or he was concealing any anger remarkably well. "Maybe not twangy country so much, and he's not into hip-hop, but he likes rap. For some strange reason, this spring, he discovered Broadway musicals."

"I saw the CDs. What's that about?" Liam set his plate on the table, then held her chair while she sat.

She smiled over her shoulder at the courtly gesture, remembering how he'd always been such a gentleman around her. It still made her heart beat faster. "It's a weird phenomenon. He cycles through music, really getting into something for a while, then moving on. Over the winter, it was Ben Folds and classic rock like the Beatles and the Stones. After his school put on *Guys and Dolls* in April, suddenly he was all about Broadway. *Cabaret*, *Rent*—even *The Music Man*." She laughed. "He sings with the CDs in the car, so conversation is out of the question."

Liam grinned, shaking his head as he dug into breakfast. They ate in companionable silence for a few minutes.

Carrie inclined her head toward the album sitting on the table near him. "That's for you."

"Really?" Liam hefted the album. "Are these pictures of Jack?"

She nodded, taking up a forkful of eggs.

He opened it. Staring at the first page, he ran a finger over a photo of newborn Jack. He started to reach for his glasses in his shirt pocket and appeared puzzled for a second when he realized he didn't have either glasses or a pocket. Carrie got her own wire-framed reading glasses from the bar.

"Here," she handed them to him. "Try these, but eat. Your food will get cold."

Liam put them on, giving her a strange half-smile that sent a prickle up her spine. As he ate, he stared at the first page—Jack as a newborn in the hospital bassinette. Noah and Margie swinging a toddling Jack between them. Eliot smiling tenderly at the sleeping baby in his arms. She could tell he didn't even taste the food, so absorbed was he in the photos. He didn't comment at all, just kept studying the pictures, almost as if he were trying to memorize them.

Finishing the meal in record time, he carried the album to the window seat. "Thank you. That was good. Do you mind if I take a minute here?" His voice was raspy as he settled in, back propped against the wall, his long legs stretched out on the cushion.

Carrie nodded as she sipped her coffee, mentally preparing herself for whatever reaction might come as he slowly turned the pages of the album. With his head bent over the book and her reading glasses perched on his nose, he concentrated on each page, examining each photo. Every so often, he'd pull a picture from its vinyl envelope and hold it up to the window. Fifteen minutes later, he shut the album, hugging it against his chest. Removing her glasses, he laid them carefully on the window seat beside him.

Carrie watched him cautiously, unwilling to be the first one to speak.

His face was closed up—no smile, nothing. A muscle worked in his jaw, his lips tightened into a grim line. Massaging the bridge of his nose with his thumb and forefinger, he took a deep breath. "He plays the piano?" His voice was deadly quiet.

"Yes."

"How long has he played?"

"Since he was little." She raked her fingers through her curls. "He's very gifted, Liam. He's–he's a–prodigy." The word wrenched from her.

"Shit, Carrie!" Liam burst out. "When were you planning on mentioning *that*?"

"I'm telling you now." Her hands shook. The eggs churned in her stomach. She swallowed once and then swallowed again. "He's been studying with Eliot for years, and he finished his first year at Interlochen last month. In September, he starts there as boarder."

"A prodigy?" Dull color flushed his cheeks. "Seriously a *prodigy*? Not just a kid who plays well?"

"Yes. One day when he was about three or so, he began picking out notes. He's incredible." She held her breath. Liam hadn't moved, but she could tell he was beyond upset. He was angry—red-hot, fire-breathing furious.

Why would hearing that his son's a gifted pianist make him so mad?

"He's like my mother," she added, trying to explain.

Finally, he stood up and ran a shaky hand over his face. "I need to go." His voice sounded rough.

"Liam?" Carrie rose from the table, but he held the photo album up in front of him like a shield.

"No." He was in full retreat. "Goddamn you, Carrie. I'm so pissed at you right now, I don't even want to see you. I've missed so much. Almost his entire childhood." His face twisted. "He's a teenager. And a pianist. But he's a stranger to me. My *own son* is a stranger."

"I'm trying to fix that—" Carrie stood still, searching desperately for the right words to say.

"Well you can't! I don't get that time back." His voice rose, the pain so evident it cut through her like a scalpel. "Jesus! He's *fifteen*. I don't *ever* get to change a diaper or rock him or read to him or teach him to play scales or Mozart. That's done. It's gone. *Over*." Tears shimmered in his eyes. It alarmed her that he was so close to breaking. "And by God, I resent the hell out of you for that."

Turning his back on her, he left, letting the door slam behind him.

CHAPTER 12

S tunned, Carrie hurried to the window in time to see Liam hop over the rail of the *Allegro* and disappear inside.

Her stomach tied into nervous knots as she slumped onto the window seat. The album was meant as a gesture of goodwill—so he could see Jack's childhood. She truly thought he'd receive it as the wonderful gift she intended, that he'd be glad to have it. Instead she'd made him angry. *Again.* And this time, he was good and pissed.

Damn, damn, damn, now what? How do I fix this?

That thought took her by surprise, because she *wanted* to fix it. Now that he was here, there was no hiding from the hunger he created in her. Not only that, it was time to think about Jack and his relationship with his father. She didn't want to blow whatever chance her son might have of knowing his dad. And yes, she wanted to find out where she and Liam were going, to see what— if anything—was possible. However, *nothing* was going to be possible if they couldn't spend an hour together without the hostility. Seemed like all they'd done in the last forty-eight hours was snarl at one another.

Or paw each other.

Instinctively, she reached for her phone to call Julie and hash it through. But as her finger swiped the screen, she paused. There was no need to call her lifeline this time. She knew exactly what her best friend would say.

Time to step up, dolly. Get your butt down there and talk to him.

She gazed down at the boat for several moments, and then taking a deep breath, straightened her shoulders and headed out the door.

W ill looked up from his laptop when Liam strode into the salon. "Hey, man, what's up?"

Liam slammed the album down on the table. "Fifteen years of my son's life, conveniently condensed into twenty pages."

"What the hell?" Will reached for the leather album. "What's going on?" Thumbing through the pages, he examined the pictures of Jack, all the while glancing at Liam who was pacing and seething. "Okay, I'm lost. I guess I don't get why this isn't a good thing."

"Goddammit, I missed *everything!* She kept him from me and I missed it all. *She* spends fifteen years with him. *I* get a fucking photo album." Liam threw himself onto the sofa. "Guess what else came out today. Jack's a piano prodigy. Do you believe that?"

"Yeah, I believe it," Will replied. "His gene pool is full of gifted musicians. I'd have been more surprised if you'd told me he was tone-deaf. His grandmother was Beth Ann Halligan, for God's sake."

Liam glared at him, but Will went on. "Look, Liam, I get why you're pissed. It's sad you missed so much of Jack's childhood. But you can't change that—no matter how much you rant and rave. It is what it is, man."

"I hate it when people say that." Liam snarled. "What else would it be?"

Will stood and warmed up his coffee. "Frankly, I can see why she kept it to herself. Can't you see it through her eyes for even a minute?"

"No! It was a crappy, cowardly thing to do. Hell, if Eliot hadn't forced the issue, I *still* wouldn't know Jack existed. She had no intention of *ever* telling me."

"Are you absolutely certain of that?" Will came around and sat down in the big club chair, cradling his coffee mug in his hands. "Yeah, you missed a lot. But your world is hell and gone from hers. Try to see why she'd be a little reluctant to come into it with a kid. Or bring you into *her* life for that matter. I can see why she'd be afraid."

"Stop defending her," Liam snapped.

"Then stop being an ass," Will retorted. "Last night you were so hot for her that you had your hands all over her and now, you're too pissed to even be in the same room with her?" He took a deep sip of coffee. "Get a grip, pal. If you want to *find out what's possible*—and those are your words, not mine—you're going to have to forgive her for hiding Jack. It's done, and she's trying to make it up to you. This photo book is an olive branch, not a trump card."

"How could *you* possibly know what her motivation is in giving me these pictures?" Liam was trying to calm down. The anger he'd spewed at Will was misplaced, but he hurt. He glared at the album on the table—a cruel reminder of what he didn't have—would never have. "You don't know a fucking thing about her."

"Well, you *do* know her. She might be closed up, but is she malicious? Is she the kind of woman who would deliberately hurt you?"

Liam gazed at him for a long moment, then shoved his fingers through his hair. "No. Not deliberately. Not even me."

"I'd be more inclined to say *especially* not you," Will said. "The woman clearly has feelings for you. Of course, that's only my humble opinion—based on the fact that when Tony and I came back last night, we couldn't have gotten a postcard between the two of you." He paused, tilting his head to peer into Liam's face. "Her world is as wrong-side-out as yours right now. I seriously doubt she gave you these pictures out of spite."

"He's right, Liam. I meant the album as a gift." Carrie stood in the doorway, her voice soft but firm. "I thought you might like to have some pictures of Jack—to see what he's been doing. You know, to start to know who he is."

They both stared silently at her as she came further into the salon.

"I'm sorry, truly sorry. I never meant to hurt you." She shrugged, her dark eyes shimmering with unshed tears. "Seems like that's all I've said to you in the past twenty-four hours."

Will stood up and grabbed his cell phone from the table. "Hello, Carrie." He smiled and patted her shoulder as he walked by. "Well, folks, gotta run. Gotta go see a man about some music. No, no, please, don't ask me to stay." He slipped out with a wave.

Silence yawned between them as the sound of his footsteps faded up the docks.

Liam sighed and rubbed his face.

Carrie trembled, but her eyes remained locked on his as she came around the chair to him. Leaning down, she ran a gentle thumb over his lower lip, resting her other hand over his heart.

Could she feel it pounding? Closing her eyes, she touched her lips to his in a whisper of a kiss that left him longing for more.

No. Dammit, no.

"Don't do that." He moved his head away and leapt up, putting as much distance between them as he could in the close quarters. "What are you trying to do? Channel your inner vamp? Get me off guard? Seduce me to ease your conscience? A quick fuck and I'm supposed to forget you hid my son from me for years?"

The blood drained from her face as she sucked in a quick breath.

He immediately regretted the cutting words. "I'm sorry. I'm sorry," he mumbled, his eyes sliding away from her stricken expression. "I didn't mean that."

Carrie stood frozen beside the club chair, her dark eyes huge, her lower lip caught between her teeth. When she finally spoke, her voice was so small he almost didn't hear it. "Jack is a counselor at Lawson this summer." She swallowed hard but continued in a more normal tone. "I'll go get him today. Or if you want, we can both go up there... right this minute." Her last words came out even louder, but haltingly.

Liam stared at her, his heart hammering in his chest. The tears that had been threatening since she walked in the door rolled down her cheeks, but she didn't bother to wipe them away. She looked so vulnerable. So delicate. So beautiful. In spite of his anger, he couldn't help wanting her.

Maybe she really is trying.

"Aww, shit," he groaned.

In two strides, he had her in his arms. He took her lips softly at first and as she began to respond, more fiercely. Thrusting his fingers into her hair, he held her head still for his mouth, tasting her salty tears as he increased the pressure. Then she was returning the kiss, opening her lips to his, meeting his tongue stroke for stroke.

When he lifted his head, their eyes met. They were both breathless.

She gave him a feeble smile. "We've got to work on our communication, Maestro, because this isn't going well." Her voice quavered. "So far, it seems like we've spent all our time being mad at each other. Oh, and making out. We seem to be doing a lot of that."

"Making out?" Liam scoffed. "Maybe we should stick with that part." He hugged her close and she relaxed in his arms. Rubbing his cheek on her hair, he said, "Carrie, I appreciate your offer, but we don't have to go get Jack right now. I'm dying to meet him, but I promised you five days. I'm not going to break that promise. We've got to figure *us* out, that's for damn sure."

"I'm really am sorry you resent the time I've had with him." Carrie smoothed her hands up and down his back. "I don't blame you for being angry, but all I have to offer you is that album and the here-and-now. I can't give you back Jack's childhood. I'm sorry, but I can't."

"I know, and I'm sorry for yelling at you." He rested his chin on the top of her head. "There aren't any more secrets, right? Jack doesn't have a twin? No husband or fiancé who's going to suddenly appear and challenge me to a duel?"

She hid her face in his shirt front as she shook her head. "No," she whispered.

∾

Carrie knew she would have to confess at some point, but not now. Not when she was practically back in his good graces. Besides, what if they couldn't make a go of it? What would be the point in telling him about the money if they were just going to be estranged parents sharing custody of a teenager?

He pressed his lips to her forehead. "That's good to know, and listen, thanks for the pictures. I'm glad to have them." He sighed. "I don't deny there's still a little part of me that's resentful. Guess I'll have to work on that, huh?"

"You're entitled."

More than you know, Maestro, more than you know.

She tipped her chin back to smile at him. "If we can leave the resentful part here, would the rest of you like to go to the lighthouse with me? I thought we might try relaxing and having some fun together. We can take a picnic and eat on the beach."

"Fun? You and me? Huh. I vaguely remember having *fun* with you." He dropped a kiss on her nose. "Don't you have clients today?"

"Nope, not a one, and the phone can go to voicemail. I don't keep regular hours at the studio since all my work's by appointment." She took his hand, pulling him toward the door. "What about you? Anything you have to do today?"

"No. Tomorrow we drive up to Traverse City to meet the orchestra. I was going to go over the rest of the scores for the benefit today, but we still don't have a couple of the pieces. Will's going up there to see about getting them. I'll need to work on them tonight, but for now, I'm all yours."

CHAPTER 13

They strolled along the Lake Michigan shore to Willow Bay lighthouse. Carrie's insulated backpack, filled with a picnic of wine, bread, cheese, and fruit was slung over Liam's shoulder. As they explored the lighthouse, she regaled him with stories about her volunteer work there. Since restoring the old structure was her favorite cause, it touched her beyond words when he not only took an envelope to make a donation, but also bought sweat-shirts for Will, Tony, and himself to help support the restoration effort. After the tour, she spread a blanket out on the sand, and nestled in the cleft of the dunes, they ate their lunch. The beach and the water were only a few yards away, and she let the waves whispering on the sand help her relax.

Carrie shared anecdotes about Jack as a baby and a youngster, delighted as Liam laughed, his eyes sparkling when she told him about Jack's first full sentence. "It's his first birthday and we're all in Noah and Margie's kitchen. Jack's in a high chair. He's stuffed himself with cake and ice cream. His little face covered in strawberry goop, and there's Eliot next to him. 'Say Elliot,' he says. 'Say Eliot.' He's drawing it out for him. 'El-li-ot.'" She demonstrated. "Finally Jack looks him right in the eye and clear as a bell says, 'No, Elly, I don't want to.'" She grinned. "He's been Elly to Jack ever since, and the kid never went back to baby talk."

"So you knew early on how bright he is?" Liam leaned back on his elbows.

"Yes, he's done everything fast. Walked at eight months. Talked really early. His vocabulary's always been extraordinary. He's got an unquenchable thirst for learning anything new." She couldn't help the pride in her voice. She wanted Liam to be proud of him, to be proud of *her*. To believe she was doing a good job parenting his son.

"And the music?" His eyes narrowed.

"That's pretty much his life." She paused for a moment. What would he think about her choices? Would he agree? "I kept him in public school until freshman year. He studied piano with Eliot and went to summer camp at Lawson. But last year, he was a day student at Interlochen. This fall, he goes in as a boarder."

"Why did you wait until freshman year for Interlochen?"

She expelled a breath, then turned to meet his eyes. "Partly selfish, I guess. I wanted him with me. But also I thought he needed balance, to have some friends who weren't completely absorbed in the arts. He needs to be at Interlochen, though. He's too gifted not to focus on the music."

Liam continued asking question after question, particularly about Jack and the piano. A tiny qualm niggled in the back of her mind as she detailed Jack's musical history. Liam was immensely curious about Jack's gift, about where he might be headed with it. That worried her. Jack needed to stay here and finish high school at Interlochen. Then maybe audition for Juilliard or the New England Conservatory. Surely Liam would never consider taking him on the road. His life was so different from theirs, her doubts about how they would ever fit into his world were too numerous to count. Yet she sat fascinated as he talked about touring, about the concert halls and venues he'd been in. About the orchestras he'd conducted.

"I wish you could have seen the open-air theater in Athens. So incredible! Full of ancient history and yet bursting with new life."

Carrie watched him, captivated by how he gestured broadly when he spoke, almost as if he was conducting. Enthusiasm shone in his expression, his zeal almost a palpable thing.

"In Europe, people cut their cultural teeth on classical music and opera. The kids are as jacked up about Mozart and Puccini as teenagers here are about rock music. They love rock music over there too, but they also appreciate classical."

"You spend a lot of time in Europe, don't you?" Carrie tipped her head back to feel the sun on her face. The breeze ruffled her hair.

He nodded, taking a sip of wine before he replied. "About every two or three years, I do a tour over there. We sort through and add cities or take some off. I always go to London, Paris, Venice, Vienna. Athens was new this past year. We did Moscow three years ago. God, was *that* ever fascinating. And three weeks in China, which was completely surreal. I'd love to take you and Jack there, you'd be overwhelmed."

"No doubt," Carrie chuckled. "I sometimes get over-whelmed in Traverse City. I can't even imagine China or Moscow."

"When did you become such a homebody?" Liam reached for her hand. "You used to travel with your dad, didn't you? And with Eliot to competitions?"

"No, my dad never traveled much after my mother died. We stayed at the farm. His agents took care of the horse sales." Carrie glanced down at their entwined fingers, too aware of the bolt of electricity that simple touch created. "And until Montreal, I hadn't been any further away from Louisville than Chicago. The competitions I played in were small time, pretty much all in the Midwest."

"You're kidding?" He seemed genuinely surprised. "I guess I assumed you were well-traveled since your dad dealt in race horses and you planned to play professionally."

"Nope. I was only a couple of years out of college when I came to McGill. I've been here in Willow Bay so long, I can't even imagine going so far away."

He eyed her for moment. "Tell me about the piano bar. What's that about?"

Heat flushed her cheeks. It was inevitable he'd bring that up. She was surprised he hadn't asked her about it at dinner the night before. "I don't know. A way to stay connected to my mother, I guess."

"Too easy. Your mother played Carnegie Hall, not hotel bars. Come on." His gaze burned straight through her.

"You'll laugh."

"I won't. I promise."

She dropped her gaze. "When I play there I'm… I'm someone else. Another woman."

"Who's the other woman?"

"A figment of my imagination." Carrie stopped, at a loss as to how to explain it. "A–a parody of the woman I should've been. The woman my father wanted me to be."

"Aren't you being a little hard on yourself?" Liam stroked one finger down her cheek. "You play beautifully and you bring plea-sure to the patrons. What's wrong with that?"

"It's not Bach or Beethoven or Schubert."

"No." He peered into her face. "But does it always have to be?"

"When I auditioned at the bar, I picked the songs my mother listened to, the ones she and Dad loved to dance to. I don't remember very much about her, but I have a vision–a memory of them dancing in our solarium to Jim Croce's 'Time In a Bottle.' Over the years, it's been something that's *mine*, you know?" When she looked up, he was staring at her with eyes so tender, her heart melted. "And in a small way, the dressing up, the makeup—it's a kick. A step outside of my life here."

"Ah, so the little homebody really *is* looking for adventure?" He grinned. "You'd love Europe, Carrie. Everything there reeks of history and beauty. The photographer in you would have a field day. Munich's incredible and Vienna—" He stopped and tilted his head like a curious child. "What?"

"Don't you ever get overwhelmed?" His experiences made him seem larger than life, leaving her both fascinated and terrified as she wondered again how she'd ever fit into his world.

"*You* overwhelm me," he replied after a long moment of silence. He moved closer, pressing her back as he leaned over her, one hand on her belly. "You scare the holy hell out of me, Carrie. You've had this hold over me ever since the first time I saw you in that rehearsal hall in Montreal. Remember? It was raining that day. God, you were soaked and haughty and so incredibly beautiful." His wistful smile shot fire through her. "Sitting there at that harpsichord, you looked... untouchable, and all I wanted was to touch you."

Almost unconsciously, she brushed back the lock of hair that always fell over his forehead. "I didn't think you saw me as an actual human being that day, the way you hauled me up onstage and plopped me down." She chuckled. "At first I couldn't believe you expected me to just fill in when I'd never even seen the music or knew who you were. But you kept staring at me." She touched his beard and then his lips. "I could barely concentrate on the notes because I couldn't take my eyes off you. Honestly, I was ready to jump you right there on the podium." When she blushed at the confession, Liam laughed—a deep throaty laugh that made her want to jump him all over again.

He brought his mouth down on hers, pulling her to him, pressing his whole length to her. Her lips parted as her tongue met his. When she put her arms around him, he devoured her, demanding that she give him what they both wanted. All thought, all reason fled at his touch. His hands moved to her hips and then cupped her behind, tugging her to his hardness.

Straining against him, she couldn't get close enough.

He's the one who has power over me.

Her hands moved lower to seek the warmth of his denim-covered hips. All the memories she'd clung to so desperately didn't begin to prepare her for the actual sensual onslaught of his touch. She thought she'd remembered, but she wasn't even close.

"Liam," she whispered against his mouth. His lips explored her cheek, her ear, the sensitive skin of her throat. He dropped nibbling kisses over her collarbone as she thrust her fingers through his hair, loving the thick, silky feel of it. "I woke up so many nights, frustrated beyond belief because I couldn't reach out for you." She pulled his head back up to press kisses on his beard and his face. "I never imagined in a million years I'd be touching you again."

"Oh God, Carrie…"

Liam's strong hands swept over her body. His fingers explored under her shirt, curving around her breast, stroking, pinching gently through the fabric of her bra. He reached behind her, released the hooks, and then covered the soft flesh with his hands.

"Touch me," he begged huskily in her ear. "I want to feel your skin on mine."

She tugged his shirt up, caressing the warmth of his back, massaging the muscles. When he wrenched her shirt up, his crisp chest hairs tickled her nipples. His fingers traced her spine. She never knew her back was an erogenous zone until Liam's hands brought the fact to light. Slipping his hands around, he stroked and caressed her breasts. His lips tasted her throat. Rolling over on top of her, he nestled his rigid arousal against her belly, his lips moving lower. Fire licked at her nerves, sizzling her skin wherever his hands touched. Her fingers reached for the snap of his jeans.

Laughter and voices sounded in the distance.

"Liam," she gasped, sliding her hands up his chest. "Someone's coming."

He lifted his head and blinked, appearing dazed. Exhaling a shaky breath, he yanked both their shirts down, then rolled to his side, taking her with him. Breathing heavily, she sat up, clumsily attempting to fix her bra. His eyes were stormy with passion as he groaned and pulled her back against him, settling her between his legs. Her backside pressed firmly against his rock-hard erection, as he wrapped his arms around her. With his face buried in her hair, Carrie felt his heart pounding as several tourists tramped past them down to the water, chattering and laughing. She wondered if he could feel hers.

After the group passed, Liam let out a huge breath. Turning in his arms, she gave him her best version of wide-eyed innocence, while he grinned at her, raising one brow suggestively.

"God, I don't think I've unhooked a bra under a girl's shirt since high school," he said, chuckling. "We really are *making out*, aren't we?" As she started to move away from him, he grabbed her. "Ah. Don't move. Not yet."

"Are you okay?" she asked, concerned about the pained expression on his face.

"No, I'm pretty uncomfortable actually." He squirmed. "We just need to sit still for a few minutes, okay?"

"Okay." With a contented sigh, she leaned back against him. His finger traced a line from her elbow to her wrist as she stroked the soft hair on his forearm.

How many times were they going to do this before stopping would no longer be an option?

He'd opened a Pandora's Box of sexuality with that first kiss on the beach. If they could manage to spend more than two hours together without erupting into a fight, she was certain she'd be in his bed before the week was out.

And she was pretty sure they both knew it.

CHAPTER 14

Snug in her yoga pants and Michigan State hoodie, Carrie lounged in the Adirondack chair on her deck, a glass of wine in hand, basking in the red-orange glow of a spectacular Willow Bay sunset. She couldn't help sneaking a peek at the gleaming boat in Berth Thirty-Eight, where Liam was working on the music for the benefit. Her mental image had him at the keyboard, glasses down on his nose as he made notes on a score. It didn't really matter how she pictured him, the effect was the same. Heat. Lots and lots of scary, wonderful heat. Hadn't today proven that?

When they left the beach at the lighthouse, she drove the twenty-odd miles to Sleeping Bear Dunes National Lakeshore, where they hiked up the giant sand dune. He was breathing hard, his face damp with sweat when they reached the top, although they'd taken it at a pretty even pace. She couldn't help laughing as he'd flopped down on the sand, groaning.

"Good Lord, woman, are you trying to kill me?" Yanking a bottle of water from her pack, he drank it down in one long gulp. "If this is some weird, sadistic method of keeping my libido under control, guess what? It's working!"

"How can you have a body that's probably illegal in several

states, but you can't hike up a sand dune?" She opened her own water bottle and sipped it slowly as she walked around him "You're going to get a cramp if you don't keep moving. Trust me, I learned that the hard way."

"There's a huge difference between my treadmill and weights or jogging on Lakeshore Drive and this giant mountain of sand." His chest heaved and his shirt was sweaty. He pushed up to a sitting position, swiping uselessly at the sand sticking to his damp clothes. "Cripes, Carrie, sit down. Y*ou're* giving me a cramp."

Grinning mischievously, she dumped her water bottle on his head. "You need to cool off, old man."

He'd grabbed her calf and yanked her down on the sand, shaking his head like a wet dog, splattering her with water. Holding her down, he rubbed his wet hair on her face and then on her shirt, while she screeched in half-hearted protest.

"Old man?" The question was muffled in the front of her shirt. He lifted his head. "Make up your mind, sweetheart. Old man or fantastic body? Which is it?"

"I didn't say *fantastic*," she denied, giggling. But his wet head on her breasts was incredibly erotic. "I said *illegal*."

"Yeah? Well, *this* is illegal!" Quirking one brow, he gazed down at her. She glanced down too. Soaked and clinging to her breasts, her shirt left little to the imagination. Her nipples were erect, showing even through her cotton bra. When she looked back up, the hunger in his eyes melted her as he dipped his head down again.

With Herculean effort, she grabbed his hair to stop him. "Liam," she gasped, breathless at the thought of his lips on her sensitive nipples. "People are coming up the dune." Squirming away from him, she stood up and grabbed her pack, then held out her hand. "Come on, Maestro, you have to work tonight. And I need to go to the studio and get some proofs ready."

With a sigh, he got to his feet. "We've got to find a more

private place to get reacquainted," he grumbled as she swept sand off his backside with her open palm. He did the same for her, but not without more groping and touching.

Their chemistry was explosive. Carrie was almost embarrassed at how they couldn't seem to keep their hands off each other. He nuzzled the back of her neck as he brushed her off, and she shivered at the touch of his lips. Heat continued to build as he put one arm around her, pulling her back against his muscled chest.

"Old man?" he whispered. "Really?" His hot breath in her ear sent another quiver of longing through her.

"Excuse me, are you Maestro Reilly?"

Liam's head shot up at the feminine voice coming toward them.

A trim, grey-haired woman trudged up the dune, waving her hand. "Aren't you Liam Reilly, the symphony conductor?"

"I am." Liam moved back, releasing Carrie, and reached for the woman's outstretched hand. "Hello. And you are?"

"Carl! Everybody! It *is* Maestro Reilly!" The woman turned to her companions, huffing and puffing up the dune behind her. "Maestro, I'm Barbara Hall, this is my husband, Carl. And our friends…" The woman went on to introduce several others in her party. Liam smiled, shaking hands with each of them.

"This is Carrie Halligan," he offered. Carrie smiled a greeting, but stood back, allowing him time with the little clutch of fans.

Barbara chattered on. "We just got our tickets for the Lawson benefit. We're all subscribers to TSO and so thrilled we'll get to see you conduct. They're a wonderful orchestra." The other women in the group clustered around him. The men were less zealous, but still seemed to be very pleased to meet him.

"They are," Liam said with a nod. "I'm looking forward to working with them. How long have you been subscribers?"

Carrie watched him slide easily into celebrity mode, chatting with the group as if he'd known them forever, giving them his undivided attention for the short time they stood together in the sand. After he'd autographed the backs of several park maps and thanked them warmly, they moved on. The women were grinning like star-struck teenagers.

"Does this happen often?" she asked as they made their way slowly down the dune toward the parking area.

Smiling, he said, "Well, probably not as often as it does to say... Bono or Mick Jagger. But sometimes people recognize me. I imagine this had to do with the press the orchestra's put out. Or maybe whatever benefit promo Dave Lawson's doing in the area."

"How does that make you feel?" Carrie was still processing the encounter. "I've never been with someone being asked for an autograph before."

"It's nice," he admitted. "I like it when people recognize me and appreciate what I do." They walked in silence for a few minutes before he added quietly, "I don't get mobbed by fans, Carrie."

"You sure about that? How many women constitute a mob in the world of classical music, Maestro?"

"I don't know the exact number, but for what it's worth, female symphony patrons rarely toss their panties up on the podium." He winked and gave her a grin.

"I'm not worried about *that*. Well, okay, maybe I *am* a little worried about that." When he raised one brow, she elbowed him. "I don't mean the panties, you idiot, I mean the attention you get."

"Why does that worry you?" Having reached her car, Carrie unlocked the doors with her remote. Liam opened the driver's side door, but stood in the way so she couldn't get in, obviously waiting for her to answer.

"How do you handle that?" she asked and then added in a whisper. "How do *I* handle that?"

"Graciously. Like we did today." He tipped her face up with a finger under her chin. "I admit, at first, years ago, I *didn't* handle it well—too taken in by my own press. But not anymore." He dropped a kiss on her nose. "Look, I'm just a guy who wants to make beautiful music and is fortunate to be able to do what he loves. Okay?" He peered down at her face. "Okay?"

"Okay," Carrie agreed. But another seed of doubt had been planted. That encounter had been a very real reminder of how different life would be if they continued.

Even now, the doubt lingered as she sipped her wine, watching the sunset. All in all, it had been a good day. They'd actually spent the better part of it together without a single harsh word between them. She'd expected him to lapse back into hostility whenever the topic turned to Jack, but he didn't. The vast silences she'd worried about never occurred. Conversation progressed almost as easily as it had in Montreal—art, books, movies, his career, her photography. But always the subject came back to Jack. Liam's questions were endless.

What kind of grades does he make? What are his favorite subjects in school besides music? When did he learn to sail? What sports does he enjoy? What are his favorite foods?

His questions regarding his son came fast and furious, but surprisingly, there were no questions about her—well, about her dating relationships. She was dying of curiosity about him and the women he'd known, but his apparent lack of curiosity made her own feel juvenile, perhaps even a bit petty. She'd seen photos of him with several different women. Most recently at the Grammy awards with Ella Grant, a tall willowy actress about twenty years his junior. Carrie was fairly certain that was who he'd been talking to the night before. But if he was involved with Ella Grant, why was he pursuing *her*?

Rod Stewart singing "Maggie May" interrupted her musing. Pulling her cell phone out of the pouch in her hoodie, she squinted in the dim light at the screen. *Jack!* "Hey, honey!"

"Mom, hi! How's it going?"

"It's good, baby. How are you?" God, it was fantastic to hear his voice. "Tell me you miss your ol' mom."

"I miss my ol' mom," Jack replied dutifully.

"You're such an obliging kid. I miss you too." She stretched her legs out, settling in for a nice long chat. "How's camp?"

"Great! Tessa and I have five kids. The youngest is only six, but wow, she's gonna rock. Already plays jazz almost like Eubie."

"No way! At six years old?"

"Yeah, she's cute and super talented." Jack's enthusiasm came through loud and clear. He was obviously having a blast. "We've also got a little guy who's eight and wants to be a conductor."

"No kidding?"

A conductor?

Carrie's stomach lurched, and she took a sip of wine.

He chuckled. "Serious. The kid brought a *baton* with him. Some conductor in Indianapolis gave it to him when he went backstage last winter. It's all he talks about. Keeps asking me if he'll get to meet Maestro Reilly when he comes for the benefit."

"Who else do you have?" Carrie wanted to get off the topic of conductors—Maestro Reilly, in particular.

"A pair of twins who do, um, fairly well, but they always want to play together—you know, like duets? I've been all over the Web looking for stuff for them to play."

"Boys or girls?" she asked. "How old are they?"

"Boys. They're seven. Our other kid is a little girl who's six. She's from Japan, but man, she speaks, like, perfect English. She keeps calling me *Sir.* It's kinda weird."

"Did you say *Tessa*? Tessa Nolan, the flute player you accompanied in spring recital?"

Carrie's curiosity was piqued. Jack hadn't paid a lot of attention to girls yet, although they were certainly interested in him. Several girls from Willow Bay High School had been hanging around the marina that spring, talking to him while he manned the bait shop for Noah. Julie had teased Carrie unmercifully about them, warning her about the dangers of having a "hunky son."

"Yeah," Jack replied. "Dr. Lawson put us together since Miko, the little Japanese girl, plays piano *and* flute."

She couldn't resist. "So how's that working out for you? As I recall, Tessa is really pretty."

"Yeah, well... she... um... she's okay."

She knew her son well enough to know that his feeble attempt at nonchalance probably meant he liked the girl.

Good Lord, am I ready for Jack and girls? Probably not.

So she simply said, "Just an observation."

"Tessa's cool." He left it there and hurried on. "I wanted to ask if you could come up on Sunday for the kids' first recital. Tradition is Dr. Lawson picks one of the counselors to do the finale at each recital and he picked me for the first one!"

"Honey, that's wonderful!" Carrie exclaimed. "You bet I'll be there." No need to tell him she'd already planned to be there and why. That certainly wasn't a conversation for the telephone.

Coward.

Her conscience nudged her. But she'd become brilliant at ignoring that particular inner voice. Hadn't she disregarded it earlier today when Liam asked if there were any more secrets?

"He said I could play anything I wanted, so I'm doing Jelly Roll Morton's 'King Porter Stomp.' It's awesome! I'm totally psyched..."

A chill went through her at his eagerness. Right now, the most important thing in his young life was getting to play jazz at a recital. But Sunday, his life would be changed forever.

How do I to tell him about Liam? What if he can't forgive me? What if he never forgives me? What if he wants to go with Liam and—

"Mom?" The question in Jack's voice brought her back to the conversation. "You still there?"

"Yes... Yes, I'm still here."

"You okay?"

"Yep, I'm fine," she reassured him. "I can't wait to see you. You'll be brilliant in the finale—better than Jelly Roll."

"Well, I don't know about *that*." His chuckle was exactly like Liam's. A bell sounded behind his voice. "Whoops, that's fellowship. Gotta go, Mom."

"Okay, good night, honey. I love you." Tears pricked at her eyelids.

"Love you too. See you Sunday!" The line went dead.

"Yeah. Sunday." Carrie said to the now-silent phone. She clicked it off and blinking back tears, took a long drink of wine.

CHAPTER 15

After he returned from rehearsal on Friday afternoon, Liam simply followed Carrie around. Loitering in the background as she photographed kids at the Methodist church vacation Bible school. Carrying her tripod and gig bag for a quick shoot down at the sailing club. Later, relaxing on a beanbag chair in the corner of the studio with his Kindle while she did a sitting of senior pictures.

"You're staring," she accused him as Heather Harmon and her mother left the studio, outfits and paraphernalia over their arms. It had been a good session—Carrie loved working with a subject who had fun with the experience. Locking the door behind them, Carrie flipped the sign to *Closed*, then stood at her desk to enter the invoice information into her computer.

Liam rose in one lithe move, coming over to stand behind her. "You know, you're very good at this." His warm breath on her neck sent a tingle through her.

Shivering, she tried to concentrate on the task at hand. "Does that surprise you?" Finished, she shut down the computer and rubbed the back of her neck.

"Not at all." He replaced her fingers with his, massaging her skin. "Did it surprise *you?*"

She turned around to find herself staring at the open neck of his shirt. He slid his fingers into the curls at her nape, lifting her chin with his thumb. The current between them sparked and flashed every time they were within twenty feet of each other. She swallowed with effort, breathing deeply to control the rapid beat of her heart.

"Honestly?" she said. "It surprised the hell out of me."

"Why?" He resumed the massage, letting his fingers knead and caress her shoulders, his thumbs only inches from her breasts.

"I'm not like you... or Jack. Both of you have always known what you wanted. From the first moment you touched the keys of a piano. But n–not me." She was stammering. His touch made thinking practically impossible.

Just breathe.

Inhaling, she tried to find the words. "I–I did what I thought other people wanted me to do. In particular, my dad. I think I was trying to live up to my mother's memory. The piano. Horses. Always someone else's dream."

"When did you start taking pictures?"

"When Jack was born." She smiled up into his eyes, loving how curious he was about everything and happy to see no judgment reflected there. "Eliot gave me a nice digital camera, and from the first shot, I knew I'd found my true talent. I photographed everyone and everything. Took some night classes at Northwestern in Traverse City. Read voraciously. Invested in equipment, a Mac, software."

Please, please don't ask me where the money for the equipment came from. Not yet. I can't tell you about that until I'm sure we're going to make it this time.

He pivoted her back around as his fingers found the knot that inevitably developed between her neck and shoulder after a long day's work. "When did you open this place?"

"About four years ago." Apparently it hadn't occurred to him to wonder how she afforded the cameras and computer. She allowed his hands, his heat, to relax her aching muscles. *Good God, the man's fingers are magic.*

"Mmm... I won a few photo contests. People began asking me to take pictures for them—weddings and events. Then Paul McCann over at the newspaper asked me to do some of his photo work. The portraits sorta came along after that, I guess." Leaning her back against his muscled chest, she tilted her head. "Oh, there. Yes. You found it."

"All your stress lands right here, doesn't it?" His fingers prodded.

"Yep." She rolled her head forward as he worked the sore muscle. "After a day like today, I'm ready for a hot bath and the percussion massager."

He dropped a kiss on the very spot he'd been rubbing. "I hope I'm at least as good as a massager."

"Oh, you'll do." She swiveled and found herself in his arms. "You've certainly been good for business. I swear, senior pictures are going to be done in no time. All the moms are booking June appointments on the off-chance you might be here to drool over."

"Perhaps you should keep me around." He ran his thumb across her lower lip.

"There's an idea." Desire curled inside her. "Maybe I'll keep you in the corner. Stuffed and mounted."

Quirking a brow, he laughed. "My, what a sharp tongue you have, Ms. Halligan." Liam brought her face to his with a slight pressure on the back of her head. "We're going to have to do something to sweeten your disposition." His mouth closed over hers, opening her lips with an exploring tongue before she had a chance to react.

Senses reeling, Carrie's arms lifted automatically to encircle his neck.

How does he do this? Turn me completely to mush every time he so much as looks in my direction. And how will I ever live without his hands, without these kisses when he cruises back to Chicago?

Liam's hands slipped down to her hips, pulling her hard against him while his tongue sought hers. She ran her hands across his wide shoulders, longing for closer contact, for skin-to-skin connection. His mouth explored her cheek while his uneven breath caressed her ear. Dropping her head back to allow him greater access to the skin of her throat, she tangled her fingers into the thick hair that curled over his collar.

He reached for her buttons, releasing the first few. His hands skated over the tops of her breasts while his teeth nipped gently at her skin. Her nipples tightened and tingled within the confines of her bra. Pressing closer, she touched her tongue to the stubble beneath his chin. He shivered, then his mouth was on hers again —demanding, teasing, caressing—and then demanding once more.

Sliding her hands down his ribcage, yearning to feel warm male skin, she found the hem of his shirt.

But before she could tug the fabric up, he released her lips abruptly and grabbed her hands. "No." He was breathing hard. His eyes were stormy, reflecting her own unsatisfied longing. "Not again. I can't. Not without... not without finishing it." Peering into her face, apparently he found what he was looking for because he whispered, "Meet me at your place in about an hour. Okay?"

Carrie could only nod, even though what she really wanted was to grab him, throw him down on her desk, and do something delicious and naughty to him. Shaking, she buttoned up with clumsy hands, then smoothed her shirt front. "I need to get to the bank before it closes." She realized how inane she sounded, but what else could she say?

No wait! Lock the door and screw me stupid right here, right now?

Well, that was one possibility, but he was already heading for the back door.

"I'm going to the market. I'm cooking supper for you," he tossed over his shoulder. "Will and Tony are entertaining on the boat tonight."

"You're kidding." She shook her head to clear it—they'd moved from practically tearing each other's clothes off to talking about Will and Tony? And Liam was damn near out the door. *How'd that happen? Crap.*

She shifted gears. "Who are they entertaining?"

"Couple of servers from the Fishwife." He stopped with one hand on the doorknob. "I think Will said they were sisters."

"Hey. Hey, wait!" Carrie seized her tote bag and shoved her laptop and checkbook into it. "Are you talking about the Arnott twins? Deanna and Dinah?"

"Am I?" A breeze swept in the open door, ruffling the curtain to the back room. "Yeah. Actually, that sounds right."

"Huh. Those two have broken about every male heart in the county." She chuckled and followed him out the door, stopping to lock it and set the alarm.

"They're legal, aren't they?" Liam's brow furrowed.

"Completely legal," she assured him. "They'll be seniors at Michigan State in September. They're a couple of heartbreakers, that's all."

"Well, they'll have their hands full with Will and Tony." He grinned. "They've broken a few hearts themselves."

She stared as he jogged down to the corner, waiting for the beach trolley to pass before he crossed to the market. This was all moving so fast again—a replay of Montreal, sixteen years later.

But this time, it was different. There was more at stake, and she should be cautious—even though she was still helpless to resist him. The man was driving her insane, and fact was, thanks to his kisses and touches, she didn't have to go too much further to get to crazy.

An hour later, Liam, swathed in her red chef's apron, poached salmon on the stove, while she lifted the lid of another pot to admire steaming carrots and snow peas.

"I'm thinking of stealing your apron," he said as he ladled lemon juice and herbs over the salmon. *If music be the food of love, play on!* Shakespeare's words were scrawled in white letters across the front of the apron. "That's from *Twelfth Night*, right?"

"Yep. A Mother's Day gift from Jack." After her shower, she'd donned soft jeans and a yellow cotton tunic. "Did Aunt Margie come by?" She glanced at the plump strawberries piled in a colander in the sink.

"No, I met her on my way up here." Liam steered her away from the kitchen, sitting her down on one of the stools by the granite bar. "Tony has an apron that says, *Friends don't let friends drink white zinfandel*, but this one is much cooler." He started putting together a salad. Handing her a tomato, a serrated knife, and a small cutting board, he winked. "Make yourself useful."

Carrie's heart almost burst with that one gesture. He looked incredibly sexy even with the apron covering his knit shirt and jeans. She would've been satisfied to just sit and look at him. Actually, she would have been *more* satisfied to rip off the apron and everything underneath it. How amazing that he was in her kitchen cooking for her. He was all she'd thought about for almost a week—oh hell, for *way* longer than that. Was it even right to want someone this bad?

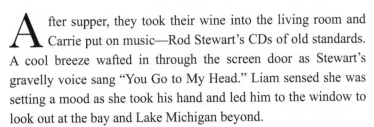

After supper, they took their wine into the living room and Carrie put on music—Rod Stewart's CDs of old standards. A cool breeze wafted in through the screen door as Stewart's gravelly voice sang "You Go to My Head." Liam sensed she was setting a mood as she took his hand and led him to the window to look out at the bay and Lake Michigan beyond.

"This is my favorite time of day," she said. "The sun makes a gold and red reflection in the water that fills my house with color and warmth." She held her wineglass up to the dying light. He shifted to stand behind her, and she tipped her head back to smile at him. "Watch, the sun will just be gone, like it simply drops into the lake."

Liam put his arm around her shoulders, holding her close as he watched the sun disappear from sight. The music, the breeze, the wine, the sunset, the lily and musk scent of Carrie's hair combined to send a blaze of sensual hunger through him. He knew where they would end up tonight. He'd come prepared with several foil packets, purchased earlier in the week, tucked in his jeans pocket. He ran his hand up and down her arm, feeling goose bumps rise at his touch. She leaned back against him for a moment, then shivering, stepped away.

"Liam, there's something I have to tell you."

CHAPTER 16

L iam's heart sank.
Where was this going?

He wanted her so much. How was he going to leave again without making love to her?

"I've changed."

"I know that." His tone was rougher than he intended as desire welled up in him.

"I mean, physically." She dropped her gaze, turning away. "My body's not the same as it was before."

"After sixteen years, whose is?" With a sigh of relief, he followed her as she paced. "Hell, my hair's getting grayer as we speak. And I thought I was going to have to be resuscitated after we climbed that damn dune."

"I'm older. I'm fatter. Gravity has started taking its toll..." She glanced at him over her shoulder, and he was certain she didn't realize how beautiful she appeared. The lights on the docks glowed through the openings in the shutters making dappled stripes across her hair and the rosy skin of her cheek.

"We're *all* older and fatter." He smiled down into her eyes. "You look delicious to me, and you're right, you're not the same."

He put his arms around her waist and pulled her against him. "You're curvier, more womanly... sexier, if that's even possible." He whispered the words in her ear and felt goose bumps chase up her arms again. "I'm not looking for some anorexic little twenty-something. In fact, I'm not *looking* at all. I've found who I want. Right here. Who I've *always* wanted."

"Oh, Liam..." Carrie trembled against him as he tasted the soft skin behind her ear. "Wait... please."

"*What*, Carrie?"

She walked away from him again, crossing her arms over her belly. "You said you wanted to give us a chance to try again. Right now, I want you so bad I can't even think straight." With a deep breath she faced him. "But there's something else you need to know before we go upstairs."

Warily, he waited for her to continue, holding onto the fact that she was indeed expecting to go upstairs.

"Something went wrong when Jack was born. I hemorrhaged and, and they had to do a hysterectomy after he was delivered." Lifting her head, she looked him straight in the eye. "I can't have any more babies. Jack is it for me. I don't know where we'll end up or if this thing between you and me will work, but if you're looking to start a family... well..." She gave him a little shrug.

Liam didn't move or respond as he processed this new revelation, which made him both sad and exhilarated. It was too bad she was unable to have any more children, but whether she meant to or not, she was telling him she wanted a future with him. "Oh, honey, I'm so sorry." He gathered her close, pressing his lips to her temple. "That must have been terrifying."

"It was. I was a mess for a while. But I've learned to live with it." She wrapped her arms around his waist, resting her forehead on his chest. "And frankly, all that time, I've thought this was how my life is going to be. A big family? More children? Those things never even entered the picture. And *you* in my life again?

That was... *past* fantasy. I'm so grateful to have Jack. But Liam, whatever happens with us... well, I thought you should know, that's all."

～

F or a long moment, he was silent and Carrie held her breath. What if this was a deal breaker in spite of his kind words? What if the fact that he'd missed Jack's childhood made him want more children? At last, he spoke. "I have something to tell you, too. Six years ago, I was diagnosed with testicular cancer. I went through radiation treatments. They got it all. Everything works just fine, except..." He paused, swallowing hard. "...except I'm sterile."

"Oh, Liam." She leaned back, but he was gazing at the horizon above the bay, clearly avoiding eye contact. Her heart ached. Little wonder he was so devastated that she'd kept Jack from him. "How awful. I'm so sorry."

"Honey, I'm forty-eight years old. Until a few days ago, I believed I'd never be a father." When his eyes finally met hers, tears shimmered in their depths. "I'm so overwhelmed just knowing about Jack that I can't even wrap my mind around actually meeting him. Whatever happens between us, Jack is an unexpected treasure, okay?" Threading his fingers through her hair, he stared into her face. "But don't ever think that all I want from you is Jack. He's a gift, but I want *you*. Right now, it's about *us*—not babies, not starting a family. Not even Jack." His mouth closed over hers, opening her lips with an exploring tongue.

She clung to him, sliding her hands up his back, meeting his tongue with her own. A low moan escaped her lips as Liam lifted his mouth to drop tiny kisses across her cheek, his tongue caressing her ear. She couldn't stop her next words. "Oh, God, Liam, I love you. I've loved you forever."

"And I've always loved you. Even when I hated you for leaving me. And even with all the resentment I'm working through, I love you." Liam ran his hands over her back and down to her hips, pulling her to him. "You're all I want."

His arousal ignited a fire in her that, for some odd reason, made her want to grin like an idiot. She tipped her head back, laughing with the sheer joy of having him in her arms. He hugged her close, chuckling with her, dancing with her to the soft music. They drifted around the couch and swayed together. He sang quietly in her ear, and his heart pounded against hers. Twirling her, he pulled her close, then deftly dipped her, before dancing her toward the open staircase.

At the bottom step, she stopped and turned to him, a sober expression on her face. "There's just one more thing."

"What is it?" He raised one brow, giving her a look of genuine distress. "Whatever it is, *I do not care.*"

"I wear contacts now." She tried with little success to keep a straight face. "And reading glasses."

Liam chuckled as he turned her around to head her up the steps with a firm hand on her behind. "Honey, I've worn contacts since I was fifteen years old. If I didn't, I wouldn't see past the first row of strings. Now, if we're done cataloguing our vast array of physical inadequacies, can we…?" He cocked his head toward the loft.

When they reached the top step, Carrie turned to him. "Come love me, Liam."

Reaching for her, pulling her roughly against him, he groaned, "Are you sure? Be sure, Carrie. I don't want to stop again."

"I'm very sure." The words were barely out before Liam's mouth covered hers. His hands slid across her back, tugging her shirt up. Her arms crept around his neck. She met his tongue, sliding her own against it to taste the wine-sweetness of his mouth.

Moaning into her kiss, he pulled away slightly, covering her face, ears, cheeks, throat with nibbling kisses. Tangling one hand in her short curls, his other one found the swell of her breast, stroking through the satin of her bra. His mouth moved to her open collar, his breath hot on her skin when he spoke. "Carrie..."

Her name sounded more like a plea, so she took his hand and led him to her bedroom.

L iam stopped at the wide French doors as she moved ahead of him, crossing over to turn on the bedside lamp. He watched as she pulled back the quilt, his heart speeding up at the graceful sway of her hips, the gentle loving way she folded back the old coverlet. He fought the urge to rush over and toss her on the bed, because, as much as he wanted to ravish her, he also wanted to watch her.

This was what he'd been waiting for, and he wanted it to last forever. Apparently, so did Carrie—she moved slowly around the room, lighting several candles and opening the window, building the romantic tension to an almost unbearable level. When she turned with an invitation in her eyes that took his breath away, he knew.

Tonight wasn't simply about sex. Or even about finally making love with *her* again. It was about coming home.

At last.

Unbuttoning the three buttons on her tunic, she brought it over her head in one smooth movement. Warmth flooded his insides. His groin tightened, but he waited and watched. This moment had been so long in coming, he was almost afraid to go to her, afraid to touch her for fear she would dissolve like all his fantasies. His breath caught in his throat as her fingers moved to the zipper of her jeans. When she slipped out of them, her eyes locked with his.

The inexperienced girl was gone. In her place, a confident, luscious woman smiled. The passion in her eyes as she came toward him set his heart racing. He opened his mouth to speak, but nothing came out.

~

C arrie was amazed to realize that the great Maestro Reilly was as nervous as she was. Clad only in her bra and lacy underpants, she went to him and slipped her hands under his shirt. His flesh was hot. Warming herself against him, she pulled the shirt higher so their skin touched.

Unlike their first time that long-ago April afternoon, he was letting her take the lead, in spite of his obvious arousal. First, she put her lips to his throat, then moved lower to the furred skin of his chest, touching her tongue to his flat nipple.

Groaning, he framed her face with his palms. "You have no idea how much I've missed you, Carrie."

Then he was devouring her, kissing, nibbling, nuzzling her neck and throat, dropping kisses over her cheeks, eyes, nose, and finally taking her mouth hungrily. Letting go of her lips just long enough pull off the offending garment, Liam yanked his shirt over his head. His tongue thrust into her mouth and she parried with her own, wrapping her arms around his neck.

Reaching behind her, he unclasped the confining satin bra and brought his hands around to capture her breasts as the wisp of fabric dropped to the floor. Carrie allowed a moment of doubt to edge her consciousness as he bent his head to her body. Would he notice the small ravages of time? The slight weight that wasn't there sixteen years ago? The pale silvery streaks—evidence of pregnancy and nursing Jack? The almost-invisible scar low on her abdomen left from the surgery after Jack's birth?

But all thought fled as his mouth touched her.

She shuddered as he explored her curves, teasing his beard toward the crest of one breast and then back to the valley between. At last, his lips closed over one aching nipple, drawing on her with a sensuality that was light-years away from the mere memories she had lived on for so many years. Pressing his head closer to her, she urged him to take more of her into his mouth, desperately needing the stroke of his teeth and tongue.

Carrie's hands dropped between them, working the buckle of his leather belt, then the snap and zipper of his jeans.

With a moan, he moved his mouth back up to hers, taking little stinging bites from her lips as he spoke. "I wanted this to be perfect. I've loved you so many times in my mind—long—and so thoroughly." He sucked in a breath as her exploring fingers dipped below the waistband of his jeans, reaching for his erection. "But if we don't move to that bed this instant, I'm going to explode right here in the doorway."

He toed off his deck shoes and shucked out of his jeans and boxers in one smooth step. Then he backed her the few feet to the bed. Sliding his fingers into the lacy band at the top of her panties, he removed the last barrier between them.

Erection thrusting against her soft belly, he pressed her back onto the cool sheets. His big body covered hers. His mouth took her lips with a ferocity that inflamed her senses. His hands created magical sensations on her breasts, her belly, then lower. Crying out, she clutched his shoulders. Flames scorched wherever his hands touched, and he followed that path with his tongue.

Licking hungrily at her tingling nipples, his fingers sought the sensitive flesh between her legs. "Carrie... Ah... my love," he murmured against her skin, "You are so much more delicious than I remembered... so much more..."

White-hot hunger blazed between them as her fingers slid down his stomach to capture him. Carrie ran her fingertips up and down his rock-hard erection, relishing the silky heat before wrapping her hand around him. His fingers found her core, and she gasped at the vibrations he created deep inside her. She was on fire, wet and hot and so, so ready for him.

"Liam, please, now." She opened her legs wider, guiding him between them.

～

He knew there was one more important question. Pushing himself up on his elbows, his eyes swept her flushed body, glowing with the sheen of perspiration. Swallowing hard, he glanced down at the floor. "I... I have protection, if you... if you want me to use it." His voice was raspy with need.

Please say no.

The thought of any barrier between them was almost more than he could stand, but he would do whatever she wanted.

Tugging his head down, she put her lips next to his ear. "Is there any reason?"

He gazed into her huge eyes, beseeching her to trust him. "No."

Squirming sensuously, she slid her heels up his bare legs. "Then we're good... like this," she whispered. "Just you and me." With her hand behind his head, she brought his lips to hers, using her tongue to show him what she wanted.

That husky voice so full of promise was almost his undoing. "God, I wanted us to savor this, but..." Then he was filling her, pulling back slightly as she gasped at the sensation, and slowly, sliding deeper.

～

C arrie wrapped her legs around his hips, her muscles tightening around him. "Ahhh... yes. You feel so wonderful... so... wonderful." Trembling with want, she ran her tongue along his collarbone, the blood surging in her veins.

With astonishing urgency, he slid his hands under her to clutch her behind and lift her to him. With a few whispered words, they found a rhythm, and she arched up to meet his thrusts, taking him in as deeply as she could.

Liam's warm skin against hers, his heat filling her emptiness was all Carrie needed. His hands and mouth were everywhere. Kissing and sucking her tender nipples, his tongue laved her breasts. Lifting himself on one elbow, he put his hand between them, and his thumb found the hardened nub of her desire. She clung to him, relishing how he knew exactly where to touch. How to move inside her. She opened her eyes to find him gazing at her, his gray eyes almost black with passion.

"Carrie, my love," he murmured.

She spiraled closer, her muscles contracting as she fell over the edge. His words turned into a moan and then he tensed as he cried out his own release.

CHAPTER 17

"Hey?" Liam whispered against her breasts.

Carrie raised passion-drowsed lids long enough to see his dark red hair against her skin. "Hmm?" Answering was an effort. She didn't want to let go of the sated lethargy they'd fallen into in the aftermath of loving.

He ran one finger down the slope of her breast, then traced the curve of her belly. "I'm sorry. I know I've been a shit about Jack. I guess I see why you did it." Liam's breath warmed her skin. "Don't like it, but I get it."

"I don't blame you for being angry, but I don't think we could have made it back then."

He raised his head and frowned but, when he drew in a quick breath of protest, she stopped him.

"No, listen." She touched his lips gently with hers, then slid away from him to sit up. Braced against pillows and the padded headboard, she tried to explain. "I was too young to deal with your life. I could barely handle my own. You never could've given me all the security I needed after Dad died. I would've been insanely jealous of every concert, every fan, anything that took your attention away from me."

"You wouldn't have been so silly." He stretched, then piled pillows to settle in next to her, his hand on her thigh. "You were way too mature."

"No, I wasn't." She gave a short laugh. "Honestly, I don't even know if I am now. And with a family in the picture, you couldn't possibly have had the career you've had so far. That magical aura? Not with a wife and baby backstage. Surely you know that."

"I'd have given it all up in a heartbeat to have you and Jack with me."

"I'm glad you think so." Carrie kissed him. "I'm also very glad you didn't have to make that choice."

"Why?"

She leaned back against the pillows, running her fingers through her tousled curls. "You would've always wondered what could've been. Maybe one day you might've started to resent me. You keep saying I was so mature, but obviously, I wasn't or I wouldn't have tucked tail and run." She watched fascinated as his fingers brushed her thigh.

Abruptly, he leapt out of bed, his damp skin glowing in the candlelight.

Her breath caught in her throat.

I've said too much. He's leaving.

Panic set it. "What's the matter?"

But he was reaching for his jeans, digging in the pocket.

"Liam what are you doing?"

He knelt on the mattress beside her. "Marry me, Carrie. We'll make it work. Marry me." In his fingers a perfect pear-shaped diamond solitaire set in platinum glittered in the soft light. "I want you. I want my family."

"Oh, Liam." Carrie's world suddenly tilted on its axis.

"I love you. I've *always* loved you. I don't even know what I expected when I saw you again. But you're what I want. Your grace, your intelligence, your humor, your sexiness. You're essential to me." He gazed into her eyes. "For a long time, I pretended that wasn't true. But now I know I need you in my life. I don't want to spend another moment without you. I want the three of us to be a family."

Closing her eyes, she took a deep breath, then swallowed hard to keep the tears from escaping. The effort was futile since she was both thrilled and scared to death. Wasn't this exactly what she'd been dreaming of for years? Why did it suddenly feel hasty and overwhelming? Because it was so obvious he was afraid of losing her...and Jack. And could she blame him?

It may seem rushed, but was it? Truly? Hadn't this been simmering for years? Why wait? They weren't getting any younger, and besides, they had a son to raise. Why not do it together here by the lake? He could move here and they'd be a real family. Jack would have his father and she'd have Liam... at last.

Liam gently brushed her cheek with his thumb. "I sorta hoped you'd be happy about this." He tipped her chin up and made her look at him.

"I *am* happy." Her voice choked with tears. "I want to say yes to you. More than anything in the world."

"Okay, then say yes." Taking her left hand, he started to slide the ring onto her third finger.

But she grasped his hand, holding it both of hers. "I can't. Not until Jack knows everything." Bringing his fingers to her lips, she kissed them softly. "And not until... until *you* do." She reached up to pull his head down to her kiss. "There's something else you have to know." Sniffing, she reached for a tissue on the bedside table before pulling the sheet up to cover her nakedness. It was a defense mechanism, but somehow it gave her courage.

"Really?" He clutched the ring in his fingers, his knuckles whitening as he visibly braced himself. "What else is there?"

Dear God, had she done this to him by not being honest from the first? Was he going to tense up, anticipating trouble, every time she needed to tell him anything? She gazed at him, her heart bursting with love and yet sick at what she was compelled to reveal. If she didn't, she'd never be able to look him straight in the eye again, and that was no way to begin the rest of their lives together.

"What is it, Carrie?" The smile disappeared. "You said there were no more secrets."

"I–I accepted money from Marty."

"What?" His eyes narrowed. "You what? When?"

"After I found out I was pregnant." She swallowed hard, determined not to sob her way through this. By God, she would hang onto some shred of dignity. "I called you in Vienna, I was going to tell you about being pregnant. But Marty answered." She clutched the sheet closer around her as he watched, his face impassive. "I was confused, devastated, scared... Dad had just died, my life was falling apart, and Marty was... he was cold."

"Did you tell him you were pregnant?" Liam asked sharply, color rising to his cheeks. "Has *he* known all this time?"

"No." She shook her head vehemently. "I just asked to talk to you, that's all. But he went off on me. Told me to leave you alone. Called me your protégé. Laughed at me. Even said that I wasn't the first and I wouldn't be the last."

Liam's jaw dropped and he started to speak, but she held up one hand.

"Wait. Let me finish."

He nodded wordlessly. The ring caught the light from the table lamp as he clenched and unclenched his fist.

"I hung up on him. I knew then that we were done, and I was going to have to do this on my own. But a week later, I got a twenty-five-thousand-dollar check in the mail. Maybe he suspected. Maybe it was just insurance that I *would* leave you alone. I don't know." She laughed grimly. "I almost tore it up."

Keeping her gaze on his face, she tried to read his expression. "I'm not proud of the fact that I kept it, but I had *nothing*. Not one single dime. Everything was sold to pay off Dad's gambling debts. Eliot rescued my mother's piano and Noah and Margie offered me a home here. I used some of it when I moved, but after Jack was born and I started playing at the bar, I replaced it. It's been in an account in Jack's name all these years. I thought about returning it to Marty, but I was scared if I did, he'd find me and—"

"And then *I'd* know where you were?" Liam's voice was quiet.

She nodded and caught her lower lip with her teeth to keep it from trembling. "I never dreamed I'd be with you again. I couldn't see any way Jack and I would fit in your life."

"That bastard!" Liam slammed his fist on the bed before jumping up to pace. "That son of a bitch."

"Liam, it's done. You're here." Carrie extended her hand. "Now I can give it back to him."

"Hell no, you're not giving it back to him." Liam's face flushed as he stalked from the door to the bed and back again, dropping the ring on the mirrored tray on the dresser as he passed it. "He's done, he's out. I've already told him that, but this? It's just one more time he manipulated me, interfered in my life to suit his own purposes."

"*I* took the money." Carrie yanked on the sheet and wrapped it around her. It trailed on the carpet behind her as she went to him. "*I* ran. *I* hid. My choices. Not his."

He spun around, towering over her naked and powerful, his eyes shooting silver fire. "Forget the money. Keep it, donate it to charity, do whatever you want with it, but don't give it back to Marty. That self-serving bastard. He knew you were different.

You scared him to death because he knew I wanted you." He grasped her shoulders, peering into her face, his gray eyes stormy. "I wanted you, Carrie. Do you hear me? You never left me. Not once."

Carrie stared at him, the lump in her throat so big she couldn't even swallow, let alone speak. He brushed the tears from her cheek with his thumb and pulled her against his chest, holding her as she wept.

When the storm passed, he stroked the hair off her face and gave her a puzzled smile. "Why were you afraid to tell me about the money?"

With a hiccup, she wiped her eyes on the corner of the sheet. "I didn't want you to think I was the kind of woman who… who could be paid off like that. That I was a terrible person or a bad mother. The money seemed like… I don't know… ammunition if… if…" She slid her eyes away from his, heat rising in her cheeks.

"If what?" He tilted his head to peer into her face. "If I'd decided to fight you for custody?"

Nodding slowly, she met his eyes again. "Yes."

"Oh, baby." He tugged her back into his arms and rubbed his cheek against her hair. "How did I turn into such a bad guy over the years? Have you been tucked away up here playing Dr. Frankenstein with your memories of me? Did you forget the day we made that kid?"

"No." She slid her arms around his waist and breathed in the warm male scent of him, letting the crisp hair on his chest tickle her nose. "*That* day is crystal clear, but I've seen your life since then and what you've become. I'm so proud of you, so in awe of what you've accomplished. Your life is enormous. My own reality is very different. And quite small."

With a sigh, he swept her up in his arms, carried her to the bed, and curved his body around hers. "We can expand your reality, Carrie," he whispered. "Just say yes."

"Slow down, my love." She turned in his arms, untangling the sheet and tossing it aside. "You need to know Jack first." Carrie longed to fling her arms around him and cry, *yes, yes, yes*, reassure him that she and Jack were his forever, but the very thought of blending their lives overwhelmed her. Apprehension about how Jack would react on Sunday nipped at her mind even as she cuddled closer to Liam. "We've got time."

"Okay, we'll wait for Jack to make it official," he said. "God knows I'm hell at waiting. I'll wait forever if I have to. But for the record, I'd rather not wait another minute." He captured her lips in a fierce kiss.

She met his tongue with her own as she curled her fingers in his hair. Several long blissful moments later, he lifted his head. Touching his lips to her cheek and then her ear, he murmured, "You are planning on saying yes, right?"

That deep, sensual voice sent a zing of rapture straight through her, quashing those tiny seeds of doubt that had already started to take root in the back of her mind.

This can work. I'll find a way to make it work. I can't lose him again. After we tell Jack, we'll figure it out.

Sliding down in the bed, she pulled him over her, wrapping her arms and legs around him and drawing his lips down to hers.

"Come here, Maestro." She kissed him and then kissed him again. "The only thing I've got planned at the moment is making love to you."

CHAPTER 18

"Good, I'm nervous as hell."

Liam's gut twisted with apprehension while Carrie parked her Jeep in the pine-encircled lot at Lawson Music Camp. Pulling down the visor, he checked himself in the mirror, shoving his hair back, smoothing the collar of the lightweight tan sports jacket he wore over a brown T-shirt and jeans.

"Maybe I should've worn a tie."

"Not with that outfit," she teased as she pulled the key out of the ignition and gave him a bracing smile. "Come on, Liam, you've had dinner at the White House. This is one teenager. It'll be fine."

"I wasn't the missing father of anyone at the White House."

Sweat was trickling down his ribs. *Damn.* Opening the car door, he stepped out onto the gravel and inhaled the pine and cedar-scented air. Michigan smelled great—at least this part of it. He'd never been in a place so fresh. Another deep breath.

He was ready to face his dragons.

Why does it feel like that? I'm more terrified than I've ever been before any performance.

But this wasn't a performance—it was real life. He was

meeting his fifteen-year-old son for the very first time, and he had no idea what to expect.

Carrie—dressed in an airy tie-dyed skirt that swirled around her calves and a soft yellow shirt tied at the waist—met him behind the car and took his hand. "Take it easy. Or you're going to make me nervous too."

"Why should *you* be nervous?" he asked, squeezing her hand. "You've already met him."

"You're cute." Wrinkling her nose at him, she gave his arm a pat. "I'm the one who kept him from you all these years. He may decide I'm the wicked witch of western Michigan." Her smile faded. "Oh great. Now I *am* nervous."

"Good. At least I'm not alone."

He slung his arm around her shoulder as they walked slowly toward the rustic log structure that housed Lawson's dining hall and offices. He scanned the area. They were early, so not many parents had arrived yet. Kids clustered around an open-air band shell perched on a hill behind the dining hall. Tidy cabins flanked the log building, nestled in the pines.

"Damn," he said. "This is a terrific facility."

"The lake's down there." Stopping on the gravel path, Carrie pointed to the right of the band shell. "Basketball, tennis courts, and a baseball diamond are back there." Turning, she indicated an area below the parking lot. "Dave encourages a lot of physical activity because most of these kids are more artistic than athletic. He tries to get them young so he can help them have some balance. Jack learned to play basketball and baseball here, as well as how to canoe. He loved it as a camper. He's been so excited to be a counselor this year."

Shoving his hands in his pockets, Liam tried to look as if he belonged as they approached the dining hall. Happy voices drifted out the screen door.

You do belong here. You do belong here.

The mantra looped in his head as he watched a curly-headed boy talking eagerly to a man who was obviously his dad. The meeting with his own son would be very different from the other fathers here today. A chill shuddered through him as they made their way around long tables to the offices at the rear of the building.

"Hey, you okay?" Carrie peered into his face as she pulled him into the hallway that led to Dave Lawson's office. She had already called Dave from the car to ask if they could meet privately with Jack for a few minutes. "You're white as a sheet."

Standing arrow straight in the middle of the hallway, Liam shook his head. "All the confidence I worked up on the ride here has suddenly abandoned me. What if he hates me? What if he hates both of us? He's fifteen. Duncan says they're very strange at fifteen."

"It'll be okay," she reassured him. "I know Jack. If he could go into a department store and pick out a father, it would be you." With a wink, she added, "Well, or Eric Clapton or John Williams... or maybe Dirk Pitt." Lifting up on her toes, she planted a kiss on his lips. "Liam, he's a warm, loving, generous kid. Just like his father."

He hugged her and their lips met briefly again. "I hope... Dirk Pitt?" His brow furrowed. "Clive Cussler's superhero? Seriously?"

"You might think about taking up scuba diving." Giving him a wide-eyed innocent smile, she turned as Dave Lawson came out of his office.

"Hey, Carrie! Maestro! Great to see you!" He extended his hand to Liam. "My office is yours. I sent someone to get Jack. He'll probably come in my back door. He's up at the center." Dave's head tilt indicated the open-air band shell on the hill behind the big dining hall. He had to be curious, but he didn't ask any questions, merely patted Carrie's shoulder and left with a quick smile.

After clearing his throat with a little nervous cough, Liam said, "I'm gonna wait out here so you can just... you know... prepare him..." Crossing his arms over his chest, he leaned his back against the wall near Dave's door.

She touched her lips to his cheek, then went in to see her son.

Their son...

"Hi, baby," she greeted Jack as he came through the back door of the office.

His auburn hair unruly, he was dressed in cargo shorts and a Lawson T-shirt, scruffy flip-flops on his feet. One of his big toenails was bruised. *Flip-flops.* Every summer, the kid had a black-and-blue toenail from stubbing his toes while wearing the silly things.

"Mom, hey!" He hugged her. "You're early. Where's Elly? Will he be here for the finale? Jelly Roll Morton." His gray eyes, so like Liam's, shined. "'The King Porter Stomp.' It's epic!"

"I can't wait to hear it. Eliot's coming on his own. I need to talk to you, Jack." She nodded to the sofa. "Let's sit down, okay?"

"What's up?" His eyes narrowed. "Is everyone okay? Uncle Noah? Aunt Margie?"

"Everybody's fine, honey. I need to talk to you, that's all. Can you sit?" Smiling, she patted the cushion next to her. "You're towering over me."

He obeyed. "What?"

Picking up his hand, she turned it over, matching it to her own. It was so much like Liam's with a wide palm and long fingers. She was trying to find the right words. Swallowing, she started to speak but stopped.

In typical Jack fashion, he immediately began worrying about her. "Are *you* okay?" He asked the question, peering into her face, obviously trying to read her downcast eyes.

He was getting scared, she could tell, so she gave him a quick hug. "Yes, I'm fine. S–something's come up that I need to tell you about." With trepidation, she dove in. "I know I've never told you anything about your father, and now... well, now I need to tell you about him, okay?"

"Ohhhkaaay." Jack sat back on the sofa, his legs stretched out in front of him, as he stared at her expectantly.

Carrie stayed perched on the edge of her seat. "This is harder than I thought it was going to be." She gave a small nervous laugh. "Oh, hell, that's a lie. I knew this was going to be difficult."

"Maybe I can make it easier for you." Jack crossed his arms over his chest.

When she gazed at him uncertainly, he simply gave her an enigmatic smile. "All right." The knot in her stomach grew tighter. "Why don't you?"

"Is Maestro Reilly my father?" Jack's voice was husky.

Astonished, she almost fell off the sofa. "How do you know that?"

"Ha!" He pointed a finger at her. "I didn't! But I thought I'd figured it out a couple of days ago. You just verified it for me." Rubbing his face, he sighed deeply.

A sigh of relief?

Exactly the same stress move that Liam uses—rubbing his face, sighing.

Good God...

"How did... how did this even occur to you?" Carrie was still reeling from his revelation.

"Um... Mom... You don't know this, but I'm sorta always on the lookout. Like when I see a guy about your age with dark red hair, I wonder if he could be my father."

She caught her breath at that admission. Jules was right, Jack *was* curious.

Why shouldn't he be? He had every right to know about his father.

Her throat tightened.

Jack stared at his feet as he spoke. "Dr. Lawson has posters plastered all over the camp of this guy who's coming to conduct the benefit. I couldn't stop thinking he looked, like... familiar, you know? Not only 'cause we've seen him on *Great Performances*—we never really saw that much of his face." Putting one hand back on the table behind the sofa, he grabbed a large sheet of shiny paper and held it up.

Liam, his hair brushed back, one stray piece hanging over his forehead, smiled in a posed publicity photo.

She met Jack's eyes over the poster.

"See?" He shook the picture. "Look at him. He's familiar because he looks like *me*." Jack set the poster down. "I got on the Web in the computer lab after I realized that and Googled him. And I—I found a bio that told where he grew up in Canada, that he'd graduated from McGill in Montreal, and *when* he taught there." Turning sideways, he tipped his head to stare at her. "I knew you were auditioning in Montreal when your dad was killed." He shrugged. "I did the math. There was a picture of him on the Web. From like, when he was a freshman at Juilliard." Jack's eyes got bigger. He shook his head as if to clear it. "Mom, seriously, it could have been a picture of me."

He was smiling a little twisted smile that wrenched her heart. "Oh, Jack... Honey, I'm so sorry you had to figure this out by yourself." In her lap, her fingers were laced together so tightly, they ached. She opened her hands and wiped them on her skirt. "I wanted to tell you. I did. So many times. But it seemed too complicated, andand I didn't want you to thinkto think..." She choked on the words.

They sat quietly for a moment, then he scooted over to put his arm around her. "C'mon Mom, it's okay." His big hand patted her curls.

Another Liam gesture.

"Oh, Jack..." She squared her shoulders—she needed to mom up and face this with dignity.

"Really. I'm okay with it. Honest. I'm glad it's out." He gave her a squeeze. "I've been trying to figure out how to ask you if I was right. I wasn't sure what to do. I know you don't like to talk about that time. I kinda thought I'd ask Elly today when he got here." He patted her head again as if she were a child. "I guess I don't have to now, huh?"

Carrie wiped her eyes. "I was wrong. I should have told you about Liam years ago. I guess I got too comfortable with just us. Andand I knew if I told you, I'd have to see him. I'm sorry." The tears threatened again. Sniffing, she rolled her eyes in exasperation. "I was being a wuss, honey. I hope you'll forgive me."

"Forgive you?" He gasped. "That's so messed up!" Shoving up from the low leather sofa, he paced across the small office, staring out the back door before he turned around to face her. "Mom, for me, finding out my father's a famous symphony conductor is kinda like a kid on a basketball team finding out his dad plays center for the Bulls. I mean it's weird, but it's... awesome!"

"Seriously?" She blinked back tears and dug in her bag for a tissue.

"Well, yeah. But are you cool with him coming here? It's been a long time since you've seen him, and I don't know what happened between you two."

He's worried about me?

She couldn't help feeling a twinge of parental pride mixed with a large dose of guilt as she blew her nose on the tattered tissue she'd discovered in her purse. "I'm fine with it. Really."

"It's kinda freaky him showing up here, isn't it?" His eyes darkened.

"It's not a coincidence. Eliot brought him here... for the benefit, but also for you. He wanted you two to meet," she admitted. "He thought it was time. He's right. It *is* time—past time."

"So I *am* going to meet him while he's here?" He sounded hesitant.

"Do you want to meet him?" She stared directly into his face.

"Yes," he answered, but backtracked an instant later. "But... not if you have a problem with it. Really, we don't know anything about him. It's been a long time since you saw him. Maybe he's a big douche who thinks he's too cool for us."

God, how I love this kid. Nobody has my back like Jack.

"He's not a douche." She shook her head. "What a word!"

"Why didn't you tell him about me?" Now his curiosity had kicked in. "What happened? Were you in love or was it... just... like a... a hook-up?"

"A hook-up?" Carrie was a bit surprised at her son's supply of information about the world. "We were in love. It definitely wasn't a *hook-up*. He wanted me to go to Europe with him that summer, but my dad's death changed everything and..." Pausing, she remembered the time with Liam in Montreal.

"What happened?" he asked again. Suddenly he snapped his fingers. "Hey! All those CDs? Your classical CDs? I just realized he's the conductor on most them. The Mozart one with the London Symphony. Mahler with the New York Philharmonic. The Strauss waltzes in Atlanta. They're all *his* recordings!"

Flushing in spite of herself, she smiled. "Not *every* one, but a lot of them. I guess it was a way for me to be connected to him." She paused, debating about how much to tell him. "Liam and I only knew each other a short time. I didn't trust what we had. I didn't believe we could make it work." She decided against including Marty Justice in her story. The bare facts were that she'd made the choice not to trust what they'd shared and she had to own it. "I'd already broken up with him when I realized I was pregnant with you. I thought I was doing the right thing by leaving him to his career and coming up here to raise you alone." She shrugged with a little smile. "Okay, not *all* alone—with Uncle Noah and Aunt Margie and Eliot and the entire village."

Jack laughed—a deep throaty laugh that always charmed her right down to her socks.

His father's laugh.

"We've been okay without him, Mom. I know that." Eyes averted, his voice softened. "I don't want to hurt your feelings, but... I kinda miss having a real dad. Uncle Noah and Elly and Charlie have all been great but... if this guy's okay, I'd like to meet him. Do you think Elly could arrange it?"

A couple of cleansing breaths later, Carrie stood up, walked to him, and smoothed his hair back from his face. It was getting long again, parting in the middle and hanging over his ears. "You can meet him right now, if you like. He's outside."

"Outside?" Jack's eyes widened. "Here? *Now?*"

She nodded. "He arrived a few days ago... on a yacht. It's docked at home."

"So you've talked to him? Did you tell him about me?" He paced back and forth, his fingers raking through his hair. "What did he say? Was he pissed? Does he even want to meet me?"

"Take a breath, babe." Putting a hand out to stop him, she rubbed his bicep. "He knows about you. He's dying to meet you. I asked him to wait until today. He agreed, but not very happily. Liam and I had to talk. We had a lot of stuff to clear up between us."

"Like what? I mean besides the obvious." He tapped his own chest rather ruefully.

"Yes, *the obvious* was the biggest thing," she admitted, chuckling. "He was hurt that I never told him about you. Really hurt and pretty ticked off that he's missed so much of your life. We had to talk that out before I could bring him to meet you. That's why I asked him to wait until today."

"How are you guys now?" He peered down at her. "Friends?"

"We're okay. Friends." Now wasn't the time to expand on her explanation. No point in dumping everything on the poor kid at once. "I'll go get him." She pointed to the office door. "He's right outside the door."

Jack turned away from her, staring out the window for a long moment. Then, taking a huge breath, he turned back to face her, his eyes cloudy with apprehension.

Carrie gave him a tight hug. "Come on, it's okay. This is a *good* thing."

He trembled and clung to her for an instant longer. When he released her, he took another giant breath. "Okay, let's do this."

CHAPTER 19

Outside in the hall, Liam paced, his heart pounding, palms sweating.

What's going on in there? Confessions? A confrontation? An ugly quarrel?

He hadn't heard raised voices, but he'd resisted hovering at the door. His stomach roiled with both excitement and apprehension.

This is what it's like being a parent? Alternately terrified and overjoyed?

It was a new sensation.

His head shot up at the sound of the door opening, and Carrie crooked a finger. Straightening, he took a deep breath as she approached to take his hand in hers. His own were like ice. When she pressed her cheek to his palm, her soft skin felt almost feverish. With a gentle squeeze of her hand, he stepped into the office.

Jack was rooted in the center of the room as Liam walked in. They gazed at one another. Liam walked closer and Jack met him halfway. The boy was taller than he expected, although he loomed over Carrie in the picture that he kept in his pocket. Staring into

Jack's eyes was like seeing a younger version of himself in a mirror.

Liam's stomach clenched.

This child was his son. This tall, handsome, accomplished, young man.

My son!

They stood barely a yard apart, still staring as if neither of them could bear to take their eyes off each other. Moments ticked by, but they didn't speak.

I should say something.

But nothing intelligent came to mind. He only wanted to gaze at Jack, maybe touch his face. Put his fingers in the dark red hair that parted down the middle and hung over his ears.

Does it have the same texture as mine?

His full mouth? That was all Carrie, as well as the firm chin. But the dimples? Definitely Reilly.

One of us needs to speak.

Finally, Liam cleared his throat. "Hello, Jack."

"Hello, it's... good to meet you, sir." His response was little guarded as they shook hands.

Liam held on, appraising his son up and down for a moment. The boy—who was almost tall enough to look his father directly in the eye—returned the scrutiny as he tossed his long hair out of his face.

"I–I can't believe I'm standing here with–with you." Liam faltered, inwardly cursing his own awkwardness.

"Me, either." Jack's voice cracked, but he kept his grip on Liam's hand.

Liam raised his other hand. "May I?" He tentatively reached toward Jack's hair.

Jack nodded, a question in his eyes as his father sifted his fingers through his silky mop.

It's like touching my own hair.

He ran a finger over Jack's cheek, feeling the soft teenaged stubble there.

What was he like as a toddler? As an infant?

The pictures Carrie had shared with him flashed through his mind as he studied Jack's features. His nose, that fine narrow nose. Liam recognized it—it looked like his own mother's.

A sudden longing for his parents coursed through him. How delighted they were going to be, finding out about a new grand-child. And how sad, too, that they missed this boy's childhood— missed holding him, cuddling him, watching him grow and develop. So much time had passed already.

Jealousy flared hot inside him for a moment. Carrie had Jack to herself since his birth—not even attempting to contact him to let him know he had a son. The Reillys were a close family. Her cowardly choice had robbed them all—Jack, too—of a powerful connection.

Jack's fingers tightened on Liam's. Tears shimmered in his eyes. His teeth worried his lower lip, but he kept eye contact.

"You're so like your cousin Jamie." Liam moved his hand to Jack's shoulder, squeezing. "It's almost eerie."

"I have cousins?" At last Jack released Liam's hand.

"Lots of them." Smiling in spite of the tears beginning to trickle out of his own eyes, Liam nodded.

"How many?"

"Um... ten, I think, at last count." Liam brushed his hand across his eyes. "And aunts and uncles—" His voice broke.

Jack threw Carrie a helpless glance as she stood in the door-way. Then as if it were the most natural thing in the world, he reached for Liam and put his arms around him.

With a choked sob, Liam enfolded his son in an embrace and they were both crying... and smiling.

When Liam glanced back at Carrie, tears were streaming down her cheeks as well.

Jack broke the hug first.

Clearly ravenous for information, he began peppering Liam with questions. "Do I have grandparents? Are your parents still alive? Where are they?" He offered Liam a box of tissues from Dave Lawson's desk, and they both wiped their eyes. "Where are my cousins? In Canada?" Jack tossed the tissue box over his shoulder without even looking at Carrie. "Heads up, Mom."

Liam gave her a strained smile around Jack's head. "My parents are still alive. Doing great." He blew his nose. "They live on a farm near Toronto and—" Abruptly he stopped. "Hey, how'd you know I was from Canada?"

"I Googled you," Jack admitted. Blushing, he let his gaze fall away.

"Why?"

Jack glanced over at his mother.

She nodded.

Jack shrugged. "I thought we looked alike. You know, from Dr. Lawson's posters? So I started trying to find some information about you. Your website said you were from Canada and you were teaching at McGill when Mom auditioned there." He paused. The color staining his cheeks became even rosier. "I've been wondering for a long time who my father... I mean, about... who... he..." Stumbling over the explanation, his eyes shifted to Carrie. "I mean... who you..."

Liam gasped. "Good Lord. You mean you had this figured out before we ever got up here?"

"Yes, sir. At least I *thought* I had. This afternoon I was going to ask Elly—Eliot—if I was right."

"Well, that's... incredible." Liam tousled Jack's hair before putting his arms around him again for another quick hug.

Jack grinned and shook the hair off his face. "Does your family know about me yet? Can I meet them?"

"Of course. You can meet them whenever you like," Liam said, avoiding Carrie's eyes. "They're your family too."

God, the kid's longing for family.

Resentment surged up in him again.

I could have had him with me. He'd know his cousins, his grandparents... his father.

Jack seemed to pick up on his reactions because the boy's eyes widened as he sucked in a breath. "Will they be pissed? I mean about Mom and me?"

Mom and me.

The boy's protective instincts for his mother came through loud and clear.

"I promise they'll be thrilled." Liam patted his shoulder and smiled.

This time his eyes darted over to Carrie. Tears still glistened on her cheeks, but the expression on her face was pure joy.

He sighed inwardly.

What was the point in being angry now?

What's done is done, as Will had so logically pointed out a few days ago.

She'd given him so much in the past few days—opened herself up and let him back into her life. Today, she'd stayed in the background, granting him full access to the one person dearest to her heart. That took courage and trust and yes... love.

He claimed he'd forgiven her for keeping Jack a secret.

But had he?

Now, standing in a room for the first time with his son, he was forced to make that choice all over again. Already, he saw how well she'd raised him—what a fine young man he'd turned out to be—even without his influence. Inhaling a deep breath, he let it out slowly and with it, released the last vestiges of the anger.

Now, we truly move forward.

He met Carrie's gaze with a bracing smile.

"What should I call you?" Jack asked Liam bluntly.

Baffled, Liam gave Carrie a raised brow before he responded with his own question. "What do you *want* to call me?"

Shuffling his feet nervously, his brow furrowing, Jack stammered. "I–I don't know."

Thankfully, Carrie stepped in. Crossing the room to put her arm around her son's waist, she offered, "Why don't you call him *Liam* for now?"

Jack turned to his father. "Is that okay with you?"

"I'm good with that. Beats the heck out of *sir*, don't you think?"

Jack chuckled and put his arm around his mother's shoulders, but he was still gazing at Liam in wonder.

Speechless again, emotions raced through Liam as he stared at his son, whose fingers tangled nervously in the curls at the back of his mother's neck.

His hands are exactly like mine—long fingers, wide palms. A pianist's hands.

All of a sudden, he was dying to hear Jack play.

Dave Lawson stuck his head around the door. "Sorry to interrupt, folks. But Jack, you need to go get your kids ready. Tessa's backstage with them." He opened the door further. Glancing at the three of them standing together in the center of the room, Liam could tell by the expression on his face, he'd figured it out in less than ten seconds. But all he said was, "Maestro, you're staying for the recital? Jack here is our finale."

"Yes, I'm staying." Liam turned to Jack. "You're playing the finale?"

"Yes, sir—" Shaking his head, he corrected himself. "—um, Liam. Jelly Roll Morton."

"So *Jack* is Eliot's star?" Liam remembered Dave's reference from earlier in the week.

Dave nodded with a grin. "Yup. We're all very proud of him."

"I can't wait to hear you play." Liam squeezed the boy's shoulder, letting his hand linger there. Tenderness tightened his chest as tears threatened again. He just wanted contact, any kind of contact.

Jack gazed from one adult face to the other before releasing Carrie. "'Scuse me. I gotta go backstage." Dropping a kiss on her hair, he made it almost to the door before he pivoted to face them again. "I'll see you after the recital?" The question was directed at Liam.

"I'll be right here," Liam replied. "I'm not going *anywhere*."

Jack's hair fell down into his eyes as he nodded. Stopping again in the open doorway, he met his father's gaze. "Liam... I– I'm glad you're here." His voice trembled.

"So am I, Jack." Liam's own voice was husky with emotion. "So am I."

CHAPTER 20

The recital was charming with the children playing the pieces they'd worked on as their teenaged counselors stood offstage encouraging them. Jack closed the program with the Jelly Roll Morton number. Liam was clearly bowled over by his son's technique and talent, sitting spellbound through the piece, his eyes glued to the stage.

Jack played with an intensity and drive that Carrie had never seen in him before. This one was for his father, and even she felt the natural gravitation they had toward one another. The music was already creating an almost palpable bond between them. It was both exciting and disconcerting.

Dear God, how is this going to change the life we've built up here?

All in all, the afternoon was a huge success, including the post-recital reception. Jack squired Liam around the big dining hall, proudly introducing him to his camp friends and former instructors. The room buzzed with talk as folks recognized Liam and clustered around him—parents introducing themselves, campers anxious to meet a famous conductor. Even the local newspaper nabbed him for a quick interview that was sure to find its way into the Traverse City paper.

Jack's eyes were huge as he stood at his father's side while Carrie watched more or less from the sidelines. Smiling that thousand-watt smile, Liam chatted as he autographed programs and napkins. But he kept Jack near him with a hand on his shoulder or an arm around him.

Is this how life is for him? Crowds always aware of his every move? Always wanting his attention?

Her heart rose to her throat as she watched him glide effortlessly through the crowd, greeting fans, pen in hand. Could she live like this? Constantly being recognized and scrutinized? Could Jack?

At the moment, Jack seemed to be soaking up the attention like a sponge, sticking to Liam, acknowledging introductions, and graciously accepting congratulations on his own playing. Several times, she caught Liam or Jack scanning the small throng.

Were they looking for her? Did they need to stay in visual contact the same way she needed to see them?

When they spotted her, she smiled and waved. Until they all got comfortable together, she was the anchor.

"This is an unusual situation, Carrie." Will's voice in her ear interrupted her musing as if he'd been able to read her mind. He'd ridden to Lawson with Eliot and was sipping from a paper cup as he walked up beside her, offering a second cup of punch.

"Is it?" She gave him a wry smile, accepting the drink.

He nodded. "This is a venue where people will know him immediately. He's a celebrity here—kind of like in the theater lobby after a performance. He always signs autographs then. But he doesn't constantly get stopped on the street in Chicago or New York."

"He doesn't?" Her eyes were on Liam as he bent down to listen to an attractive young woman standing next to him. He laughed at something the woman said, and she lit up like a Christmas tree as she handed him her program to sign. Carrie glanced back at Will. "This happened at Sleeping Bear the other day. A woman stopped him for an autograph."

"Honey, his picture's plastered all over the county, thanks to Dave Lawson. He's in TSO's program right now. Plus there are posters all over Interlochen."

"I know, but it's a little... daunting. This is all foreign to me —*and* Jack." She gazed back at her son, who was now deep in conversation with two other young men. One of them vigorously played air piano while Jack grinned and nodded.

"Jack's having the time of his life." Will tossed his cup into the trash bin near the door. "He's been floating ever since he took that third bow."

"I don't want him to—" Carrie stopped, biting her lip.

Will gave her a long look. "To be like Liam?"

"That's not what I meant to say." She expelled a long frustrated breath.

Crossing his arms over his chest, he leaned against the log wall. "What's wrong with being like Liam? He's a fine musician. A fantastic conductor with an incredible career. And he's a good man."

"Jack's a fifteen-year-old *boy*, not a worldly wise celebrity. He needs time to grow up. Time to be a kid."

"Liam has no intention of taking that time away from him," he reassured her as Liam and Jack headed their direction, talking a mile a minute.

Carrie's heart swelled at the sight of them—both tall and handsome, their features so much alike—moving easily between the tables and chairs, being stopped by fans as they chatted.

"Carrie, you gotta let this happen." Will patted her shoulder. "Relax. Give them time to get acquainted." Will's expression was kind, but deadly serious.

He was right. Jack and Liam deserved some time together. Maybe she just needed to stop worrying. She scanned the crowd for them again, but this time found only Jack talking animatedly to his friends.

What had happened to Liam?

When she turned to ask Will, his attention had been caught by something he'd noticed beyond her head. "Excuse me for a minute, Carrie." Patting her shoulder, he scooted past her, heading in the direction of Dave Lawson's office.

⁓

"What the hell are you doing here?" Liam's temper detonated as soon as he and Marty Justice hit the door of the office.

He'd spotted his former manager hovering at the edge of the crowd as they all made their way to the dining hall. He'd deliberately ignored him, hoping he'd get the point and disappear. However, Marty—never one to pay attention to a subtle hint—had stopped Jack when Liam's back was turned. He was talking fast and in the process of handing the boy a business card when Liam stepped between them.

Gripping Marty's bicep, he practically frog-marched him away from Jack.

"What's happening?" Will appeared in the doorway before Marty had a chance to answer Liam's question.

"Nothing that concerns you, Brody," Marty snarled. "Buzz off."

Will stood fast. "Um, Liam?"

"Don't leave, Will." Liam paced the office, so angry the blood pounded in his ears and temples. "Marty, we had this conversation on the phone. You're fired. Peter messengered the papers to you yesterday."

"That little ambulance chaser left about a dozen voicemails trying to get me to sign those fuckin' papers." Marty dropped onto the sofa, sweat beading on his brow.

"Well, why didn't you?" Liam gave him a hard stare.

"I'm not signing anything until we talk."

"We *did* talk. Didn't you listen to a word I said?" Liam threw his hands out in front of him, palms down. "We're finished. You got a hell of a severance package, which I wasn't obligated to give you. What are you doing here?"

"When I realized it was that old fart Raines who'd contacted you about this gig, I knew something was up. Then you called all bent out of shape. I came back here to see what was going on and goddammit, I was right. Carrie Halligan? A kid, Liam? Seriously?"

"Stay away from my son, Marty." Liam fought to control his anger, although he'd seen red when he spotted Marty talking to Jack.

"Stay away? Hell, this is exactly what we've needed to jump-start your career, man." Marty slapped one hand on the arm of the leather sofa. "At first, I thought this could be a real mess. What does this chick want after all these years? More money? Publicity for her little photography business? But then I saw the kid play. What a fan-fucking-tastic story!" His eyes gleamed in the harsh fluorescent light overhead. "Let me run with it. We'll set up some interviews—maybe *Fresh Air* or *All Things Considered.* Put you on to tell the story of finding your long-lost son, and then bring the kid in and let him play. If it hits on NPR, we might get a shot at *ET* or the *Today Show.* The European press will go wild over it." He pulled out his smart phone and began tapping the screen, still talking a mile a minute. "We could have him onstage at Town Hall by the end of summer and Carnegie Hall by Christmas with you conducting the orchestra behind him. Is that perfect or what?"

Liam wavered between punching the man's lights out and

bursting into hysterical laughter. He shook his head as he met Will's gaze. "Do you believe this guy?"

"Nope." Will sauntered into the office to stand shoulder to shoulder with Liam and gave him a reassuring smile.

"I don't think a DNA test is necessary." Marty glanced up from his phone. "No doubt in my mind the kid is yours. Hell, he's a fuckin' clone."

"Marty, what part of 'you're fired' do you *not* understand?" Liam asked. "Your services are no longer required here. As a matter of fact, meet my new agent." He jerked a thumb at Will.

"New agent?" Marty's face reddened, but he kept his tone even. "Liam, come on. We've had too many years together to just bag it. What's *she* been telling you?"

"The truth, which is more than I've ever gotten from you."

Marty made a fist before releasing it with a visible effort. "Jesus Christ, you'd known her for a week. She was gonna drag you down, man. She'd have destroyed everything I... *we'd* started. You'd have gone *nowhere*."

"This isn't about what happened with Carrie and you know it. It's about *you* having no idea who *I* am!" Finger stabbing the air, Liam glowered at him. "You've been making money hand over fist with this maestro-playboy crap. I told you years ago it wasn't me, but you refused to listen."

"Bullshit!" Marty exploded. "I suppose *you* haven't enjoyed the money? Or the attention?" His voice grew even more caustic. "So what if I profited from it? We *all* made a pile of money." He threw Will a pointed glare. "Look how far you've come. If it weren't for me, you'd probably be assistant director of music at some high school in the fucking Yukon. Where would you be now if you'd gotten tangled up with that little nobody?"

"I'd have been with my wife and son." Liam's voice was quiet even though inside he was seething. "Carrie was different. You knew she was special and that scared the hell out of you. So you thought you had to lie to her... and to me. You were afraid she'd fuck up what *you* had going. We had different agendas, Marty. More different than I ever imagined. Today just reinforces it."

Brushing imaginary lint from his impeccable suit jacket, Marty stood up. "Come on, *Maestro*. Convince me that what I did for your career wasn't exactly what you wanted. The money, the parties, the tours. TV appearances, celebrity... the women. You've just *suffered* through that because you'd lost your one true love. And all you had left was the music." He snorted with derision. "What a load of crap."

"I was a fool for too many years." Liam clenched his fists, battling the urge to go after Marty. "I let you run me because all I wanted to do was conduct, and you made that happen. Okay, I appreciate that. But I told you years ago, I was done with the games. Now it's really over. I want you *out*."

"Liam, you've gotta stop thinking with your dick. You can't stay up here and play house." Marty voice rose about half an octave. "Your career's headed straight for the shitter, and Brody's clueless about how to handle you."

"Excuse me?" Will protested. "*I've* been on the road with him for the last few years while you've been lounging on a beach in LA."

"Big fuckin' deal." Marty dismissed him with a brusque wave. "I built this career and by God, you're not going to destroy it."

"You no longer have any say in what happens to *my* career, so just get out." Liam pointed to the door.

Marty stared at him for a long moment, then stalked across the room. Stopping at the door, he turned around. "We're not done, pal."

"Yes, we are." Liam felt his temper rise even further. "And Marty, stay the fuck away from my son, or I'll slap a restraining order on you so fast, you won't know what hit you."

CHAPTER 21

Several days later, Carrie came home for lunch to find Jack at his grandmother's baby grand, entertaining Will and Tony. The only thing missing from the picture was Liam, but he was in Traverse City with the TSO. With Jack taking a break from his duties at Lawson to spend some time getting to know his father, the past few days had been filled with so much activity, she never knew who or what to expect when she walked in her apartment.

Her heart rose in her throat as she stood discreetly at the screen door, watching her son's fingers dance across the keys of the piano while Will busily tapped the screen of his phone.

Her stomach clenched.

They already know he's talented. Keep an open mind. Trust them as Liam trusts them.

Will surely wouldn't exploit his dear friend's only child.

Perhaps not deliberately, but now he's a promoter of talent. That's his job. Is he seeing dollar signs?

Swallowing the tiny bud of fear, she waited for Jack to finish the Chopin Mazurka before she pulled open the screen door and joined in the two men's applause. "Bravo!"

Will grinned as he set the phone on the table and stood. "This is one incredible kid, Carrie."

"He's great!" Tony added while Jack beamed shyly.

"He's his father's son." She smiled, going over to put her hands on Jack's shoulders.

"It's more than that," Will replied. "His talent is unique, far and away more than—" He stopped at Carrie's warning look.

"Honey?" Carrie tousled Jack's hair. "Could you please run up to Aunt Margie's and grab the produce she got us at the farm stand this morning? I thought I'd make BLTs for lunch. Tony, Will—stay and eat lunch with us?"

"Sure, Mom." Jack jumped up from the piano bench and headed out.

Tony glanced from Carrie to Will. "I have a fruit salad and sauvignon sauce downstairs. How 'bout we add it to our lunch?" At her nod, he followed Jack out the door. "Be right back."

Will waited for them to get down the stairs before he crossed over to Carrie standing next to the piano. "What's up?" He dipped his blond head to peer into her eyes. "Have we got a problem?"

"No, we don't," she replied. "Not yet. But I don't want you making comparisons between Liam and Jack. Especially not in front of Jack."

"That's ridiculous. Even Liam says the kid is better on piano than he ever thought of being. Do you think Jack's not aware of that fact himself? What's *really* going on here?"

Lowering her eyes from Will's piercing gaze, she ran her fingers idly over the piano keys.

"You came in here glaring at me like I was some kind of child molester or some—" Realization lit his expression. "My God, you think I'm going to try to capitalize on Jack's talent, don't you?"

She glanced up, not even trying to hide her fear. "It would be a wonderful promotional gimmick, wouldn't it? Especially for a

brand new agent just getting started? Maestro Reilly and his
newfound prodigy son?"

He sighed and gave her a small frown. "You know what? I've
been with Liam for over six years—by his side for every performance in every city, every lonely night on the road, and every
argument with Marty about what Liam was and was *not* willing to
do to further his career. I may have taken over Marty's job, but I
am *not* Marty." His tone was kind, but his expression was dead
serious. "We're friends first. I would *never* do anything that might
hurt Liam or anyone he cares about. Got it?"

They stared at one another for a long moment.

Finally, she broke eye contact, sighing deeply. "I'm sorry. I
guess I'm a little overprotective. I have no idea what's in store for
us now. When I saw you in here watching him play, I–I kinda
flipped out."

"I'd be lying if I told you that the possibilities for Jack's own
career haven't crossed my mind." He shook his head. "But he's
just a kid. You and Liam have to make the decisions about that,
not me. I told you before, nobody intends to take his childhood
away from him."

"I know."

She walked slowly to the kitchen and he followed her. His
eyes were on her, silently observing as she took plates from the
cupboard and dug sandwich makings out of the refrigerator. She
placed a griddle on the stove and laid strips of bacon on it.

He leaned against the bar. "Keep in mind, though, your son's
bound for the stage. The question isn't *will* he play Carnegie Hall,
it's *when* will he play Carnegie Hall. He's an extraordinary talent.
Like your mother. He's gonna be in the limelight, and it won't
have anything to do with being Liam's son."

"This isn't like... like Mick Jagger suddenly discovering he
has a son, is it?" She meant the words to be wry, but they came
out a little more like desperate. "We're not going to constantly be

in a fishbowl, are we?" She poured iced tea into four glasses as the bacon began to sizzle.

"Well, it's a fishbowl of sorts. Liam's a celebrity—those are the facts." Settling down on a bar stool, he accepted the glass of iced tea she offered.

"Yeah, I've figured that out."

"Come on, Carrie, I think you're blowing this way out of proportion. Most people wouldn't know a symphony conductor if he walked up and hit them with his baton. Only his own public is curious about him. They're going to be even more curious now." Will shrugged with a grin. "There's nothing wrong with getting attention and admiration for being good at what you do. That's all this is. Liam keeps it in perspective. He really does. Things *are* going to be different, but stop expecting the worst. It could be fun, ya know?" He gave her a wink as Jack came clattering up the stairs.

≈

"Liam! Hey, Liam!" Jack's voice carried down the beach. Carrie kept an eye on him as he stood waist-deep in the cold water of Lake Michigan, waving frantically at his father who was swimming several yards out past the sandbar.

"They're getting good now. Come on," the boy shouted. He was teaching Liam how to body surf in the waves, amazed that there was anything at all that Liam *didn't* know how to do. They'd been at it for about an hour, and Liam had spent more time under the water than riding on top of it.

Although she'd been in the lake earlier, she now sat on the beach, her royal blue tank suit drying in the warm breeze. Liam and Jack rode a small wave close to shore, laughing and shouting to one another. She couldn't help chuckling as Liam ended up underwater again, but they swam back out to catch another one.

Even after only a few days, anyone would assume they'd always been together. They seemed as comfortable with one another as any father and son could be.

Glancing down at her arms and then up at the sun, she dropped the bottle of SPF30 into her beach bag. There was no more need for sunscreen. She'd have to think about supper soon, but instead of calling out, she watched them for a few more minutes. Their wet hair gleamed in the sun, Jack's young body a coltish duplicate of Liam's mature brawny frame. With her book at her side, she laid back on the beach towel, closing her eyes against the late afternoon glare.

Maybe a few minutes longer.

The three of them had spent time together every day, and Jack and Liam were practically inseparable. While Carrie took senior pictures, Jack went to Traverse City with his father to rehearse the upcoming benefit concert. Every evening, he bounded home full of enthusiasm for the orchestra and the music. They shared meals, at the apartment or at Margie and Noah's or on Liam's boat. Liam fit into their little family unit like the missing piece of a puzzle.

Jack followed him around like an eager puppy, inundating him with questions, and it seemed as if Liam asked Jack just as many about his own life there in Willow Bay. They were learning to know each other, feeling their way, and each had insatiable curiosity about the other. Neither of them appeared to be looking forward to Jack's return to camp.

Jack delighted in taking Liam, Will, and Tony on what he referred to as "field trips," including canoeing down the Platte River one afternoon, climbing the rocks at Willow Point Light-house, and taking the *Penguin* out for an early morning sail. Will and Tony gave Jack free rein on the boat, treating him like one of the guys.

In spite of Will's reassurances, another tiny seed of doubt started to take root as she watched how fascinated Jack was with

Liam's career. She tried to quell it, but the concern niggled in the back of her mind as she lay on the beach. Raising her head, her gaze followed Jack and Liam riding the waves. They were out past the sand bar. Seeing them play together eased her doubts a bit, so she smiled and went back to sunbathing.

A shadow blocked out the late afternoon sun. When she opened her eyes, she expected to see clouds coming in from the west. Hadn't the weather forecast predicted rain for tonight? Instead she saw a pair of elegant Italian loafers and, as her eyes traveled upward, an expensive designer suit.

Sitting up, she shook her hair free of sand to rise and pull on her terry cover-up. The man was darkly handsome, his tie perfectly knotted, his white shirt crisp. He pulled off a pair of mirrored sunglasses—his eyes were the truest sapphire blue she'd ever seen, but they glinted icily at her.

"Are you lost?" she asked, giving him a friendly smile. "Are you looking for the bait shop?"

"No, I'm not *lost*." The man's eyed her up and down, appraising and dismissing her with one glance. "And I do believe I've found the *bait*."

A sudden chill in the pit of her stomach telegraphed trouble, and she knew instinctively whom she faced. "Marty Justice. I'll be dammed."

"Carrie Halligan, as I live and breathe." Marty's voice was as cold as his eyes. "Frankly, I'm a little disappointed. I guess I wasn't expecting the paragon of virtue Liam's been pining after for so many years to be a dumpy little *hausfrau*."

The full frontal assault set her back on her heels. When she caught her breath, she spoke as evenly as she could. "C–can I get Liam for you?"

"No, thanks." He lifted one elegant loafer out of the sand and shook it. "I'll wait for him on the boat. Send him up when he's done... playing." He turned away, started toward the marina, but ambled back to gaze at her coolly for a moment. "Don't think you've won any battles here, lady. You'll never fit into his life. He pulls this shit all the time. Gets wrapped up in playing out one fantasy or another." He eyed her before relentlessly continuing the attack. "This time it's the *daddy* fantasy and it won't end any differently. Being on a podium is his life. He may *think* he wants you and the boy now, but in a few months, he'll be bored with you and ready to move on, just like with every other piece of ass he picks up."

Stepping closer, he invaded her space.

Carrie moved back, but he continued in the same distant, icy tone. "Do yourself a favor, Carrie. Take your son and get the hell out. This isn't going to work now any more than it would have worked the first time. Let Liam get back onstage where he belongs." He stared at her, his tone growing even more calculating. "I can make it worth your while… but you already know that, don't you?"

With that, he strode off across the sand.

L iam and Jack dove together into the waves, letting the momentum of the water carry them closer to the beach. Liam struck back out toward the sand bar, leaving Jack standing in the shallows at the shore.

"Liam."

Liam thought he heard his name as he swam away, but when he glanced back, Jack wasn't facing him.

There it was again, louder. Jack's voice calling, "Liam. Dad."

Splashing as he rolled over mid-stroke, he searched in the direction of the voice.

Dad? Jack called me Dad?

But the boy was pointing to the beach where Carrie stood

listening, her head bent down, her arms folded across her waist. The man talking to her whirled suddenly and hurried away.

Jack glanced over his shoulder as Liam swam up next to him. "Who's the suit with Mom?" he asked, jerking a thumb toward the beach.

Liam thrust his fingers through his wet hair, brushing it out of his face. "Oh, dammit," he muttered. "Come on, Jack, let's go in."

"Who is he, Dad?"

At the word, Liam's heart soared as they headed toward Carrie, in spite of the anger that had started burning in him at the sight of Marty Justice striding down the beach. "Just someone I used to know," he replied more brusquely than he intended. "Head back home. I'll take care of it."

Liam kept an eye on Marty disappearing in the distance.

Carrie began folding beach towels, snapping them out in front of her.

He jogged to her while Jack lagged behind.

"You okay?" He picked up a towel from the short pile she'd accumulated and ran it over his hair and face.

She gave him a tight smile. "Me? I'm fine." She leaned down to stuff sunglasses, her book, and Jack's watch into her tote.

"I can't believe he showed up here after I'd warned him to stay away." He glanced back at Jack, who stood a few yards away watching them warily.

"You *are* kidding, aren't you? I can't believe it took him this long to get here." She trembled, fists clenched at her sides as she gave a grim laugh. "Did you honestly think he was just going to let you go and not put up some sort of fight? You've been a hell of a meal ticket, *Maestro*." They stood in the sand, tension crackling between them.

Liam brushed sand from his legs and dropped the towel back on the pile. "He's been here since Sunday. He was at the recital."

"*What?*"

"I grabbed him when I saw him talking to Jack." He could tell his words were not reassuring her, so he tried another tack. "I'd already fired him. I think he thought he could talk me out of it."

"He was talking to Jack?" Her dark eyes turned almost black with emotion. "What's he want with Jack?"

"It doesn't matter. I sent him away."

"Then why's he still here?" Carrie's voice rose. "Keep him away from my son, Liam."

"Carrie, for God's sake—"

"Mom, are you okay?" Jack came up behind them.

Liam swung around and barked, "Dammit, Jack, I said go home. Now!"

When Carrie took a step back, her eyes huge, he shook his head, immediately contrite. "Oh, God. Jack, I'm sorry—"

She picked up the pile of towels and her tote and started up the beach.

Expelling a frustrated breath, he raised one finger to Jack, indicating for him to wait and went charging after her with long-legged strides. "Carrie, listen." He grasped her upper arm and swung her gently around to face him. "I don't know why he's here, but he doesn't have anything to do with *us*." He peered into her face. "Or Jack. Now, I'll go handle him, but you've gotta trust me. Are you gonna trust me, Car—" He broke off as Jack came up behind him and seized his arm.

"Let go of my mother." His gray eyes shot fire, his lean young frame tensed. He dropped his hand when Liam glanced back at him, but stood his ground, his lips set in a firm line.

Immediately Liam released Carrie, his jaw dropping at the intensity in his son's voice. "Jack, I–I..."

But Jack's face was hard and his eyes, drilling into Liam's, were frosty. "Don't *ever* grab her like that again."

Reaching out to touch Jack's shoulder, Carrie spoke in calm, soothing tones. "Jack, it's okay. He didn't hurt me. He wasn't trying to hurt me. We're okay." She handed him the pile of towels. "Go upstairs, honey, and get changed. Go on." She smiled and nodded toward the docks.

Jack looked over at her, then back at Liam whose gut churned as he stared aghast at his son.

"Are you sure you're okay, Mom?" The boy gripped the towels against his chest.

"I'm fine." Still smiling, she reached behind her for Liam's hand. "Go on, we'll be up in minute."

Jack trudged through the sand toward the marina, turning around every few yards to glance back at the two of them standing together hand in hand.

Carrie turned to Liam. "I'm sorry I was such a bitch. Marty really blindsided me." She put her arms around him and the sun-warmed skin of her cheek heated his chest.

He pressed her head close to his heart and buried his lips in her hair. "I lost it, too. I'm sorry," he admitted with a frustrated sigh. "It's just that I've spent days getting past your defenses, and suddenly, you were all shut down again. Now I'm getting attitude from Jack." He tipped her face back with one finger tucked under her chin. "Jesus. He really thought I was going to hurt you."

She touched his beard, running her thumb across his lower lip. "Liam, he's protective of me—it's always been just the two of us. He and I have to get used to sharing each other."

"I'd never hurt you," he said huskily. "And I shouldn't have snapped at Jack, dammit."

"He'll be fine. Don't worry about it, I'll talk to him."

"No, *I'll* talk to him." He dropped a quick kiss on her lips. "I guess these past few days have been like a father-son honeymoon. I never once thought about what might happen if one of us got angry or upset." Kissing her again, he tugged his sweatshirt from her bag.

She pulled him back for another kiss. "It's rarely a honeymoon with teenagers, even one as terrific as ours." With a little grin, she slung the bag over her shoulder. "Please go get rid of that... that *bastard,* and don't be nice, okay?"

"Shouldn't take long. I'll be up in a few." With one last kiss, he strode up the beach toward his boat and what he knew would be another ugly confrontation.

CHAPTER 22

Liam stormed into the *Allegro*'s salon, ready to take on his former agent. He rather hoped Tony and Will weren't around because they'd probably stop him from beating the crap out of Marty, which was his fondest desire at the moment. "You son of a bitch."

Marty was alone, ensconced on the deep-cushioned sofa, calmly sipping whiskey from a heavy crystal glass. When Liam stalked in, he simply raised one black brow.

His unruffled demeanor irritated Liam even more. "What the hell are you still doing here?"

"I could ask you the same question." Amber liquid splashed over the rim of the glass as Marty swirled the ice. His next words proved he wasn't as cool as he seemed. "What the hell are *you* trying to do to your goddammed career? Fuck it up completely?"

"Give it up, will you? Peter told me you deposited the check. Contracts are null and void. We're done." Liam strode to the bar and pulled a beer from the small refrigerator.

"Man, don't do this."

"Too late, it's done." Liam took a long drink, letting the cold liquid cool his temper before he spoke again. "Look, I'm sorry, but we've run our course. Thanks for everything you did for me. I suggest you go back to Malibu and take care of the rest of your clients." He paused and then jerked his head toward the door. "Come within a mile of me or my son again, and I promise you, I *will* get that restraining order."

With an exaggerated sigh, Marty drained his glass. "You're such a fuckin' loser, Reilly." When he stopped at the door, his face twisted in an ugly sneer. "Enjoy your retirement, *Daddy*. Your career is dead. Oh, and you'll be hearing from my attorney. We're not done."

Liam shrugged. "Good-bye, Marty."

∾

Carrie brushed her sandy feet against the sun-warmed wood of the dock, glancing over her shoulder at the *Allegro* as she started up the steps to the apartment. Jack's playing drifted out before she got halfway up the stairs. He was running scales with feverish intensity. As she got to the deck, he started into a crashing chord sequence.

Good Lord.

That furious playing? It was a sure sign he was upset.

Dressed in shorts and a T-shirt, he sat at the piano, his bare feet working the pedals as his fingers raced over the keys.

Shouldering the canvas bag, she crossed over to him and ran a hand through his still-damp hair. "Did you hang your wet suit on the rack?"

He nodded before abruptly changing tempo to a slow, rather melancholy melody that she didn't recognize.

"Is that one of yours?" she asked on her way to the laundry room behind the kitchen.

He nodded again. His hair hung in his face, hiding his eyes.

Back in the kitchen, she pulled a foil-wrapped casserole dish from the refrigerator and switched on the oven. "I like it, it's pretty." Passing behind him on her way up the stairs, she stopped for a second to read the notes over his shoulder. "I'm going to get a quick shower, babe. Then we'll have supper. Will you stick that casserole in when the oven beeps?"

He nodded once more.

Experience had taught her to let him play it out. He'd talk when he was ready, but not before. She slipped into the shower, washed quickly, shampooed her short curls, and then dried off with a fluffy towel. The music had stopped downstairs.

Liam must not be here yet, I don't hear voices.

Wrapping up in a thick terry robe, she opened the bathroom door to find Jack sitting on the edge of her bed, tracing the pattern of the old quilt with his finger.

His eyes clouded with apprehension when they met hers. "Is he in charge now?" His lower lip trembled ever so slightly.

Carrie sat down on the bed next to him. "Oh, come on, Jack."

"What's he pissy with me for?" He ran his hand over his face in a gesture that reminded her of his father. "He can't just come in here and take over. Can he?"

"He was upset about Marty. He really didn't mean to be short with you."

"Well, he was."

"Hey, you don't get this upset when *I'm* short with you."

"You're my mother, it's different."

She peered into his face. "He's your father. How's it different?"

With a fifteen-year-old's look of exasperation, he shrugged. "I don't know. He's only been around a little while and..." He hesitated. "It's just different, okay?"

"Honey, these past few days have been like a... a fairy tale. Real life was bound to creep in. You know, things can't be sunshine and fun all the time. Liam's a human being. And he's new at this parent thing. Give him a break."

"Who's Marty anyway? I think he tried to talk to me at the recital, but Liam interrupted." He shoved his hair out of his eyes. "What's Liam's problem with him?"

"He was his agent for years." She tried to decide how much of the story her son needed.

Just the basics. If Liam wants him to know more about the rocky relationship he had with his former agent, he *can tell him.*

"There's a long list of issues between them," she continued. "Bottom line is your dad fired him last week. I think Marty might be here to try to get his job back."

"Dad should stick with Will. He's cool."

"*Dad?*"

Jack shrugged again. "I don't know... just trying it out." He let one finger follow the stitching in the quilt, keeping his eyes downcast. "Can I ask you a question?"

"Sure. Ask me anything." She tousled his hair affectionately.

"Were you *ever* going to tell me about him?"

This wasn't the question she was expecting. Her belly clenched, and when he lifted his head to meet her gaze, she simply stared at him for a long moment. "I'd planned on it," she said finally, her voice soft.

"When?" His eyes bored into hers.

With great difficulty, she resisted the urge to look away from his steady gaze. "I don't know. I've been a coward for a long time. But I hope I could have stepped up, told you the truth... eventually. Eliot took care of it, so I guess we'll never know, will we?"

"Maybe I should have asked you sooner." He stared down at his hands.

Carrie put her finger under his chin and made him face her

again. "No, baby, this was *all me*, not you. My job. Not ever yours. I'm so sorry I wussed out on you."

"It's okay. Really it is. But what's going to happen now?"

"In the next five minutes?" she teased. "Supper, I think."

"No, I mean... you know... you and Liam? I–I think he's hot for you." Color rose in his cheeks. "He watches you all the time."

"He does?"

Jack had been so wrapped up getting acquainted with his father, she was surprised he'd even noticed anything else. They'd been deliberately holding their own feelings and desires in check while he and Liam got to know one another. Liam was sleeping on the boat, and they'd barely exchanged a few kisses—and never in front of Jack.

"Yeah, he looks at you like a guy who's been in prison for ten years and you're like... like, I don't know... some hot woman a guy his age would find attractive." Jack laid back on the bed, his bare feet dangling over the edge.

"Wow, thanks." She gave him a wry smile. "Who would that be exactly?"

"Dunno." Staring at the skylight above her bed, he pursed his lips.

"How about Angelina Jolie?" she offered, hoping for a smile.

He cleared his throat, then rolled his eyes. "Sure, yeah. That's exactly who I was thinking of." When she wrinkled her nose at him, he tucked his hands behind his head, gazing at her thoughtfully. "I saw you kissing down on the beach. Does that mean you guys are back together?"

"Yeah, we are."

"You mean you're like... dating?" His brow furrowed.

"More than that, actually." Warmth flooded her as she thought about Liam's proposal and the ring waiting in the box on the dresser. "Liam asked me to marry him."

Jack sat up, his eyes round with wonder. Then they narrowed. "Are you in love with him?"

"I've *always* been in love with him. But I never imagined being with him again."

"Is he the reason guys like Jeff and that other guy—Max Whatsis—never got anywhere with you?" He bent his head down to peer into her eyes.

"Yep."

"Wow," Jack whispered. And then a little bit louder. "Wow. So, *are* you going to marry him?"

"What do *you* think about that?"

Emotions played across his young face. He sat quietly for a moment before he bolted up. Crossing to the window, he stared out at the tall pines behind the boathouse. "Things sure would be different, wouldn't they?"

"You'd have the regulation number of parents." She wished he'd turn around. She really needed to see his face.

"Would we have to move? Or would he come here when he wasn't out touring?" He was still speaking to the window. "What would happen to us?"

Carrie crossed over to stand next to him. "I don't know. We haven't gotten that far yet."

A long sigh slipped out. "I know he never meant to hurt you, Mom. I got pissed because he yelled at me." He stared down at the rug before turning to face her. "He was all upset about that Marty guy, and I acted like a douche to him. I shouldn't have done that."

"He understands." She brushed his hair back from his face and thought—apropos of nothing at all—*the kid really needs a haircut.* "But it'd be nice if you apologized."

"I will when he gets up here." Jack started for the door. "I like him, I think he's awesome. If you want to marry him, you should do it."

She smiled at him. "I love you, Jack."

"Love you, too." He sprinted down the stairs.

"Hey. Did you put the casserole in?" she called after him.

"Yeah." His voice carried up the stairs.

The sound of the piano began again as he played his own elaborate version of an old Beatles tune.

CHAPTER 23

C arrie dawdled over dressing, applying a small amount of blush, a little lip gloss, and spritzing scent on her throat and wrists. Mind whirling, she slipped on a simple pale green tank-style sundress.

Only two weeks since they'd gotten back together and Liam's career had already interfered in their new life. She was sure it wouldn't be the last time.

Marty's appearance wasn't really the problem, but what he'd said about her not fitting into Liam's life truly struck a chord. He'd had been an active participant—even the main manipulator —in shaping Liam's career. For years, he'd basked in the reflected glory of *Maestro Reilly*. That celebrity was the part of Liam she didn't know and the part of him that worried her the most.

Right here, right now, in this small hamlet, Liam belonged to her and Jack. The town buzzed about them this week, but these folks knew and loved her. They would accept Liam with open arms if they stayed here. But if they left, what would happen?

Will I be able to share him?

Thanks to NPR, cable, and public television, classical music was available to a much wider audience. From the reaction of women around here, symphony conductors could indeed have groupies. Once again, she wondered how that might affect her and Jack. Would he be taken in by the attention and glamour and want that life for himself?

She straightened the towels on the rack, swept her makeup into the vanity drawer, and wandered into the bedroom to smooth the quilt on the bed. Glancing in the dresser mirror, she finger-styled her damp curls.

Jack had never been any further away from home than Chicago and then only for museum field trips or piano competitions. He was used to being onstage, but nearly always in front of audiences full of friends, neighbors, and schoolmates. His life was *here,* on the lakeshore, quiet and safe. So was hers.

Voices downstairs, then the sound of the piano drew her. Stopping at the loft rail, she looked down. Jack and Liam were both on the piano bench, Jack playing the bass end and Liam the upper notes as they rollicked through a Scott Joplin ragtime duet. Father and son were a natural duo.

When she came downstairs, Liam leaned his head back to catch her eye as she passed behind them. He snaked one hand out and she let him pull her to him. Jack concentrated on the low keys, but peeked at them out of the corner of his eye. He smiled when Carrie dropped a kiss on Liam's forehead.

"Are you guys about ready to eat?" she asked as they played the final notes and high-fived each other. "You can toss a salad." A head nod indicated Jack. "And Maestro, you can set the table."

"I'm putting in *both* avocados. Hope everyone's okay with that." Jack sprinted into the kitchen. "What else are we having?"

"That chicken casserole, and Eliot brought us blueberry tarts. He's been baking again." Carrie gazed at Liam. He still sat on the piano bench, his expression affectionate—the face of a father, a husband, a man content in the warm company of his family. The tenderness in his eyes practically liquefied her insides. When he met her gaze, the look changed to one of pure raw hunger.

Her knees almost buckled. Closing her eyes, she gripped the granite bar.

In that second, Liam was across the room, standing close beside her. His lips touched her ear. "I've missed you. Want to meet me on the boat later?" he whispered under Jack's clatter in the refrigerator.

"More than anything," she murmured, turning her head for a quick kiss before going to pull the casserole out of the oven.

Liam set the table, all the while laughing and joking with Jack. When they sat down to eat, the boy started to pick up his fork, but set it down again. "Liam, I'm sorry—" he began, but at the same time Liam started to speak.

"Jack, I owe you—" He stopped. "Go ahead."

"I just wanted to say I'm sorry for what I said out on the beach. I was out of line." Jack's eyes met Liam's.

"I'm sorry too, son. I shouldn't have snapped at you."

"No sweat." Jack shrugged. "Don't worry about it."

"I'd like to talk about it, Jack." Liam accepted the salad from Carrie, dished some onto his plate, and then passed it to Jack.

"Mom already told me who the suit was." Jack helped himself to salad, obviously avoiding Liam's gaze. "Did you get rid of him?"

"Yes."

"Well, good," Jack said briskly, reaching for the casserole dish.

"Marty isn't really what I wanted to talk to you about." Liam accepted the casserole from him and spooned some onto his plate. "I don't want you to think that we aren't ever going to have problems." Jack frowned as Liam continued in a matter-of-fact tone. "We're going to get on each other's nerves sometimes. You'll get mad at me. I'll get mad at you. It's all part of being a family. Take it from me, kid—family life can be really messy."

Jack grinned. "You should know, I guess. You had like... a platoon of kids in your family."

"You're right. With eight brothers and sisters, it could get pretty chaotic," Liam chuckled. "Son, we've gotten to be good friends these past few days and I'm very glad. But I'm also your father and I'm not going anywhere, so now you have two parents to drive you crazy. Aren't you lucky?"

Carrie smiled, her heart nearly bursting with pride as Liam took the parenting reins with honesty and kindness. She was surprised at how lovely it felt to have someone share this journey of raising a gifted child. No jealousy or guilt, just relief and unspeakable joy.

Liam took a couple of bites, watching Jack absorb what he'd been saying before he continued. "I'm brand new at this parenting thing. You're brand new to the dad thing, so I guess we're both in uncharted territory."

"I guess so," Jack mumbled around a mouthful of salad and then glanced at Carrie, who scowled affectionately at his lack of table manners. "'Scuse me."

"Your mom, over here, stuffing her face"Liam jerked a thumb Carrie's direction as she returned his teasing with a goofy expression that broke Jack up completely"is an old hand at parenting, but you're going to have to allow me some mistakes. And trust me to never ever deliberately hurt either one of you."

Jack flushed, but he met Liam's eyes straight on. "I'm sorry, Dad. I never really thought you were going to hurt her. I was being a douchebag."

"It's okay." Liam reached out to ruffle Jack's hair. "And son, thanks for calling me *Dad*. I like the sound of that."

"Yeah, well, it feels better than *Liam*."

"I think so too." Liam smiled. "*Douchebag?* Really?" He quirked a brow at Carrie, but she only smiled and shrugged.

Douchebag was Jack's newest word and she had no idea where it came from. That was another teenaged thing that Liam was going to have to grow accustomed to. She eyed him as he frowned, clearly struggled with something before he blurted, "Jack, there's something else I need to tell you."

What on earth?

Carrie gazed at him, a little shiver passing through her as she tried to figure what else he could possibly have to say. She thought he'd handled things very nicely.

He took a breath. "I'm in love with your mother." Reaching across the table, he took Carrie's hand. "And she's in love with me."

Her heart soared. Blinking back tears, she smiled and nodded, afraid to speak for fear of blubbering.

"Yeah, I kinda figured that out." Jack blushed to the tips of his ears.

"How'd you figure that? We thought we were being pretty discreet."

"I'm gifted." Jack grinned. "And perceptive."

"And modest," Liam said.

"You forgot handsome and charming," Jack added.

"Oh, is charming what you were being when you were chatting up that cute little blonde at the canoe rental place yesterday?" Liam winked at Carrie. "What was her name? Lanie?"

After wiping her eyes on her napkin, she said, "Jack? You like Lanie Palmer?"

"Geez," Jack groaned. "Thanks a bunch, Dad." Liam snickered as Jack pointed at his mother. "We're not going there, okay?" He got up from the table to take his plate to the sink. "Anyone want dessert?"

Inwardly, Carrie breathed a sigh of relief as the silliness

continued throughout the rest of the meal. Thank God, they'd weathered a small family storm.

Jack served the blueberry tarts with a flourish, right down to the folded towel over his arm. He even started a pot of coffee before he left to go night fishing with Tony, Will, and Noah.

"There you go, 'rents." He pushed the switch on the coffeemaker. "I'm outta here, so you two can stay put and do whatever you were planning to do *down on the boat later*." With a knowing smile as he quoted Liam's earlier whispered proposition in a low intimate tone that sounded remarkably like his father.

"Lord, is nothing sacred around here?" Liam's brows furrowed in mock dismay.

Jack only laughed. "Hey, if you want sacred, don't whisper indecent proposals to my mother right in front of me."

"I can't believe you even heard that."

Hot color crept up Carrie's neck. "We weren't planning anything in particular," she denied, but Jack held up his hand.

"No details, please." He clasped his hands, rolled his eyes skyward, and the brogue was right on. "Lest ye defile me boyish innocence." He headed out the door. "I'll be back late." His wicked grin was so much like Liam's, it took Carrie's breath away.

The two of them sat at the table, staring silently at one another as the sound of his flip flops slapped on the deck, then faded down the stairs to the docks. Shaking his head as if to clear it, Liam got up to carry dishes to the kitchen. "You've got a weird kid." He grinned over his shoulder.

"You mean *we*," Carrie retorted, following him to the kitchen with the rest of the plates.

"This may work yet." Liam gave her a tender smile. "Carrie, he's calling me *Dad*."

"So I heard." Filling two mugs with coffee, she moved to the living room, gazing out the window overlooking the bay. The lights of a freighter flickered in the moonlight. After a few moments, Liam joined her and they snuggled together on the sofa.

"I was afraid he hated me after that little fiasco on the beach." Liam wrapped his arm around her.

"You were great with him," Carrie said, running her hand up his denim-covered thigh. "It will be easier when we're settled and he has the security of all of us being together all the time. I think he's not sure what's going to happen next. Everything's kind of up in the air."

"It doesn't have to be." He caught her hand, pressing a kiss into the palm. "Put on the ring. Let's set a date."

"I guess we *could* spend the rest of the summer trying to find a house or maybe get a builder." Carrie shivered at the magic his tongue created on the sensitive skin of her wrist. "Eliot owns the land on either side of his place. Maybe he'd sell a lot to us. It would be so great to live next door to him. Jack adores him. Outside of Noah and Margie, Eliot's the closest thing he has to a grandparent."

Liam set her hand down slowly. "He has a complete set of grandparents in Toronto. And I have a house in Lincoln Park."

"You want us to move to Chicago, don't you?"

"It's where I live. It's where Will and Tony live." He put his cup on the blanket chest and turned to her. "My house in Chicago is plenty big for all of us. There are wonderful schools there. Jack could study with Eric Currado at Northwestern. He's the best there is. He could get him ready for Juilliard."

"Interlochen can get him ready for Juilliard." Carrie scooted to the end of the sofa to set her mug on the lamp table. "You've been thinking about this a lot, haven't you?" It wasn't her intention, but the words came out sounding like an accusation.

"Of course." His brow furrowed. "Carrie, the city just makes more sense for *all* of us. We would be together for one thing. Jack wouldn't be boarding, he'd be with us. Northwestern has a wonderful music academy. There're tons of opportunities for him there. And summers, we could come back up here and he could go to Interlochen."

"Liam, I don't want him in some huge urban high school." A chill developed in the pit of her stomach at the very thought. "He's used to a small town school and the intimacy at Interlochen. He'd be lost in Chicago. And he... he needs the lake. He's always lived on the water." Her conscience prickled as she spoke.

Who exactly am I talking about here? I need the lake. But so does Jack. We can't leave.

"Then we'll sell the house in Lincoln Park and buy one on the North Shore. He can still sail and swim. Same lake, other side." His voice dropped into that low persuasive timbre she'd grown accustomed to hearing from Jack when he wanted something special from her. The power of his gaze drew her in.

She didn't want to have this discussion tonight, not when she wanted him so bad she was trembling. "Liam, let's not waste our time alone tonight on *this*." Moving over beside him, she started on the buttons of his shirt. "Can't we just wait until you're done with the benefit before we make any decisions?" Her hands found the crisp hair on his chest, the warmth of his skin, the hard nubs of his nipples. She pulled his mouth down to hers, seeking the warm coffee-sweet cavern with her tongue.

CHAPTER 24

Liam met Carrie's lips fiercely, opening his mouth to her searching kiss, meeting her tongue with his own. Desire rose in him. Several long nights had passed since they'd made love—he was aching to be inside her. Sliding one hand down her leg to the hem of her dress, he slipped it under the fabric to stroke her soft thigh. She moaned, reaching for the snap of his jeans. His mind clouded, his senses became intoxicated, but a voice inside him wouldn't be silenced.

No! We need to talk about this. Now! Tonight!

Easing away from her, he ran his thumb over her full lower lip. "Talk to me, baby. What are you so afraid of?" he murmured. "Do you think I can't have my career and take care of you and Jack, too? Are you so terrified of change that you'd be willing to stay in this little town forever and keep him from the world?" He caught her hand in his, lacing their fingers. "Can't we find a way to compromise?"

"How?" Her voice was husky as she pulled away from his. "I don't want to live in the city. I love living in Willow Bay. What's so wrong with that?"

"Nothing's wrong with this town. It's wonderful. But I need more, and Jack does, too. He's got incredible talent. He should be developing it. I'm certain Currado would take him on, but he's in Chicago."

"What about baseball and sailing and all his friends here?" She asked, a tear edging out of the corner of her eye. "I don't want anyone in the city trying to put him up on a stage. He's too young for that. I couldn't face fighting drugs and alcohol and those kinds of problems. *You* know how show business is!" She choked, then swallowed hard. "And yes, I'm scared I'll lose him... and you, to touring and audiences and all the... celebrity."

He was touched by how she struggled not to cry. "Carrie. Sweetheart. Listen to me." Liam pressed a gentle kissed to her lips. "First of all, this is the symphony. You know? Classical music? As far as I know, drugs aren't a big issue with conductors or pianists. And I swear to you, I've never seen a violin section trash a hotel room." He added a wink, "Um... the horns, I'm not so sure about." Grinning, he was encouraged that she smiled through the tears. He pulled her closer. "Besides, Jack isn't nearly ready for touring. He has years of study and preparation ahead of him. I'm not going to let anyone exploit him."

"I know that, but—"

Pressing his finger to her lips, he stopped her words. "Stop creating mountains and monsters. My career is pretty innocuous as entertainment careers go."

Liam watched her closely as she knit her fingers in her lap, her eyes downcast. She was clearly scared and confused—but he was dammed if he knew what to say to convince her how groundless her fears were.

She's closing up again. Shit.

He blew out a frustrated breath. "What did you think was going to happen after I got done with the benefit?" With difficulty he kept his voice even. "Did you think we'd get married and just continue to divide our time between this apartment and my boat?"

She sat straight up, hugging herself. Her dark eyes flashed. "Frankly, I hadn't gotten that far yet. I'm still working on believing that you aren't just going to cruise away after the benefit."

"Okay, now that was below the belt."

"I really don't care."

He went on offense. "Dammit, I have a career to consider here."

"I have a business to consider *here*." Her tone turned even cooler. "And my son."

"*Our* son!" he snapped. After a long moment of silence, he raised both hands in surrender. "Okay, I'm sorry. I'm sorry. I'm fully aware of your business." It seemed impossible to address this without sounding patronizing, so he started over. "I love this town too, but *I* have to go out into the world to make my living. I can't do it here. I also love you and Jack. I want you with me, not sitting up here waiting for me to make an appearance between concerts. You're a wonderful photographer. You can make a living taking pictures wherever you are. Jack deserves the best. I can do that, but I need to keep working."

"I'm sorry, too." Carrie leaned over to put her hand his chest. "I want to be with you. I want us to be a family, but it's important to me for Jack to be *here* where kids fish and sail, not in a big city where there are drugs and gangs and guns and violence. *And* there's my studio. I worked hard to make it a success. I'm not ready to go out and start over in a new place. The competition in Chicago would be fierce." Sliding her hand over his belly, she stroked the hair there, raising goose bumps—and more—with each touch. "Besides, what about my own playing? Where would I do my lounge act?" She gave him a sly smile.

That drew the chuckle he was certain she'd been going for,

and with a sigh, he put his arm around her, resting his chin on top of her head.

God, I never expected this much of a battle. Would the conversation have been the same sixteen years ago? Am I being selfish expecting her to just pack up and come with me?

But he *was* thinking of her and especially of Jack—he needed a master like Eric Currado and the stimulation of the city. On the other hand, the kid loved it here. This was the only home he'd ever known and he'd already been thrown for a loop by meeting his long-lost father. Was it fair to pack him up and take him away from everything familiar while they were getting to know one another? Interlochen would give him what he needed for now, probably as easily as studying with Currado.

What about after he graduated from Interlochen? Could Carrie handle it if Jack went as far away as, say, New York?

She slid her fingers under his unbuttoned shirt, running her hands over his ribs and reaching around to massage the tense muscles of his back. Moving almost automatically, his fingers traced her spine down to her waist. Thoughts tripping over one another, his mind raced as both sides of the argument tumbled around and around in his head.

Her breath warmed his neck. The soft mounds of her breasts pressed into his chest as he settled back on the sofa and pulled her against him.

Everything *was* perfect now—the three of them together in this lovely place. Turning his head, he stared out the big window at the moonlit bay. Carrie pressed feather-light kisses into the hollow of his throat. Hell, he already had enough money invested to keep them more than comfortable for the rest of their lives. The concert circuit *was* getting tiresome—rehearsals, airplanes, lonely hotel rooms, bad room service...

Maybe retirement isn't such a bad idea.

She explored the waistband of his jeans, her fingers dipping below the low-riding denim to find his burgeoning erection, her fingertips stroking his heated flesh. He relaxed deeper into the cushions, taking pleasure in her warm breath on his skin, her hands on him.

It isn't fair to ask her to pull up stakes and follow me.

She obviously needed the security of being here. All *he* really needed was her and Jack. It would be great to have time to work with Jack himself. The kid was like a sponge, absorbing everything set before him. He smiled as he thought about the piece they'd been working on together since his trip up to Lawson—a little surprise for Carrie. He knew she'd be overwhelmed—just thinking of her reaction excited him.

I'll retire. Let the touring go.

Will mentioned a movie score—he'd been dying to try that. And didn't he say he had other ideas? Maybe he could teach at Interlochen. How great would it be to be near Jack every day? He could do some more composing and arranging—try his hand at some choral music. He didn't *have* to be on a podium anymore. He had plenty of other ways to use his talent.

As her tongue touched his nipple, a lightning bolt of desire shot through him and any attempt at clear thinking was over. His hands moved to her head. He tangled his fingers in her hair, gently pressing her head down while she kissed and nipped his belly and opened the snap and zipper of his jeans. When she'd freed him and her lips and fingers were on him, all clear thought took flight. Her mouth and tongue worked magic.

He was hard as a rock, in a throbbing heavenly haze, mindless with the stroke of her tongue and the rasp of her teeth. "God, Carrie, how do you know—" He gasped.

She lifted her head long enough to glance up at him, dark drowsy passion in her eyes. "I read." Her voice was sultry, turning into a little moan as she returned to the task of driving him completely wild.

He slid his hand down her hip to bunch the knit fabric of her sundress in his fist and got the shock of his life.

As thrilling as her mouth was, his prim and proper Carrie panty-less was impossible to resist. Groaning, he tugged her head up. "I can't believe you're going commando, you wanton wench."

She gave him a mischievous wink as he hauled her onto his lap. "Not all night, just for the last hour or so. I thought I'd surprise you." Kneeling over him, she straddled his thighs.

"I'm surprised... very pleasantly surprised."

He groaned as he guided her hips down. She settled onto him, rotating sensuously while he skimmed his hands up under her dress, sliding his fingers beneath the soft built-in bra. The hardened tips of her breasts pressed against his palms.

She dropped her head back, catching her breath as he brushed her nipples with his thumbs, then rolled them between his fingers. He kissed her, his mouth opening to hers while his hands moved around, down her warm spine to her pumping hips. Her tongue met his and he rose up to grind his pelvis against her.

He was dangerously close to bursting, trying to manage that heat until he was sure she was closer to climax. But it was impossible to regain control. She was in charge, leaning back as she moved on him, slanting into him slightly to change position and allow him to drive deeper into her.

Pulling her mouth away from his, she found his ear with her tongue and whispered, "Now, Liam..."

His name was a caress. The breathy sound tipped him over the edge. Gripping her hips, he exploded with a tortured cry while he held her down. Seconds later, she contracted around him as she moaned and whimpered against his neck in her own release.

He slumped back against the sofa cushions, eyes closed. Her head was on his shoulder, her lips on his neck. Still connected, they were both breathing hard. He didn't speak, simply enjoyed the quiet, sated aftermath, the warm woman surrounding him.

It might be perfect to have only this forever. Carrie, Jack, this peaceful, beautiful setting. Perhaps they could even think about adopting more kids. Plenty of kids out there needed good homes, and she was such a great mom. Liam cupped her face, tunneling his fingers into her hair.

"Carrie, I need you," he said hoarsely. "I love you. I want you. Let's do it—let's just stay here. I'll retire from conducting. We'll build a house up by Eliot. Jack can go to Interlochen. You can keep your studio open." He pulled her face down to kiss her. "Hell, I'd hate to disappoint your fans at the bar. They might come after me with tar and feathers."

"Liam." She frowned. "Wait. What are you talking about? Retirement? I'm not asking you to *retire*. I just want this to be your home base."

"No, listen for a minute. This makes sense." His eyes focused somewhere past her head. "If we stay here, Jack can go to Interlochen—either as a day student or a boarder. If he boards, we'll go get him on weekends. I can work with him. Eliot, too and even Dave Lawson if we need extra help. Touring's getting old anyway. I think I'm ready for a change and—" He broke off, gazing out at the moonlit water. "This is a beautiful place. I see why you love it."

Carrie sat up and moved off of him. Curling her legs under her on the sofa, she watched in silence while he zipped up. Finally, she took his chin and turned his face toward hers. Biting her lower lip, she looked him full in the face. "You would stay here for *me*?"

"I would stay here for *us*." His voice was husky with residual passion.

"Are you sure that's what you want?" Her brow furrowed. "You're ready to let go of the audiences and the orchestras and the travel? It'll be a huge change."

"I'm ready. I can handle it." A heady sense of abandon filled him as she brought his mouth down to hers for a deep kiss.

He *could* handle it. Conducting had been his whole life for too many years. Now it was time for Carrie and Jack to be his life. Her lips parted under his, their tongues met, and that faint niggling of doubt got shoved to the furthest corner of his mind as intoxicating pleasure took over again.

CHAPTER 25

"You were right to bring Liam here," Carrie told Eliot one evening as they shared a bottle of pinot noir on his deck above Lake Michigan. "I'm amazed that they've only known each other a few weeks. It's like they've always been together. Their connection is almost... I don't know... spiritual." With a smile, she pressed her hands together in an attitude of submission, offering him a small bow. "I bow to your superior knowledge in all things. Jack didn't just need a father figure. He needed Liam."

"Their relationship has blossomed nicely, hasn't it?" Eliot took a sip of wine.

Carrie wandered restlessly around the redwood deck, jingling her keys in the pocket of her hoodie. She simply couldn't sit still. It was as if Liam's energy was contagious. Even though she worked hard at the studio every day and got little sleep thanks to passion-filled nights with him, she still woke up each morning galvanized for action, full of anticipation. It was a new and heady feeling.

"Sometimes, I think they're almost reading each other's thoughts," she said. "Jack's not even sure he wants to board next year. He's talking about doing another year as a day student so he can spend time with Liam."

"When are you getting married?" Eliot asked. "And will you please sit down? Your pacing is exhausting me."

"After the benefit. August thirteenth." She perched on the end of his chaise. "Just a quiet ceremony on the beach with a reception on the boat. Julie and Aunt Margie are in hog heaven. They're thick as thieves with Tony planning it. With senior pictures and the two weddings taking up so much time, I've gladly turned it over to them. Liam's bringing his family in that week. Jack and I can't wait to meet them. I arranged for a couple of condos down by the harbor for them." Tilting her head, she smiled at him with affection. "I'm hoping there won't be a mess of publicity around this. We want to keep it quiet. Will says he'll save announcing it until after the wedding."

"Liam drove up yesterday to talk to me about buying one of my side lots." He gave her a long look. "He told me he's retiring and that you're going to live here."

"We are. Isn't it wonderful?" she said dreamily. "I hope you'll give me away at the wedding, Eliot. It would mean so much to me."

"I should refuse you." Eliot's blue eyes were icy.

"Why on earth—" Her jaw dropped and she shot to her feet.

"I wish you happiness in your seclusion, my dear. I only hope you can live with this decision." He stood up stiffly, then walked to edge of the deck. "I'm sure there must be some measure of feminine satisfaction in knowing you've seduced one of the great musicians of our time into your private little corner of the world."

She stood in stunned silence as her dear old friend continued in the same acid tone. "No doubt Jack will become a wonderful music teacher one day. Maybe Noah can put a piano in the snack bar at the marina for Liam if retirement proves to be a bit slow for him."

"Eliot…" Carrie reeled at the unexpected attack. "What a sucky thing to say."

He gave a snort of disgust. "No *suckier* than what you're doing. Liam is no more ready to retire than you are, and Jack deserves an opportunity to fully develop his talent. Interlochen is a fine place for him now, but what happens when he graduates? Are you going to lock *him* away up here like you are Liam? How can you do this? I'm utterly ashamed of you."

"Retiring from conducting is Liam's decision." She kept her voice quiet, but her heart pounded and her palms grew moist.

"Bullshit."

She took a step back. Eliot resorting to profanity was almost as shocking as his angry accusations.

"He's doing what he thinks *you* want. Maybe he's ready to stop touring ten months a year, but he's not ready to retire. For his sake and Jack's, you should be encouraging him to be onstage. You should be packing to move to Chicago right now."

"Dammit, Eliot, why don't you get it? All I want is for my son to have a normal life."

"He's not a normal child. Why don't you see that?" He put one veined, trembling hand on the deck rail. "He could be at Carnegie Hall *today*, for God's sake. Liam can help him achieve great things. But not here."

This wasn't the conversation she'd expected to have when she'd walked up here. "I'm not stupid—"

"Oh, really?"

How can he be so insensitive? Doesn't he understand anything at all?

She swallowed hard, determined not to succumb to tears. "I know what Jack is. He's incredibly gifted, but I want him to stay grounded. I won't have him turned into some… some sideshow freak. I don't care who his father is. 'The Maestro's new-found son... and he's a prodigy.'" She indicated little air quotes. "I can see the Internet buzz now."

"Sideshow freak? I think you're being melodramatic, don't you?" His teacher voice only irritated her more. Clearly ignoring her grimace and eye roll, he charged ahead. "There isn't a more grounded kid in the country than our Jack, but he loves music. Piano is his life, and he deserves the opportunity to share his extraordinary gift. When you have a child like Jack, you owe it to the world to share him. And not just Jack, but Liam, too. Neither of them can be your exclusive property."

"My exclusive—" She gaped at him.

Who does he think he is, talking to me like this? My father?

This hurt more than any sneering comment from Marty Justice ever did—so much more. She held up one hand in warning. "Okay, stop now. This isn't any of your business."

"The hell it isn't." Eliot's gentlemanly demeanor disappeared. "I'm up to my neck in this situation, starting with my foolish promise to help you hide from Liam for such a long time. Well, I brought him here, so I'm going to have my say."

He paused and his expression softened as he limped across the deck to her. When he touched her cheek, the tremor was evident, and when he smiled fondly, she noticed more lines around his eyes and mouth.

Dear God, when had he become an old man? How did I miss it? And what will I ever do without him?

Eliot sighed before he spoke in a loving tone. "Honey, I'm so glad you fell in love again and I'm thrilled you're so happy. It's what I hoped for when I invited him here. But I also hoped you'd open up to some new experiences, and get out of the little box you've been in since your dad died." Eliot dropped heavily onto the settee, and patted the cushion next to him. "Besides, you've never seen Liam in front of a live orchestra. I have. He's brilliant. It's who he is. He may adore you, my child, but his *life* is on a podium... conducting. If you take that away from him, you'll regret it every day for the rest of your life. Because one day, he'll start to resent you for it."

"What about *my* life, Eliot?" Carrie met his frank gaze. "What about *my* career and *my* studio and everything I've built here for Jack and me? Doesn't that matter too?"

"Of course it does." But you need to find a compromise that will work for both of you, and maybe, just maybe, consider that this phase of your life is ending and a new, more exciting one is beginning."

"I don't know." Carrie curled up beside him offering him a half-hearted smile. "I'm so happy and yet so scared of what all this will mean to Jack and me. I'm only trying to maintain some shred of normal for us."

"Breathe, Carrie. Talk to Liam. Stay open to change." Eliot put an arm around her shoulders and kissed her cheek. "And yes, child, I'd be honored to give you away."

Later as she trudged down the beach toward home, Eliot's words of warning burned a hole in her heart. When she crossed the docks and passed the *Allegro,* soft lights and the sound of Jimmy Buffett's music told her Tony was probably onboard, making something delicious for when Liam returned from rehearsal. The tears hit, blinding her as she hurried past the boat and jogged up the steps to her apartment. She almost ran over Julie who was turning away from the door.

"Hey, I just got back from the Marshall's shoot. I wanted to show you pictures of some wedding dresses I found." Julie grinned, waving a sheaf of shiny photos in the yellow light from the docks. "These are simple, elegant—perfect for a beach wedding and— Caro? What is it, sweetie?"

Wrapping her arms around Carrie, Julie held her as she wept, patting and comforting as she would have comforted a hurt child. Leading her to the bench overlooking the bay, she fished a tissue out of her pocket. "Hmmm, it's mostly clean, I think." She offered it with a wry smile. "Now what's up? Where's my happy little bride?"

Sniffling, Carrie wiped her eyes. "Jules, am I wrong to want us to stay here after we're married?"

"I'm not the one to ask. If I had my say, you'd never leave here. I want you near me." Julie hugged her again. "What does Liam say?"

"He says he wants to retire from conducting and stay here with me."

"He does?" Julie frowned. "You mean retire and stop conducting altogether? Forever?"

Her heart dropped. Apparently, Liam in retirement was something no one else could fathom. Was she so wrong in wanting to stay here where it was safe? Where her life and business were? Where everything was familiar?

Julie sat next to her on the bench, deep in thought, her eyes on the blue-gray water of the bay. Finally, she turned to Carrie. "What are you scared of? What's got you so spooked?"

"I don't know." Carrie caught her lower lip with her teeth, then sighed. "Dammit. What if I'm not really what he wants?"

"Oh, honey—" Julie began, but Carrie held up her hand.

"What if we go out there and I travel with him and follow him and wait backstage for him like some damn groupie? Then one night, someone else... someone younger or prettier or more glamorous or more talented suddenly shows an interest in him?" Swallowing hard, she shrugged. "Then what do I do? How do I survive that?"

"You're such an idiot." Julie let out disgusted snort. "Do you think that same thought doesn't occur to me every time Charlie goes to some heart seminar or medical conference? What if some young sexy doc or med student suddenly starts working on old Charlie's ego?" Julie's laugh was full of disdain. "So what if some hottie cello player goes after Liam?"

"Yeah. What then?" She blew her nose, blinking at her friend.

"Marriages don't come with warranties. That's why you gotta have faith. You can't keep him tucked away up here. That's no guarantee he'll never stray." Julie took her by the shoulders and shook her gently. "Caro, you've got to decide right here and now that it's okay for the great *Maestro* Liam Reilly to love *you*."

Tears shimmered in Carrie's eyes as she bit her lower lip. "How did you know?" she whispered.

"I know you like I know my own kids," Julie replied, stroking Carrie's cheek. "You've been walking around here all summer, looking like a kid who got caught with her hand in a cookie jar. Somehow you're convinced you don't deserve a guy like Liam. You think he should he be with some young, rich, hot babe with boobs out to there and legs up to here." She gestured expressively.

Carrie nodded, her heart aching. Deep inside, the idea of traveling with Liam was very appealing, mostly because it meant being with him, but also because she'd see places she'd only dreamed of seeing. And what a glorious experience for Jack to be immersed in the world of a classical conductor. The adventurous woman who played piano in the bar wouldn't have hesitated for a moment, so why was the photographer so frightened?

With a chuckle, Julie continued, "Listen, he's a great guy, but he ain't perfect. I've yet to meet the man who is. The good news is he has that ego under control. He's realistic about his celebrity. I think he knows it could be gone tomorrow. He's a good man, but let me tell you, *he's* the lucky one. And he knows he's lucky... to have *you*."

"I want to believe that, and–and when we're together... you

know... in bed? I almost do." Rosy color heated Carrie's cheeks. "But I'm *so* not like the other women he's known, not even close."

"Exactly." Julie grinned. "You're not. You're warm and caring and funny and smart and so beautiful, inside and out—no, don't look at me like that. You know it's true." She jabbed a finger at her. "You're what he's been waiting for... for *years*. He needs *you* and he needs Jack. But he also needs the music. You give him home, and you can do that whether it's here or at the Plaza in New York or the Ritz in Paris or his house in Chicago. Stop thinking you have to stay here in Willow Bay to keep life perfect. Life will never be perfect. But it can be so damn good. Just let him love you and love him back. That's all you need to do."

Carrie sat still for a long moment. "I love you, Jules," she said, hugging her close.

"I love you too." Julie leaned back and gave her a broad wink. "And honey, that man's butt? Just a great bonus."

CHAPTER 26

Carrie's life settled into a comfortable routine as summer lingered. Liam rehearsed every day before the benefit, in addition to making trips to Lawson to see Jack. Returning home euphoric, his demeanor had shifted from relaxed vacation mode to one of vigorous activity. He hit the apartment each evening still full of enough energy to sweep her off her feet, dancing her around the living room, playing the old piano, singing and teasing her mischievously as they cooked supper together.

The high he was on even affected their lovemaking—it seemed he couldn't wait to tug off her clothes and fall into bed to spend the night kissing and touching. Carrie was astonished at the passion and intensity of the feelings he provoked in her and how he absorbed her thoughts throughout the day.

Hurrying home each evening to prepare for him, she pulled out all the lingerie Julie had insisted she buy over the years—delicate, lacy things she'd never worn. It was a great pleasure to slip into something delectable she knew Liam would get a kick out of removing later.

The fervor they shared also showed in her gig at the bar in Traverse City, almost as though her reawakened libido manifested in her playing. Liam, Will, and Tony appeared one Saturday night, applauding vigorously after each number and sending up requests that kept her at the piano until well past midnight.

Later, at home, he urged her to leave the smoky eye shadow and sexy black underwear on, and then lavished so much sensual attention on her that she practically passed out from sheer ecstasy. Afterward, she couldn't help teasing him about preferring the sultry lounge player to her.

"Never," he'd mumbled, lying sated with his head on her belly. "But it's fun to play with fantasies, don't you think?"

"It is." A long shiver raced through her. "Want to be Johnny Depp for me next time?"

"Sure." He yawned as he nodded and his hair tickled her skin. "You want Jack Sparrow or the Mad Hatter?"

"Um, how about Roux from *Chocolat*?"

"Chocolate, too? Good god, woman, you're insatiable."

Curling her fingers into his hair, she tugged gently to bring his lips up to hers. "Your fault. You showed me all this delight, Maestro."

The day of the benefit finally arrived and after a hurried brunch, Liam and Will took her Jeep to drive to Lawson, where they'd pick up Jack and then go on to Interlochen. The plan was for her to drive Liam's sports car and meet them backstage after the concert at Corson Auditorium. Will hung their tuxes in the back of the Jeep as Liam handed over the keys to the Mercedes to her. Myriad instructions came with the keys, and he ran back up the steps to kiss her one more time and remind her again about the temperamental clutch on the old roadster.

She spent time on her laptop after they left. The photos from the YMCA day camp needed to be edited and a link emailed to the director. But she also had a disk full of pictures she'd taken of Jack and Liam that she was anxious to see. She'd snapped them in every possible situation—down on the beach tossing a Frisbee, on Liam's boat, swimming in the cold water of Lake Michigan, and watching the sunset at the lighthouse. There were photos of the two of them with Eliot, with Margie and Noah in the bait store, fishing with Will and Tony, and swabbing the deck on the *Allegro*. But the ones that moved her most were the pictures she took of father and son at her mother's old piano one rainy afternoon.

One was of Jack, his young face so serious, concentrating intently on Liam's instructions. And one of Liam, his glasses down on his nose, watching his son working through an intricate fingering pattern. Jack with a pencil stuck behind his ear, leaning on the edge of the piano while Liam experimented with a melody the boy had composed. Liam standing behind his son with his hand on his shoulder as he listened to Bach's "Jesu". And Jack laughing, his eyes bright with delight as his father treated him to a rowdy rendition of an old Rolling Stones tune. There had been music, joy, and excited chatter that rainy day and it showed as she clicked through the pictures on the screen.

The last photo on the disk was of the two of them together at the piano. Liam's hands were over Jack's, his own fingers guiding the boy's in a fingering sequence from a difficult Schubert piece —she could still hear the haunting melody as she stared at the screen. Jack's adoration for his father showed clearly in his expression as he looked up at him. Liam gazed down at his son with incredible tenderness. The candid moment brought tears to Carrie's eyes, and she blinked several times to clear her vision.

With a sigh, she walked to the kitchen to pour another cup of coffee, taking it over to the big window overlooking Willow Bay. Sipping slowly, she watched the gray-blue water shimmer in the noon sun. This lake had been her only source of peace since she'd arrived, pregnant and alone. Every time she was upset, tired, frustrated, or lonely and thinking of Liam, she knew she could find serenity on the lake. A walk along the shore or even just out across the docks cleared her mind and heart and prepared her to face the world again.

But now, the need was for Liam, the warmth and haven of his arms, the security of his lips on hers, the joy of his driving hunger filling her emptiness. Julie had told her that *she* was home for Liam—and maybe that was true—but the fact was *Liam* was also home for her. Not this lovely little town or this apartment or even the vast expanse of water below. And she hadn't been willing to open her heart and give as he was giving.

Dear God, Eliot's right. Can I really allow him to abandon such an elemental part of himself?

Instinctively, she knew he would never ever ask such a thing of her. Hadn't he already shown her that? It was time to consider all the good things about sharing Liam's life.

They would be together, a real family. Jack would have his father in his life, and she would have the man she'd always loved by her side. She and Jack would be part of a large loving family and holidays would be big noisy events with grandparents and cousins and aunts and uncles. Jack had missed that for so many years.

Jack's career would soar with Liam as mentor and he'd be able to reach his full potential as a pianist and musician. She *could* take pictures anywhere. How thrilling would it be to take her camera to all the lovely places he traveled to? To capture grand old theaters and concert halls? To photograph Liam in front of orchestras all over the world? And to take pictures of Jack onstage at Julliard and later, perhaps Carnegie Hall? The thought sent a frisson of delight through her.

It's time to go, time to move out into the real world, time to stand by Liam's side and be the whole, nurturing woman he deserves.

Her son needed her, too—needed her to release him and allow him to experience the marvelous things in store for such a gifted and talented young man. Jack deserved all the opportunities she and Liam could provide, whether it was finishing high school at Interlochen or moving to Chicago and studying with a new and different master. That would be a choice they would make together.

If Liam wanted to continue touring, he should. She wouldn't stand in his way. There was music yet to be interpreted, orchestras that needed his special touch. And for her, so many photographs were out there waiting to be taken, pictures of amazing and remarkable sights all over the world. Senior pictures and Sunday school picnics paled in comparison.

Carrie set her cup on the window seat and twirled around the high-ceilinged room, laughing out loud in sheer joy.

Plopping down on the piano bench, she ran her fingers from one end of the keyboard to the other. Then she began a rollicking ragtime tune, pounding the keys in wild abandon. She wanted to skip, shout, fly—this freedom of spirit came from deep within her. She was set free and overflowing with energy.

Finally, my life's going to begin! Maybe I can even do a book about concert halls around the world. How great would that be?

All of a sudden, it was vitally important to talk to Liam. Grabbing her purse from the countertop, she picked up his keys. But as she started for the door, a glance at her watch stopped her. Damn, he was probably at Lawson getting Jack. Then he and Will had meetings with the TSO director and Dave Lawson. After that, he'd have just about enough time to change and help Jack get into *his* tux before he had to be onstage. She picked up her cell phone, but set it back down.

This wasn't news for the telephone.

Talking to Liam would have to wait until after tonight's concert.

CHAPTER 27

Bursting with excitement, Carrie squirmed in her seat in the center of Corson Auditorium, alongside Eliot, Margie, and Noah. The concert had sold out, and Liam and Jack were backstage. She craned her neck, hoping to catch a glimpse of them in the wings, but people filing by and packing the enormous auditorium blocked her view. Student ushers hurried up and down, checking tickets and leading people to their seats.

When she saw Julie and Charlie coming down the outside aisle, she held up her hand to signal to them. Julie—stunning in a black wrap dress and pearls—caught her eye and hustled Charlie down to their seats.

It was a warm night for late July in Michigan so Carrie had opted for a lined, knee-length silk chemise in a deep rose color with a light crocheted shrug over it. She'd slipped the simple dress on over a lacy hot pink thong and matching bra—her first time to wear a thong. She wasn't entirely sure it was working for her, but it would probably work for Liam.

She tried but couldn't convince Jack to dress more casually. No doubt he was sweltering in the tux he and Liam had bought in Traverse City. However, Jack was adamant—if Dad was going black tie, so was he, and Liam had gotten a huge kick out of taking him up to the city to buy the new suit.

She fidgeted restlessly as the theater filled to capacity. Dave Lawson had to be thrilled—his promotion of the benefit had paid off in spades. The event even brought out the Traverse City media. There had been television vans clustered in the parking lot when she arrived.

Julie leaned over Eliot to tap her on the knee. "Great crowd. I'll bet Dave's over the moon."

"I imagine he is. He was practically bouncing around the lobby earlier."

"Hey, I saw Jack and Liam during the reception. What's with the kid's formal wear?"

"His choice." Carrie shrugged. "I think because Liam's wearing one."

"Who knew that kid would look so fabulous in a tux? Little Lanie Palmer was all over him."

"Yeah, I saw that. She was pretty clingy, but I think Tessa Nolan's going to give her a run for her money."

"Is she that tall brunette in the ivory mini-dress?" Julie asked. "Legs up to her neck?"

"Yup. She plays the flute. They've been at Lawson together for years, but this year, he finally noticed her." Carrie shook her head. "Jules, am I ready for Jack and girls?"

"You better *get* ready. He's dropping them in their tracks." Julie scanned the crowd. "Where *is* that kid, anyway?"

"Backstage. Liam told him he could watch from there."

Eliot touched her arm. "This is the largest crowd I've ever seen at one of these benefits. You'd think they all somehow knew this was his *last* concert appearance, wouldn't you?"

She shook her finger at him and frowned. "Don't start, okay?"

"Start what? He told me he was done after tonight." Eliot

brushed at his immaculate linen jacket and sighed. "The music world's losing a great treasure, thanks to you."

A twinge of guilt nipped at her for letting him get indignant so unnecessarily, but Carrie simply smiled. "You know, Eliot, if I didn't love you so much, I'd seriously consider punching your lights out. You've got a real attitude going."

"And I love you too, which is why I'm sorely tempted to haul you over my knee and give you the spanking you've so richly deserved for years." Eliot's eyes flashed sapphire blue in the house lights.

Giggling, she patted his gnarled hand. "Well, don't do it here. The concert's about to begin and I'd hate to steal any of Liam's thunder with a brawl in the audience."

Dave Lawson stepped out onto the stage, raising his hand to silence the crowd. For once, he was succinct and to the point. "We'd like to welcome all of you tonight and thank you for participating in this benefit for our music camp. We've raised a great deal of money with this event—money that will enable us to continue serving young musicians from across the country. It's all due to our wonderful guests, the Traverse Symphony Orchestra and Maestro Liam Reilly."

He extended his hand stage right. Deafening applause greeted Liam as he came out, tall and breathtakingly handsome in his black evening clothes. Carrie's stomach flipped as he shook Dave's hand and then walked energetically to the podium. With a brief smile and nod to the audience, he put on his glasses and picked up the baton.

The concert opened with Rossini's Barber of Seville Overture and moved immediately into Bach's Brandenburg Concerto No. 3. The eclectic mix of classical and contemporary music, from Dvorák's New World Symphony to a medley of songs from *Rent* and the *Lion King,* showed Carrie exactly how gifted her lover was. She was delighted with each piece he'd chosen, and her heart sang throughout the entire program.

From the first note, Liam held the enthralled audience in the palm of his hand, leading them through his own musical land of enchantment. He stopped now and then to step off the podium and speak for a moment about a composer or a particular piece of music they were going to hear, charming everyone with his impressions. Two hours had passed in a heartbeat by the time he broke for a brief intermission before the finale.

Carrie sat spellbound as the house lights came up and a hum of activity began around her. She was caught in an other-worldly kind of haze. Seeing Liam conduct on television was a fascinating experience. Watching him perform his own brand of magic live was exhilarating. All concept of time, all reality of the venue were lost as she got caught up in Liam's stirring interpretations.

She found a peculiar thrill realizing that this provocative, passionate musician brought the same allure and intensity to baton and podium that he brought to the intimacy they shared. He was a heady combination of earthy sensuality and straightforward intellectualism that would be difficult for anyone to resist. No wonder women were wild about him, and how delicious that he was hers and hers alone.

"He is exceptional, isn't he?" Eliot's voice brought her back to the auditorium and the buzzing audience.

She nodded wordlessly as the house lights dimmed, unaware they'd moved a large grand piano onstage until she glanced up to see it center right.

Eliot looked over at her, curiosity evident in his expression.

Every muscle in Carrie's body tensed, almost as if she could physically sense what was coming. She peered down at her program, but all that was written there was *Finale*.

Liam walked onstage and standing next to the piano, turned to speak to the audience.

"Ladies and gentlemen, this trip to Michigan has been an extraordinary experience for me. Working with the Traverse Symphony Orchestra has been a rare privilege. What amazing musicians." He extended his hand toward the orchestra.

The concert master rose and led them in a bow as the audience applauded loud and long.

When they quieted, Liam added, "I'd also like to thank all of you for coming out to support Lawson Music Camp, a wonderful organization working with the children who will be our future composers, conductors, and musicians."

He asked the campers in the audience to stand and also acknowledged the instructors, the parents, and Dave Lawson.

When the applause died down once again, he smiled and gave an endearing shrug, then glanced down almost self-consciously. "I found another unexpected pleasure here in this beautiful place." He paused, peering into the center section of the audience. "The woman who stole my heart over fifteen years ago."

The audience members who didn't already know about the family reunion craned their necks and turned in their seats to see if they could figure out who he was talking about as he went on.

"We discovered that absence can indeed make the heart grow fonder—we're getting married next month." He beamed at Carrie as her face flushed hot, but she gave him a shy smile to the delight of the enamored crowd. "You've welcomed me so graciously, and I'm looking forward to living in Willow Bay and counting you all as friends."

Apparently, the wedding was no longer a secret, but Carrie didn't mind a bit when the audience buzzed. She was a part of his world now and just the thought sent a tingle of excitement through her.

Julie leaned around Eliot with a big grin. "We all love a love scene, kiddo." she stage-whispered, drawing laughter from several patrons around them.

Carrie winked at her before turning her attention back to Liam onstage as he spoke to the crowd.

"Our finale is a particularly special piece of music to me personally, made even more so tonight by the fact that our guest pianist is my son."

He paused at the unison intake of breath from the audience.

Carrie's heart leapt in her chest. She glanced at Eliot who reached over to take her hand in his as Liam continued.

"I'm so proud of him. He's a gifted pianist. Besides being a student here at Interlochen, he's also a Lawson alumnus and counselor. At his request, I'm introducing him to you by the name he'll be using in a few years when he begins playing professionally." Liam accepted applause with a smile as he briefly lowered his eyes to Carrie's. He looked back at the audience, extending his hand stage right. "Ladies and gentlemen, Haydn's Concerto in C Major with the Traverse Symphony Orchestra and soloist Jackson H. Reilly."

Jack—mature and handsome in his formal clothes—walked confidently across the stage to the grand piano, settling himself on the bench. He gazed up at Liam, who had moved to the podium. But in an utterly Reilly gesture, he turned to the audience and tossed a quick nod to his mother.

Liam stepped away from the podium to turn back to the audience. "Folks, musicians are, by nature, a sappy lot and I'm no exception. I haven't dedicated a piece of music to anyone since my high school prom, but tonight"—his voice trembled slightly—"tonight, Carrie, this is for you—from Jack and me."

He stepped on to the podium and tapped the baton. With a quick smile at Jack, father and son began to weave a magic spell.

Carrie sat entranced, blinking back tears, totally unaware that the audience was almost as interested in her reactions as they were in the drama onstage. She allowed herself to become immersed in the music that had been her own swan song so many years ago.

Liam and Jack were in complete harmony, and together with the orchestra, brought all the passion of Haydn's music alive. Jack performed the piece with exquisite technique.

So caught up in the music, she was barely aware of Eliot's hand squeezing hers as the final measures were played. With her heart soaring, she was one of the first on her feet in ovation.

Liam stepped down from the podium to meet his son center stage. Side by side, they bowed low to the audience, then separated to extend their hands to the orchestra. The concert master nodded, the musicians rose as a unit to accept the recognition before Liam and Jack came together again bowing to thunderous applause.

"They look good together, don't they?" Eliot said in her ear over the applause.

She turned to him, tears glistening in her eyes. "They do. And this is just the first of many ovations for the two of them, Eliot."

Eliot's face filled with joy as he grasped her shoulders and hugged her close. "Thank God you saw the light! It's the right thing, Carrie, you know it is. "

Carrie leaned against his bony shoulder, pressing a kiss on to the old man's lined cheek. "It's what I owe the world, Eliot, remember?"

CHAPTER 28

Curled up on the sofa in her apartment, Carrie watched Liam pour wine into two glasses. The lights were dim. Candles flickered around the room. He'd seemed delighted to see the mood she'd set when he returned from taking Jack back to Lawson.

Dropping his jacket on the armchair, he'd pulled off his silk bowtie and vest, and unbuttoned the top buttons of his pleated shirt. When he removed his cufflinks and folded his sleeves back, she resisted an urge to reach out and touch him. Before he opened the wine, he'd even tugged off his shoes and socks, so now he stood barefoot on the soft rug.

"Now *this* is a post-concert party," he said, handing her a glass and tipping his toward her with a small intimate nod. "To us."

"To us." She touched her glass to his. "Okay, now I have toast of my own." She rose and walked across to close the shutters over the big window.

Liam crept up behind her to slide his arm around her, his hand warm on her stomach. Nudging the strap of her dress off her shoulder with his bearded chin, he nibbled the sensitive skin there.

She stopped him with a gentle pressure on his head. "Don't you want to hear my toast?" She smiled provocatively over her shoulder as he continued to explore her shoulders and neck with his lips.

"I'd rather hear that sexy little moaning noise you make when I touch your breasts... like this..." He demonstrated.

She stepped away from him just enough to get a hand's breadth of distance and some sanity. "No. Truly. I think you want to hear this one."

He kissed her earlobe, all the while managing his wineglass with great skill. "Go ahead, I'm listening." He licked the skin under her chin.

Arching her neck, she granted him the access he was seeking before putting her hand up to move his face away. "Liam, this is *really* serious."

"I am being perfectly serious." He pressed a kiss into her palm.

"Hold up your glass, please, and let me make my toast."

With an exaggerated eye roll, he held up his wineglass. "Remember where we left off," he grumbled. "I'd hate to have to start this seduction all over again. In about two minutes, I intend to kiss you senseless, so don't get long-winded."

Carrie raised her glass to tap his with a little click. "To my Reilly men. May they both have long and illustrious careers touching the hearts of music lovers all around the world."

Liam's eyes widened. He slowly set his glass on the table behind him, keeping his gaze locked on hers. "What are you saying?"

"I'm saying you belong in front of an orchestra, Maestro." She smiled. "And I belong with you. So wherever that is— Chicago, New York, Paris, Vienna, Moscow, Beijing... you name it. That's where I'll be."

"Are you sure?" His voice was husky with emotion.

"I've never been surer of anything in my life." She set her wine aside to pull his face down to hers for a long gentle kiss. "Do you remember back in Montreal, you told me I was the only person who never tried to separate the man and the musician?" Kissing him again, she wrapped her arms around his neck. "I've had an epiphany—I realized I was doing just that by letting you change your career because I was too much of a coward to go out in the world with you. I'm not afraid anymore. I love you and I want you. All of you—the man, the musician, the celebrity, the father, the lover—the whole damn package. I want to travel with you and take pictures of all the wonderful places we visit. I'm getting bored with senior pictures and weddings." With a tilt of her head, she gazed into his eyes. "I'm thinking about doing a book about concert halls around the world. What do you think?"

"I–I'm overwhelmed." Liam pulled her close to him, cupping her face in his hands to kiss her deeply. "That sounds wonderful. I love you. I love you so much."

"And I love you. I always have and I always will," Carrie vowed. "I can't wait for what's next for us."

He hugged her, then tipped his head back, a question in his expression. "What would you think about starting in Ireland?"

"Ireland? I'd love to see Ireland." She laid her hand on his chest and slipped open another few buttons so she could touch his naked chest. "Why? How?"

"Frankly, when Jack and I were onstage tonight, I realized I don't want to stop conducting. Not entirely. I knew we'd have to find some compromise to retirement. On the way home, Will told me the Ulster Orchestra in Belfast contacted us about filling in for one of their guest conductors for two weeks in August. Apparently, the other guy needs open heart surgery and can't make his commitment to them. It's short notice, but I'd love to do it and take you and Jack with me."

"That would be fantastic!" Carrie's sobered for a moment.

"But what about school? I don't even know when school starts in Lincoln Park. We need to check that out, don't we?"

"Nope. No high school in Chicago. Jack told me tonight on the way back to Lawson that he wants to board at Interlochen. I don't see any reason why he shouldn't do that. He doesn't start back there until after Labor Day, so we can all go to Ireland if you want to." Sliding his hands down her arms, he touched his lips to hers. "Honey, I said we had to find a compromise and I had some ideas on the way home. Want to hear them?"

"Absolutely." She nuzzled and stroked his chest before kissing his neck.

"How about if we build a house up by Eliot and use it as our home base, but we keep an apartment in Chicago? We'll sell the house in Lincoln Park. Will lives in a great building on the lakeshore. Maybe we could see if there's something available. That way we can be with Jack while he's finishing high school. And since he's boarding, we can still go on the road. But I really am ready to slow down."

She stared into his eyes, shaking her head. "Liam, no. You belong on a podium. Tonight, I watched how much of your essence goes into your conducting. It's who you are, my darling." With a soft chuckle, she ran her hand under his shirt to stroke his back. "Little wonder you turn women on everywhere you go. You are so gifted and sexy up there. You take the audience on this incredible musical... I don't know... odyssey. It's amazing."

He blushed to the roots of his hair. "Did I turn *you* on tonight?" he asked, putting his lips on her bare shoulder. "I think I must have—you just called me *darling*. I believe that's the very first time you've ever used an endearment to me."

"Really? Huh. They're always in my head, but I do love to say your name. Liam..." She shivered at the touch of his tongue on her skin. "You turn me on whether you're on a podium or not."

Toying with the silver streaked hair over his ear, she pressed her lips to his throat. "Please don't stop conducting. Promise me."

"I'm not talking about stopping entirely, just slowing down. I want time with you and Jack. Will's mentioned a movie score, which would be fantastic. And I'd love to do a workshop or two at Interlochen. I'm also looking forward to working with an architect and builder on our house and"—he touched her nose with his —"I think I want to discuss adopting another child." He slid his hands down her silk-clad back. "What would you think about that?"

Speechless, Carrie bit her lower lip as tears stung her eyes. "Oh, that would be heaven!" She hugged him close and kissed him over and over. "A little girl?"

"Do you think Jack would like a baby sister? We could start investigating when we get back from Ireland."

"I think Jack would *love* a little sister." She allowed him to push the straps to her dress down. It bunched around her waist and he smiled.

"A hot pink bra—nice touch."

Tugging his shirt out of his pants, she finished unbuttoning it as he made quick work of the bra. It fell to the floor exposing her breasts.

"Carrie, we have so many options open to us, it's incredible." His voice was jubilant as he cupped her breast and bent his head to her skin. "As a matter of fact, why don't we start exploring some of those options right this minute?"

"Right now? Like what?" She gasped when his tongue touched one hardened nipple and the other, his hair brushing against the soft flesh in between.

"Hm?" Liam's voice was muffled as he sucked and licked her nipples.

She pressed against him, feeling the touch of his tongue all the way to her toes. Putting her fingers into his hair, she lifted his head. "What kind of options can we explore tonight?"

He blinked, then grinned. "Oh. Well, we have the option of staying right here and making love on the couch." He brought his mouth down hers, opening her lips to his exploring tongue. "Or we can go upstairs and try out the bed." Another long deep kiss. "There's also the kitchen table—" He stopped when her wandering fingers found the button and zipper on his pants.

Shoving the dress down over her hips so that it made a puddle of silk around her feet, she gave him his second surprise of the evening.

The leer he tossed her made the effort worthwhile. "Carrie Halligan, are you wearing *a thong*?"

"I am." Her voice was low and sultry as she opened the button on his pants. Carrie giggled, heat flushing her neck and cheeks, as she stood in front of him clad only in the lacy pink thong.

He stood back, one hand stroking his beard. Taking her hand, he twirled her around very slowly. "Oh, good Lord. I do believe I need to write Jules a thank-you note," he said, his eyes devouring her as he shrugged off his shirt.

"I'm glad you like it, but frankly, it's a little uncomfortable," she admitted, her own eyes widening when she saw what he'd revealed when he slid out of his pants and boxers in one step. He was more than ready and so was she.

"Okay, let's get that thing off you. I'd hate for you to be uncomfortable." He peeled the thong away and laughing and kissing, they fell together onto the sofa.

She arched up to meet him as he moved over her trembling body. "Ahhh, apparently right here on the couch is where we're going to be finishing this," she murmured as he entered her with a groan. Twining her arms around his back, she stroked each muscle as he moved slowly within her. "But I'm working on adventurous, Maestro, so maybe later, we *can* try the kitchen table." She brought her legs up around his hips.

He smiled into her eyes. "You're getting downright bold, sweetheart. The kitchen table it is. Then maybe the boat or even the beach."

His mouth closed over hers and the music began in her heart.

EPILOGUE

T*hree years later...*
   "Where's Daddy?"

Carrie sighed at yet another question from her precocious daughter. "Izzy, honey, you need to sit down."

"Mom... mee," the little voice insisted. "Where's Daddy?"

"Daddy'll be out soon, but remember you have to sit still and be very quiet. Okay?"

"Is that piano for Jack?"

"Yes it is."

"It's bigger than our one at home. It's like the one at his school. Like Elly's piano." Despite Carrie's efforts to get her to sit, three-year-old Isabella Reilly was standing in her seat—Row H center—in Stern Auditorium at Carnegie Hall. Her long black hair shone in the theater house lights, her dark almond-shaped eyes sparkled. "Mommy, here's Elly and Uncle Noah and Aunt Margie." The sweet voice carried through the concert hall as the newcomers found their seats next to Carrie.

"Carrie, let me take her." Julie's voice came from behind them as she reached over the seats to lift Isabella into her lap. "Iz, honey, we have to talk softly here. The orchestra's going to play pretty soon and we want to hear."

"And Jack. Jack's going to play, too!" Isabella stared at the people sitting in the row behind Julie. "My big brovver's gonna play dat piano!"

"Is he?" The older woman smiled. "Is your big brother Jackson Reilly?" The woman scanned her program and then met the dark eyes staring at her.

Carrie watched her daughter's face light up as she nodded her head vigorously. Suddenly the child's attention was drawn to the back of the auditorium. "Mommy, here comes Grammy and Poppy and everybody!" Isabella again made her announcement at full volume as the seats around Julie filled up with Liam's parents and brothers and sisters and Jack and Isabella's cousins. Hugs and kisses were exchanged, and Carrie hoped they weren't making too much of a spectacle of themselves. Isabella was passed down the row of relatives, finally ending up back with Carrie. "Mommy, *when* does Daddy come out?"

She glanced at her watch. "Just a few more minutes, Izzy. See? The orchestra's getting seated."

"Where's Jack?"

Julie leaned forward, whispering to Carrie, "I should've brought my duct tape, kiddo."

"She'll be okay when Liam comes out."

Isabella gave Julie a look full of childish wisdom. "Everybody hafs to sit down and be quiet when Daddy comes out, Aunt Julie. Dint you know that? He's the one who tells the musi… musi… cans what to do, so everybody hafs to be quiet and listen."

"Are *you* going to sit down and be quiet when Daddy comes out?" Julie's voice was full of skepticism.

"Course I am!" Isabella's dark eyes widened as Carrie grinned. The child was clearly appalled that Julie would even ask such a question. "Daddy would be sad if I dint. Tonight, I hafta hear the… the French… French horns. I promised Daddy I'd listen for the French horns." Isabella tugged on Carrie. "Mommy, show me where the French horn people are sitting, okay?"

The audience members near the Reilly party murmured among themselves, clearly delighted as they pointed to the tiny beauty dressed in a pink ruffled dress and with the pink ribbon in her hair.

She's Maestro Reilly's little girl.

Carrie could hear the buzz around her.

Isn't she precious? They adopted her from Korea.

Putting her lips against Izzy's sleek dark head, she inhaled the sweet perfume of her daughter's hair.

The child had joined their family just over two years earlier when she was nearly a year old. They'd registered with an adoption agency almost immediately after getting married, but Isabella Grace came to them through a friend of Liam's from the International Violin Competition in Indianapolis. Her parents and two brothers had been killed in a terrible car fire in South Korea when Izzy was less than a year old. Liam's colleague's connections cut the red tape to a minimum and in just weeks, final papers were signed and they flew to Seoul to bring her home. The girl charmed them all from the moment she came into their lives. In no time, she had Liam and Jack wrapped around her little finger.

Jack graduated from Interlochen in June and, much to Carrie's pride and delight, had been accepted to Julliard. On this warm September evening, he was making his debut at Carnegie Hall, accompanied by the Chicago Symphony Orchestra. Liam would be on the podium. The two had been rehearsing for weeks, ever since she and Liam and Izzy had returned from Venice. Carrie's heart pounded as she waited for them to come onstage.

Jack seemed nervous when she'd left him backstage earlier, but he looked so handsome in his black tails. She imagined him with Liam in the wings, their heads together as they encouraged one another for the last time before taking the stage.

The orchestra was quiet now. Izzy craned her neck trying to catch sight of Liam. Finally, the house lights blinked. After a long moment, Liam entered from stage right. Carrie caught her breath as she always did when he appeared onstage anywhere in the world. His hair was a touch grayer, but he was tall and straight and handsome in his black tails. Only Carrie and Will knew that she was sometimes icing his right shoulder after rehearsals.

The announcer's voice was deep as the house lights dimmed. "Ladies and gentlemen, tonight Carnegie Hall welcomes to the Ronald O. Perelman stage in the Isaac Stern Auditorium, the Chicago Symphony Orchestra under the direction of Maestro Liam Reilly. And the debut of an extraordinary young pianist, Jackson H. Reilly.

To a burst of thunderous applause, Jack came out from stage right, walked slowly up to the piano, and sat, tossing the tails of his coat out behind him. Liam stepped up on the podium and picked up his baton, scanning the orchestra. Although Carrie couldn't see his face, she knew he was giving the musicians a goofy grin and his private thumbs-up. Orchestra members around the world talked about Maestro Reilly's traditional seven seconds of silliness before getting down to business. It was so typically Liam and endeared him to the musicians after long hours of tough rehearsals.

The people in front of her whispered to one another. Isabella leaned forward from Carrie's lap. "Shh. My daddy's on the box, so you be quiet now," she admonished in a voice that carried all the way to the stage of the huge auditorium.

Carrie closed her eyes, bit her lip, and tugged little Izzy back against her as she heard Julie and Charlie snickering behind her.

The audience broke up when Liam turned around on the podium. "Thank you, Izzy." He smiled down at his daughter, without a moment of embarrassment. He caught Carrie's eye and winked. Her heart soared.

"You're welcome, Daddy." Izzy didn't miss a beat, completely comfortable having the exchange with her father in front of over two thousand strangers. Even the people she'd shushed were charmed enough to turn around and give the child a smile as Carrie offered a slight nod and returned the gesture.

Liam turned, lifted his baton, and glanced over at Jack, who sat smiling with his hands in his lap. The orchestra members kept their eyes on the Maestro, instruments at the ready. Jack lifted his hands to the keys of the beautiful old Steinway. Then he nodded, and together, father and son began to play.

OTHER BOOKS IN THE WOMEN OF WILLOW
BAY SERIES

Sex and the Widow Miles
His life ended. Hers didn't.

Beautiful and aging gracefully, Julie Miles was looking forward to
retirement with her husband, Dr. Charlie Miles, in their idyllic Willow
Bay, Michigan home. But when Charlie dies of a heart attack, simply
getting out of bed becomes a daily struggle. Desperate for a change of
scene, she leaves her home to stay in her friend Carrie's unoccupied
Chicago apartment.

Her handsome and younger new neighbor, Will Brody, seems to enjoy
his assignment to keep an eye on her, and Jules can't help but be
flattered. She embraces life—and sex—again, until the discovery of a
dark secret shatters her world once more. She knows her feelings for
Will are more than casual, and he's made it clear he wants her, but how
can she ever trust a man again when her perfect life turned out to be a
lie? Determined to get to the bottom of it all, Jules goes in search of the
truth and discovers that there's always a second chance to find real love.

Available at <u>Amazon</u> | <u>Barnes and Noble</u> | <u>Kobo</u> | <u>Smashwords</u>

The Summer of Second Chances
It's never too late to start over...

When Sophie Russo inherits two lakeside cottages in Willow Bay,
Michigan, she thinks she can start over with a peaceful, quiet summer.

Boy, is she wrong.

First, there's Henry Dugan, the nerdy genius behind the GeekSpeak
publishing empire, who has rented Sophie's second cottage so he can
write his novel. The instant attraction catches them both off guard. He's

fresh off a brutal divorce, and Sophie's still grieving her beloved Papa Leo, so this is no time to start a relationship, but a casual summer fling might be an option...

Then Sophie's long-lost mother barrels onto the scene and opens up a long-buried mystery involving Depression-era mobsters and a missing cache of gold coins worth millions that some present-day hoodlums would like to get their hands on.

Suddenly, Sophie's quiet summer becomes a dangerous dance with her grandfather's dark past. With Henry at her side–and in her bed–Sophie needs to find a way to make peace with the past and look toward the future... assuming she lives that long.

Available at <u>Amazon.com</u> | <u>Barnes and Noble.com</u> | <u>Kobo</u> | <u>Smashwords</u>

Saving Sarah

She thought she'd never feel safe again. She was wrong.

When Sarah Bennett's abusive ex hunts her down in Chicago, her friends spirit her away to Willow Bay, where she hopes to begin again with a different identity. But terror keeps her holed up, unable to start her new life.

Deputy sheriff Tony Reynard never expected to be staring down the barrel of a gun when he enters Sarah's apartment to finish up some handyman work, but that's how the fiery little redhead greets him, and he's beyond intrigued.

After an intervention by her loving friends, Sarah becomes involved in a project to turn an old mansion into a battered women's shelter. The women work together to renovate the house, along with the help of the townspeople and the delectably handsome Tony, who is a true renaissance man. Tony vows to bring Sarah back to life and love, but knows he needs to move slowly to win her heart.

When her ex tracks her down once more, Sarah must find the courage to protect her friends and her new love from his wrath.

Available at Amazon.com | Barnes and Noble.com | Kobo | Smashwords

ABOUT THE AUTHOR

Nan Reinhardt is a *USA Today* bestselling author of romantic fiction for women in their prime. Yeah, women still fall in love and have sex, even after 45! Imagine! She is also a wife, a mom, a mother-in-law, and a grandmother. She's been an antiques dealer, a bank teller, a stay-at-home mom, a secretary, and for the last 20 years, she's earned her living as a freelance copyeditor and proofreader.

But writing is Nan's first and most enduring passion. She can't remember a time in her life when she wasn't writing—she wrote her first romance novel at the age of ten, a love story between the most sophisticated person she knew at the time, her older sister (who was in high school and had a driver's license!) and a member of Herman's Hermits. If you remember who they are, *you* are Nan's audience! She's still writing romance, but now from the viewpoint of a wiser, slightly rumpled, menopausal woman who believes that love never ages, women only grow more interesting, and everybody needs a little sexy romance.

Visit Nan's website: www.nanreinhardt.com
Facebook: https://www.facebook.com/authornanreinhardt
Twitter: @NanReinhardt
Talk to Nan at: nan@nanreinhardt.com

CPSIA information can be obtained
at www.ICGtesting.com
Printed in the USA
FSHW010950310320
68661FS